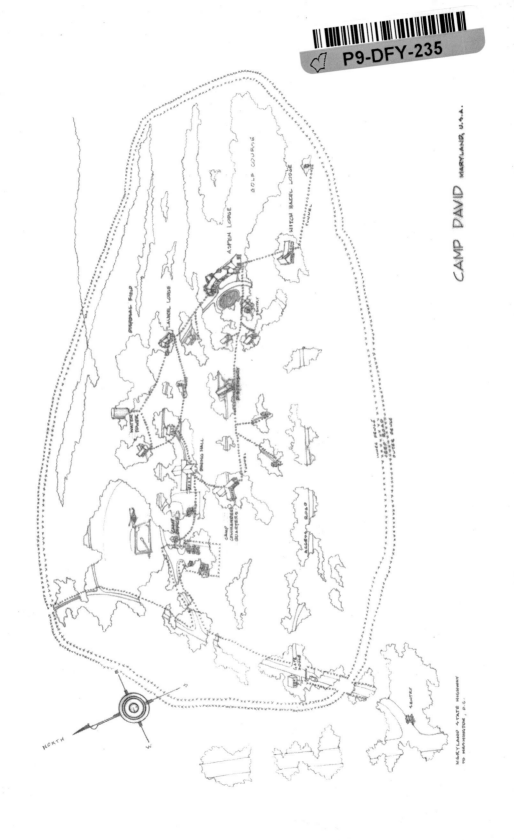

CAMP DAVID MARYLAND, U.S.A.

The Secret
of Camp David

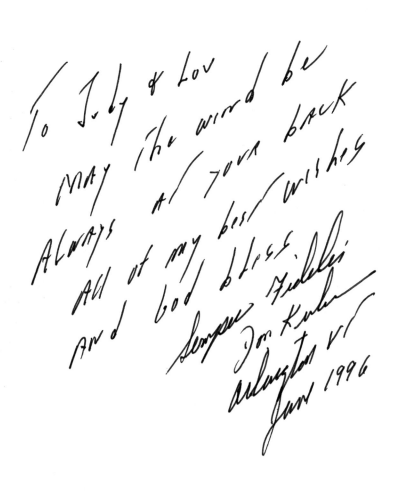

To Judy & Lou
May the wind be
always at your back
All of my best wishes
And God bless.
Semper Fidelis
Don Kuhn
Arlington VA
Jan 1996

The Secret
of Camp David

A Novel

by

Donald B. Keelan

DORRANCE PUBLISHING CO., INC.
PITTSBURGH, PENNSYLVANIA 15222

This novel is a work of historical fiction.
With the exception of historical figures
and events, any resemblance to any persons,
living or dead, is purely coincidental.

ISBN # 0-8059-3573-8
Printed in the United States of America

First Printing

For information or to order additional books, please write:
Dorrance Publishing Co., Inc.
643 Smithfield Street
Pittsburgh, Pennsylvania 15222
U.S.A.

DEDICATION

This book is dedicated to

Corporal William J. Freeman, USMC

and

Mom and Dad

and

Verrall

and to DeWitt S. 'Pete' Copp and
Christine Meyer whose persistence, dedication,
and support made *The Secret of Camp David* a reality.

PREFACE

"The disintegration of the Soviet Union has made it necessary to rewrite history. The unlocking of the KGB files has revealed untold secrets. One such secret was an event that occurred at Camp David on September 25, 1959, during Premier Nikita Khrushchev's visit with President Eisenhower. The simultaneous lifting of the State Department's thirty-five-year seal of the files, together with events in the Soviet Union, enable the Secret of Camp David to be revealed."

Mikhail Kaganovich
Former Head, Section A
First Chief Directorate
KGB

Prologue

0420 Sunday, November 4, 1956, Radio Free Kossuth:

"Attention! Attention! This is Premier Imre Nagy. Today at daybreak, Soviet troops attacked our capital with the obvious intent of overthrowing the legal democratic Hungarian government."

The Soviet Army's invasion into Hungary, spearheaded by four thousand tanks and two hundred thousand troops, was cruel and unjust, but the horrors and slaughter inflicted upon the Hungarian people during those early days of their uprising were eclipsed by the atrocities of the AVH, the Hungarian equivalent of the KGB. By November 14, the revolt had collapsed. While negotiating with Soviet General Malinin's staff on a Russian pullout from Hungary, Hungary's Defense Minister, Pal Maleter, was removed from the room by the KGB, never to be seen or heard from again.

Surrounded by the Russian Army and the Hungarian Secret Police, the Freedom Fighters of Budapest had lost the chance to leave by the main road to Vienna. The chains, welded by Nikita Khrushchev, were now completely linked and Hungary was nearly shackled. And so began the escape south for many members of the resistance: By car to Budafok, by barge on the Danube to Szta-linva-ros, by horseback to Komlo, and over the Mecsek mountains to the Yugoslavian border.

* * *

Winter had come early to the northern mountains of Yugoslavia. Trekking through snow drifts at six thousand feet was exhausting to the four climbers. Being shot in the back by their pursuers was a constant fear. Sunlight quickly gave way to darkness, and the light from the full moon was a beacon to guide the escapees as they slowly and painfully made their way up and over the ice-covered cliffs and then, for the first time, saw the entry to the pass that would lead from Hungary to Yugoslavia—from chaos to freedom.

During their escape, they had been asking, "Why had Hungary been betrayed by the United Nations?" "Why had not the United States and the other nations of the Western world come to their aid?"

Janos tripped, nearly fell. He knew he would never again have the use of the fingers of his left hand, but their loss in the fighting was a small price compared to the torture and murder of his family and the families of his companions.

Entering the pass, the half-frozen refugees—Janos and his wife Nina, together with Hanna and Laszlo Pelm—looked back for the last time towards their beloved country. The clouds were moving in and blocking the moon's illumination of the vast Hungarian plain. The four, rendered powerless, vowed to themselves that they would never forget. Although the Hungarian landscape was hidden from view, the brutal acts inflicted upon them, their families, and their country would remain with them forever.

* * *

Beneath the jagged cliffs, fog had moved in, covering the rocky beach on the Adriatic Sea coast twenty miles south of the Yugoslavian port city of Split. Distances were now measured in yards, and a steady rain complicated the rescue effort being undertaken by helicopters from the United States carrier Ranger standing two miles offshore.

Over the noise of the rotors, U.S. Marine Lieutenant Michael Fergurson shouted to the pilot of the giant Sikorsky Sea Horse helicopter. "Major, there're four more coming down the path. They'll be here in a minute! Two of 'em look like they're injured. You've got to keep the chopper on the ground."

"Lieutenant," the Major shouted back, "if I don't get her up now we'll never get it off this rock pile! The wind will carry us into the goddamned cliffs as soon as we take off—I'm moving it, so get your men in now, Lieutenant. That's an order."

Knowing that the Major would not take off without them, Fergurson, with his two corpsmen, ran toward the stragglers now within fifty yards of the helicopter.

"You've got to hurry, we have to leave," Fergurson called. "Do you understand me?" Sensing that they did not, he lifted the man with the poorly bandaged hand over his shoulder while the corpsmen aided the two women.

"Where you take us?" asked the larger of the four, able to move on his own.

"To safety, to freedom!" Fergurson cried.

"Another stunt like that, Lieutenant," the Major shouted, "and you'll be wearing stripes instead of bars! Get them in and let's get the hell out of here."

CHAPTER 1

WASHINGTON, D.C. THE PRESENT

The door leading from the Oval Office was closed discreetly by a White House aide. The highly polished brass latching made a soft sound as it engaged the lock on the door jam. Escorted by a Secret Service agent down the hallway and through several more doors, Professor Michael Fergurson felt he was taking the longest walk of his life.

His private meeting with the president had lasted nearly an hour. However it had seemed an eternity. What the president had asked him to undertake was the last thing he wanted to do—president or no president. "Who," he asked himself, "ever says no to the president?" Now, as a result, he was angry, angry at himself and the president.

The president's request to have him retrace events that had taken place at Camp David over thirty-five years ago had been totally unexpected.

As he passed through the final door before exiting the White House, he barely heard the Secret Service agent say that the car that would take him to Quantico was waiting for him under the porte cochere.

* * *

On the forty-mile drive south on Interstate 95 to Quantico, Fergurson did not speak to his driver. Instead he focused his eyes on the Virginia scrub pines now hunched over from the unexpected snow that had hit Washington the night before. As the distance away from the city became greater he thought how he and the trees had shared a similar burden—one that neither wanted. The trees' burden would soon be gone in the autumn sun, but his burden would not disappear so quickly or as easily. Over and over he kept asking himself: Why the need to disclose

1

events of so long ago? Who is it that needs to be told about that awful night? And what purpose would it serve?

He wondered what he would tell his wife, Susan. During the twenty-four years of their marriage, he had always confided in her and they never had secrets, except this one. If the world is finally going to be made aware, Susan should know first. "Maybe if there's time I'll call her when I get to the base."

The driver interrupted his thoughts as they arrived at Quantico Air Station and pointed to the helicopter. "Here we are, sir," the driver said, bringing the sedan to a gentle stop. "I'll get your bags, sir, and that officer over there will be taking over from here."

"Thanks!" Fergurson said as he shut the car door and walked over to the Marine officer.

"Welcome to Quantico and HMX-1. I'm Captain Greenberg, and I'll be your co-pilot."

Greenberg, he noted, was dressed in an orange jumpsuit with the presidential seal embossed over the left breast pocket. "A lot different than what you must have seen in your day, Professor," Greenberg shouted over the ear-shattering noise of the slowly rotating blades of the giant helicopter.

"What gave you the idea that I've been in one before, Captain?" said Fergurson, surprised.

"Oh, your facial expression when we came out onto the tarmac and, yes, we had advance notice that you were once a Marine officer," Captain Greenberg said, smiling.

"Interesting and perceptive, Captain. Yes, it was thirty-five years ago when I flew in what was known then as VH-34D or, as we called it, 'Marine One.' "

"It's still called 'Marine One,' sir, because it is primarily used to ferry the president. The outfit, HMX-1, continues to carry out testing and evaluation of helicopters for the Marine Corps."

The aircraft that was going to take Fergurson to Camp David sat majestically on the tarmac. Its white top and military green bottom contrasted brilliantly with the snow. However it was the size and shape of the aircraft that amazed Fergurson. Three decades had passed since he had been this close to a military helicopter, and he had only a passing knowledge of the advances that had been made in helicopter design and aerodynamics.

Fergurson climbed the four steps that led into the chopper. The three-striper, Sergeant Draper, said, "Let me help you buckle up, Professor. Major Rooney, our pilot and the squadron's exec, wants to be airborne as soon as possible."

Fergurson was impressed by the homeyness of the helicopter's interior cabin. The deep-piled carpeting on the floor softened the noise from the aircraft's engines and blades. The carpet's soft red colors blended in warmly with the material that was draped over the windows as well as with the deep brown leather chairs that made up the president's sitting area.

"What model aircraft is this?" Fergurson asked.

"You'll be flying in what is officially called XH59a ABC," Sergeant Draper said. "The ABC stands for 'Advancing Blade Concept.' The aircraft uses two counter-rotating blades, and they are mounted one above the other. When we get airborne, you'll see how this design gives us more lift and maneuverability. Also this dual blade concept will not only allow for a speed in excess of 300 knots, but it also eliminates the almost unbearable noise which was common on earlier helicopters due to the tail rotor, which is non-existent here."

Fergurson absorbed all that the black, muscular crew chief had to say and was impressed with the enlisted man's knowledge. His mind went back to 1959 when he had flown in what was then the state-of-the-art in helicopters—speeds of up to 120 miles per hour, ceilings of 9500 feet gave the pilot a flying range of 180 miles and had made the VH34D the most advanced helicopter developed by Sikorsky Aircraft.

The sudden lift brought Fergurson back to the present.

The aircraft, once off the ground, moved upwards as in a speed elevator on its way to the sixtieth floor of an office building. As the helicopter rose to its cruising altitude of 4000 feet, rapidly the base below became less distinguishable. At this altitude it would be tracked by Washington National Airport's air traffic control. The flight would be assigned to a priority air corridor, as is always the case when Marine One is in the air, regardless of whether the president or his family are on board.

"Professor, the skipper wants you to put on the earphones," said Draper.

Fergurson gently placed the black colored, velour earphones over his head. Attached to the set of earphones was a small circular speaker mike that cantilevered from the left earphone.

"You are now in communication with the pilot as well as with the assistant crew chief and myself," Sergeant Draper said.

"Professor, this is Major Rooney, and I want to welcome you aboard Marine One." Fergurson couldn't help noticing a Midwestern accent, despite the fact that it was coming over the "on board" radio. "Any minute now you'll be seeing the Jefferson Memorial and the Potomac River, and out the starboard window you can get a good glimpse of the Washington Monument and the Capitol," Major Rooney said.

Fergurson pressed the speaker button on his headset and said, "Thanks, Major; Sergeant Draper has made things very comfortable."

"Good. We'll be flying north/northwest with a hundred sixty degree heading at two hundred twenty-five knots and should arrive at the mountain in thirty-five minutes," Rooney said. "Visibility is fifteen miles, and we've got a strong northwest wind of fifteen to twenty-five knots, which is why we'll be in the air ten minutes longer."

To Fergurson the countryside appeared as one large, white quilt with the patches framed in black, owing to the melted snow on the roads. The series of roads that snaked below him, miles and miles of them, I-66, I-495, I-270, I-70, had not been there thirty years ago nor the rooftops of office buildings in countless office parks and the numerous subdivisions of residential developments. Just how big the Federal government had become in the thirty-five years since he had left Washington could be, to a degree, measured by the sprawl that was moving north, northwest of the city.

He could not help but think what it must be like riding in Marine One with the President of the United States on board. The comforts he had all to himself certainly befitted the nation's Chief Executive. And yet the amenities were cozy and comfortable while not ostentatious.

Once again he began to reflect that only two hours ago he had been in the Oval Office of the White House, summoned there by the president. He had all he could do, in the time since the meeting, to get ready for the mission he was now undertaking. And there was much he would have to cancel: classes at Marist College in Poughkeepsie; a speech before the New York Historical Society on the "Transfer of Power by the President" would have to be delivered by his assistant; and the exit from his wife and five children without a word of notice would not make him very popular back in his Dutchess County, New York home. "How else can you act," he thought, "when the president is seated five feet from you and is asking for your help?"

"But why me? And why now, after so many years, is it necessary to go back to Camp David?" The strain of it was beginning to engulf him. The chopper's steady movement northward signaled realization that there was no way out. He cursed himself for not having had the nerve to ask the president why the need for revealing anything. He should have told him that all parties must leave the night of September 26, 1959, buried forever, for it was hard to see what good would come from having to unearth the tragedy.

The tragedy—a world ago—when his physical and mental skills had been stretched to their limits, when his courage as a Marine officer was put to the ultimate challenge. And now, aboard Marine One, he continued to harbor self-doubts about his ability to meet the challenges with which fate had once again confronted him.

"The skipper wants you to buckle up." The assistant crew chief's order scattered his thoughts.

"My God, are we already here?" he said. "In such a short time."

Looking out the window, Fergurson could see that the snowstorm that had buried Northern Virginia had missed the northwest corner of Maryland. Here the landscape was lush in its fall colors. As the helicopter descended, he noted the corn harvest was nearly complete. A collage of colors was in evidence from the farm lands rising up the slopes that make up the Cumberland Mountains. At the higher elevations they were at their peak.

Marine One, having descended to seven hundred fifty feet while over the village of Thurmont, now rose again, climbing to the top of Catoctin Mountain. Fergurson could see the outline of Camp David marked by what appeared to be a logging road completely encircling the Camp area. He could see the outline of buildings muted by the sun's reflection off the cedar shingles that covered the roofs of some of the Camp's buildings. But the dense foliage blocked from view any observations of ground personnel as the chopper made its descent into the Camp.

"We're at Camp David, Mr. Fergurson," the pilot said. "The camp commander will be escorting you to your quarters, and it was a pleasure to have had you aboard."

Fergurson had not felt the landing at all. He unfastened his seatbelt as Sergeant Draper swung back the starboard hatch and pushed out a four-step ladder.

"Welcome to Camp David, Professor," a voice called from the bottom of the ladder. "I'm Lieutenant Commander Hoyt." He held up a fur-lined parka. "You'll need this to shield yourself from the twenty-five degree weather we have up here."

"I'm pleased to meet you, Commander, and can I ever use the coat—God, is it cold up here. Always was," Fergurson said as he carefully made his way down the steps.

"Have a good visit, sir," Major Rooney called from the pilot's window, barely audible over the sound of the double-blade rotors still spinning at low idle.

"Thanks Major, and to your crew," Fergurson shouted as he turned toward Hoyt.

Hoyt said, "Professor, let me introduce Major Michaels, United States Marine Corps and Company Commander of the Camp's Marine Detachment, and Lieutenant Colonel Watson, United States Army, who heads up the base communication systems."

"Pleased to meet you, gentlemen," Fergurson said as they helped him into the coat. "Your organization was once referred to as the Army White House Signal Agency, if I remember correctly, Watson."

"Same function today, sir, different name—White House Military Office," Watson said as he adjusted the glasses on his cherubic face.

Fergurson looked at the officers in his greeting party, surprised at how young they appeared. He could not help but reflect on where the years had gone since he too had been a Marine officer, standing at this very site. The only difference, besides age and profession, was that he was here now as the president's guest. And once again he wished it weren't so. Despite the Camp's tranquility, he would much rather be back in class before his students, lecturing on the merits of their country entering the Gulf War.

"We understand that you're not a stranger to Camp David," the Commander said, "and that you had served here during the Eisenhower Administration."

"That's so, Commander, and I can see at a glance that a great many physical changes have taken place. This landing strip, if I'm not mistaken, was our ballfield, and there were no hangers or buildings whatsoever out here."

"Under Presidents Nixon and Reagan, a considerable amount of expansion and upgrading was done," Hoyt said. "Matter-of-fact, immediately after you go through I.D., we'll give you a tour of the Camp's facilities. Then we'll have lunch at the Officers' Mess. We'll arrange to have your gear stowed at Witch Hazel Lodge."

Major Michaels interjected with a tone of concern, "Professor Fergurson, our orders from the White House are that you're to be given complete freedom to all Camp areas, and I must say that, within my recollection, you're the first civilian we have had here who has been given this type of access."

"In due course, Major, you'll see why the president has given me this latitude, and I can appreciate your concern," Fergurson replied as the four made their way off the windswept helicopter pad.

It was a short walk from the pad to the I.D. building. Fergurson followed Major Michaels into the building and acknowledged Commander Hoyt's remark that he and Colonel Watson were going for a Jeep.

"Sergeant Mitchell, meet Professor Fergurson," the Major barked as he walked over to the trim and neatly dressed NCO.

"Pleased to meet you, Professor. I gather you're here for processing?"

"It's a pleasure to meet you too, Sergeant," Fergurson said with a smile, wondering how many visitors the Sergeant got each day. Probably not many.

"Sir," Sergeant Mitchell said, "if you would stand in front of the camera, I'll take your I.D. photo, and I'll also need a thumb print and, if you don't mind, a sample of your saliva on this swab."

"Why the fingerprint and the saliva sample, Sergeant?" Fergurson asked.

"Your fingerprint will be converted into a hologram and, together with your photograph, will be made into an I.D. card that you must wear on your lapel while you're here. The saliva sample will be cross-referenced at the FBI's Forensic Science Research Testing Center at Quantico, Virginia, with the sample you provided to the Secret Service earlier today in Washington."

"How long have you been doing this procedure?"

"About four years now. The Secret Service adopted DNA, which stands for deoxyribonucleiconly, one year ago, sir," Mitchell explained, "and they believe in its almost fool-proof capabilities. DNA fingerprinting must be used to positively identify all visitors to Camp David, with one exception—the president and his family."

"How long will the process take?"

"Oh, about ten minutes," Mitchell said as he closed the cover on his DNA analysis screening machine.

"Not many people are invited to Camp David by the president," Major Michaels repeated, "and when they are, they certainly are not given the complete access that has been granted to you, so we just want to take precautions."

"I can say that your I.D. procedures are so much more advanced from the time I was here that it makes our old security procedures seem ancient."

"So you might know, Professor, we had a good idea that you are who you're supposed to be before you landed. And that was because a voice print check was being made while you were in Marine One with the one taken at the Oval Office."

"God, you people have come a long way! That wasn't too painful," Fergurson said as he left the I.D. Building with the Major and walked over to a waiting Jeep with Commander Hoyt at the wheel and Colonel Watson in the rear seat.

"You now have full clearance, Professor," Commander Hoyt said. "The Camp personnel will be informed of your visit with us."

"Good," Fergurson said as he got in the Jeep with the others and they drove down the pea-gravel road to the Camp's circumferential road.

As the Jeep moved along the Camp's main road, he noticed the extensive use of closed-circuit television cameras. The cameras were mounted on swivels which, in turn, were anchored to trees by some form of strapping tied around either the branch or tree trunk. Also perched on limbs, with others on three-foot tall ground-mounted pads, were the latest in laser sensors, constantly emitting a red beam of light to a receiver disk mounted in a similar fashion two hundred feet away.

"Where do you monitor the television and laser devices, Major? Are they always on or just when the president is here?"

"Good observation," Commander Hoyt said with a smile. "Those systems, together with the Doppler sound, smell, and pressure systems, are all under constant watch in the CC2 building. That's the communications center building."

"Well, I might as well admit it, I did not notice any sound or pressure security systems," Fergurson said. "And, from what I remember of back in the late 1950s, we were in the 'Stone Age' when one compares with what is here today."

All the sophisticated security systems had come as a surprise. Not, however, what he now saw. Two hundred feet away along an eight foot high fence were two Marines dressed in their olive green fatigues; they wore bloused boots and were warmed by a U.S. Government issue down jacket dyed Marine Corps green. Slung over their shoulders were M-16 rifles, each Marine also holstering a 9-millimeter side arm and what appeared to be a hand-held, two-way radio much like those used by city policemen.

Beyond the Marines, who were now moving westward along the interior fence, the professor heard and then saw a Marine Jeep approaching from the opposite direction. One Marine was at the wheel while the other was semi-crouched in the rear with both hands being trained on a mounted M-60 machine gun. In a matter of seconds, they had disappeared down a side path.

"Well, I guess despite all the elaborate electronic security you have," Fergurson said, "the government still falls back on the Marines to provide the ultimate protection."

"There's no way we or, for that matter, the Secret Service, would feel at ease by having only electronic surveillance, professor." Major Michaels sounded defiant. "The systems you observed are here to aid us in our mission, and in no way could anyone vouch for the Camp's security otherwise."

Commander Hoyt swung the Jeep into the side road leading to Aspen Lodge, the president's home at Camp David. "Professor," he said, glancing at Fergurson, "we feel that we would be less than frank if we didn't ask you about your mission here at Camp David. We know if you don't wish to tell us you don't have to."

"Pull over here if you will," Fergurson said, pointing to the pond. "This is a fitting place to answer your question."

Hoyt brought the Jeep to a sudden stop and pushed the floor shift in place. The four left the vehicle, and Fergurson led them toward a bench by the pond.

The pond was not much larger than that which would be found near a park statue. It was located just a few yards away from the front entrance to Aspen Lodge. Surrounded by large rocks and centuries-old oak and elm trees, it seemed a tranquil place to sit and hold conversations.

Joining them near a small, white marble bench, Fergurson took out his pipe. Smoking his pipe was his favorite way of dispensing stress and carrying on a conversation. His Savenilli brier, with a small silver band where the stem joins the bowl, was his favorite.

"What I'm about to speak of must remain with you here. Under no circumstances must any of what I'm to tell you be repeated," Fergurson said. "The president has given me permission to let you gentlemen be made aware of my purpose here, but only you three. He knew you would ask; I guess he felt it was only natural."

Commander Hoyt noticed Fergurson's hands shaking and said, "Professor, if you're getting cold we can move inside where it will be warmer."

"Thank you, Commander. I'll be fine," Fergurson said, clutching his pipe. "The reason I'm here is to gather information as well as to re-visit the area where some thirty-five years ago an incident occurred, one which has never been revealed to the American public."

He filled his pipe with tobacco from his leather pouch and flipped his Ronson lighter several times, knowing the three officers were watching him. The light wind was only partially the cause for the pipe tobacco not igniting immediately. Fergurson's hands were not at all steady.

"Please sit down, here, next to what I remember as Roosevelt's Pond." He was about to relive the events of September, 1959—the second time in one day. And now, as before, he was unconvinced as to why the story must be told at all.

10

CHAPTER 2

LATE JULY, 1959

"Sir, Lieutenant Michael Fergurson reporting as ordered," snapped the First Lieutenant as he stood at attention dressed in a tan-colored uniform with black leather belt.

"Welcome to Eighth and I, Lieutenant, and stand at ease," responded the crewcut and tanned, over six-foot tall Marine major from behind his desk. The major extended his right hand to Fergurson, at the same time holding in his left hand what little remained of a chewed up cigar.

The desk was an oversized partners' desk bedecked with many small Marine Corps memorabilia of Major Simmons, Adjutant of the Marine Barracks, Washington, D.C.

Lieutenant Fergurson noticed the four rows of ribbons on the major's chest, topped off by the blue and white ribbon signifying the Navy Cross.

Behind the major's chair, Fergurson observed the flags of the United States and the Marine Corps. On the wall between the flags hung photographs of President Eisenhower and General Randolph McCall Pate, the present and twenty-first commandant.

"I hope you had a good leave and that all is well at home, Lieutenant."

"Thank you, sir. It was good to get home and spend time with my parents, sir. But toward the end I was anxious to get back in uniform."

"Your results at the Quantico Leadership School and your platoon's success on the beach during last year's Second Division landing in Lebanon are commendable, Lieutenant," Simmons said glancing up from the lieutenant's Service Record Book. "Your assignment here at Eighth and I will be a great deal different, but, nevertheless, as demanding.

You'll be taking over the Third Platoon of the Ceremonial Guard Company. Captain Johnson is your company commander and Sergeant Kellerman your platoon sergeant. They and the platoon will be arriving by bus at fourteen hundred hours from Camp David where they've spent the last seventy-two hours with the 'Old Man'—President Eisenhower to you, Lieutenant."

"What, exactly, will my duties be here at Eighth and I, Major?" Fergurson asked.

"Sit down here, Lieutenant," Simmons said, pointing to a leather-backed chair, "and I'll give you some background. Lieutenant, would you like a cup of coffee? I apologize for not having asked—I realize that you've been traveling for almost two days."

"No thank you, sir. I'm fine," Fergurson said as he sat down.

"By being here, Lieutenant, you must be prepared to live in what we all call the 'fish bowl.' You'll see why in a minute. Your assignment and duties here at the Marine barracks will be multi-faceted. In no particular order, they'll include your leadership over a twenty-four man, silent drill team that practices approximately three hours a day, five days a week throughout the year while they're here in Washington. When you and the platoon are not here, you'll be on tour throughout the United States or, as is sometimes the situation, the world. Our Second Platoon went on a two month tour aboard the aircraft carrier Ranger, and made port-of-call visits to two dozen cities on both coasts of South America."

"I'm no stranger to the Ranger, sir. I served on her in '56."

"Yes, I see you were part of that Hungarian rescue attempt in the Adriatic. Your 914 jacket states that you did a splendid job."

"I didn't mean to interrupt you, sir."

"No, that's quite all right, Lieutenant. Where was I? Oh yes, also the platoon will be called upon to perform duties of a ceremonial nature here in the District and at Arlington National Cemetery. And, on Friday evenings between May and October, there's a sunset parade put on here at the Barracks."

"I'm familiar with the parade, Major. I was here with my class from Quantico a few years ago and found it breathtaking."

"Well, Lieutenant, you've been selected to lead a drill team platoon and much of what is done here on Friday evenings is also performed on Tuesday afternoons at the Marine Memorial in Arlington Cemetery. This, of course, is not to be confused with the five to ten burial ceremonies that the Company carries out each week at the Cemetery," Simmons said, attempting to relight his cigar which was almost completely extinguished. "Also we have assignments for officers here at the barracks, at the State Department, and at the White House, as escorts at State dinners for foreign dignitaries or other social functions."

"Major, you mentioned that the platoon is coming back from Camp David. What role does Eighth and I have there? I've heard of Camp David before but know very little about it other than that it is used by the president and his family and was supposedly named for President Eisenhower's grandson David."

"While you were on leave, Lieutenant, the Secret Service and the Office of Naval Intelligence processed your clearance papers. You're now in possession of a Crypto-graphic clearance which, if I am not mistaken from having read your 914 file, is an upgrade from Top Secret. I want you to be aware, Lieutenant, that all matters concerning Camp David are considered Top Secret and under no circumstances are you to talk or write about it to anyone unless you have positive proof that they're in possession of the same clearance that you hold. Before you complete your processing today, you'll sign a statement that, in effect, will seal your lips regarding Camp David for twenty-five years subsequent to the date you retire or resign your commission. Now, back to your question—what does Eighth and I do at Camp David?"

"Yes, sir," Fergurson said.

"We work at the direction of the Secret Service when it comes to matters regarding Camp David or, for that matter, anything pertaining to the protection of the president and his family. I might add we also are assigned to the summer White House, which, in 1957 and again last year, was a six-week detail at Newport, Rhode Island."

"What is the nature of our protection for the president at Camp David?" Fergurson asked, beginning to feel more at ease.

"Our function is to maintain constant surveillance over four miles of perimeter fence, operate the main entrance from the state park into the Camp, maintain roving patrols through the forest, secure the Camp's helicopter landing pad when the president is arriving by chopper, or if by car the numerous bridges that cover the park's mountain streams," Simmons recited matter-of-factly.

"How often do we go there?" Fergurson asked.

"Let me answer that as we take a walk outside," Major Simmons said, putting on his cap. "It's getting stuffy in here and it'll give me a chance to show you around."

Fergurson got up from his chair and followed the huge man through the outer office's side door that led to the walk paralleling the parade field. Along the way he wondered how he was going to cope with the litany of duties he was about to assume. Major Simmons led him to the center walk next to a fifty-foot high flag pole. They stopped and watched the Marine Band and a drill team practicing their marching maneuvers and led by a ram-rod looking sergeant-major who was carrying a six-foot mace. Fergurson was not paying much attention to the smart-looking Marines; he was in thought. "Why," he wondered, "didn't Major Simmons mention my brother Kevin, Sergeant Kevin Fergurson?" Why was he chosen for this assignment? Could they've made a mistake? And, above all, could he carry out the duties that Major Simmons brushed over so quickly?

Major Simmons startled him by saying, "In due time you'll get to know this place a lot better, Lieutenant. Just keep in mind that Commandant Pate lives in that house."

"Is this what you meant by the fish bowl, sir?" Fergurson said as he looked at the three-story Federal Building that filled the north end of the parade field.

"This place is hallowed ground. However you'll be more fortunate. Every fourth week your platoon is rotated to Camp David for two weeks. And, I can assure you, Lieutenant, that after four weeks of ceremonies and drill performances, you and your men will look forward to spending two weeks in utilities up on the mountain."

With a flick of his swagger stick, Simmons beckoned Fergurson to follow him across the center walk. Fergurson did not miss how immaculate the grounds and buildings were kept. Also he was impressed with the snappiness of each enlisted man's salute and the neatness of their uniforms, details that were observed at his previous assignment, but only barely.

"Let me tell you a few things about Camp David, Lieutenant," Major Simmons said as he and Fergurson continued walking down Officer Way. "Everyone involved prefers to maintain a very low profile, Lieutenant, when it comes to Camp David. We do not spend a great deal of time talking about it here and we keep the press at bay when it comes to Camp David. Mum is the word; just learn to keep your mouth shut and make absolutely clear your men do the same. To my knowledge, the only time the press was allowed in to take photographs was when Roosevelt met with Churchill to conduct strategy meetings for the invasion of Europe, and when President Eisenhower held his first press conference and Cabinet meeting, subsequent to his heart attack. The press stays in the small village of Thurmont, Maryland, at the foot of the mountains. I'm told that during World War II, the press knew that President Roosevelt left Washington on weekends. What they didn't know until late '44 was where he went. At that time Secret Service agent-in-charge of the White House, Mike Reilly, wanted a reporter charged with espionage for having come close to revealing the president's retreat."

"I had no idea, sir, just how involved this assignment was going to be. And also how critical," Fergurson said as he glanced over at the drill team now in the process of their silent drill.

"A lot more critical then you think, Lieutenant, and with precious little time for you to get up to speed."

"I'm not sure I read you, sir," Fergurson said quizzically.

"The scuttlebutt is that something big is being discussed over at the White House concerning Camp David and an important visitor to the United States," the major said.

"Who do you think it might be, Major?"

"Word has it, Lieutenant, that the Chairman of the Soviet Union is coming to the United States this fall."

The Major's remark shook up Fergurson. Bewildered, he said, "The head of the Soviet Communist Party is coming to the United States and to Camp David!"

"We don't know for sure, but this town lives and thrives on rumors, Lieutenant. If this scuttlebutt is correct, Mr. Khrushchev could be here within sixty days, and his protection and that of the president will be in your hands, Mr. Fergurson," Simmons said in a firm manner.

"Major, if I'm shaking it's because I don't think that in sixty days I'll be up to this. How can I?"

"Lieutenant, I could be corny and say that you'll do it because you're a Marine, but I won't. You'll be up to it because you've got a record that demonstrates that you can do it. Also, from the little I know of you, you're much like your brother Kevin. We served together in Korea and here at Eighth and I during my first tour, I had the same role that you're now assuming."

"Sir, I hope you realize that Kevin was someone special to me. But in no way do I feel that I could ever live up to his accomplishments."

"Don't misunderstand me, Lieutenant. However when I said that your tour here will be no less demanding than your previous assignments, I probably should have said, more so. Let me welcome you with my best wishes to the oldest post in the Marine Corps. I'll have Corporal Larson escort you to your Company headquarters. And good luck to you."

CHAPTER 3

President Eisenhower's favorite place to hold meetings with his senior advisors was the Oval Office in the White House. Its simple and tastefully laid out decorum, as well as its views of the White House gardens, provided a relaxing environment in which to conduct conferences. However, on this sultry, late July afternoon, the serenity of the Oval Office was anything but relaxing and calm. The president was in full voice. "For God's sake, Chris, where does he get off inviting himself to the United States without so much as a call to me?" he said glaring at Christian Herter, his new secretary of state.

"But, Mr. President," Herter said, "Chairman Khrushchev accepted your standing invitation to visit the United States, which he said you extended to him in Geneva four years ago."

"My invitation, if I recall, was an off-the-cuff comment while Khrushchev was being photographed with me at the conclusion of the Geneva Summit, and it was nothing more than that, God damn it. I do not wish to have it made into any more than what I meant." He turned away in annoyance looking out the window at the Rose Garden, his back to Herter. "With all that has transpired since 1955, the Chairman of the Soviet Communist Party chooses this time to want to come to America because it fits neatly into his own political and propaganda agenda."

Herter said, "We heard through the Embassy in Moscow that he would very much like to spend two weeks here, preferably in September, Mr. President."

"What are we—a travel agency?" Eisenhower swung around. "For Christ's sake, can't you see how this crafty S.O.B. is using us for his own purposes?"

"Mr. President, I should inform you that he has issued a statement to *Pravda* concerning his desire to take up your invitation. Our turning him down, short of a national disaster here at home, would be a major propaganda victory for him."

"What a situation his visit poses for us," the president said sarcastically, rubbing his hand across his bald head. "The political ramifications here at home will be nothing short of disaster. Six months ago I was crisscrossing the country campaigning for a new Congress, exposing the evils of Communism, and denouncing their leaders especially for what they did to Hungary. Now I'm inviting their chief mischief maker to pay us a visit." The president sounded weary as a knock at the door interrupted him. "Come in," he called.

James Haggerty, the president's chief press officer, said, "You wanted me, Mr. President?"

"Chris, I've asked Jim to join us because I trust his opinion when it comes to assessing the temperature of the press. And, although he can at times bring an over-abundance of optimism to a situation, the calm, honest, and reassuring manner that he projected to the American people during my heart attack was brilliant."

"Good afternoon, gentlemen," the red-haired, round-faced press secretary said.

"Jim, what can we expect here at home when we announce Khrushchev's visit? And, for God's sake, don't feed me your Irish optimism! I want it straight," Eisenhower said, moving to his desk with his arms folded across his chest.

"The hardliners in the Senate," Haggerty said, "led by Senators Dodd and Bridges will try to crucify us, with Senator Dirkson carrying the nails and providing the wood for the cross. The House side will have nothing but contempt for your decision, and I would not at all be surprised if the conservatives Keating and Halleck move for impeachment. Keeping in mind, Mr. President, that Mr. Khrushchev will be the first leader of the USSR to visit the United States, the press will have mixed opinions about the visit. Certainly, the *New York Daily News,* the *Journal American,* and the *Herald Tribune* will fry you and the State in their editorials. The *New York Times* and the *Washington Post* will be neutral if not somewhat supportive of the visit. Our biggest problem is with the leaders of the Republican Party. They're being caught off-guard and they, as well as most of the corporate and other large contributors, will perceive the visit as another spike in the coffin, as the country moves closer to socialism."

"Jim could very well be right, Chris," Eisenhower said. "And if there is a backlash to the visit, one can see the McCarthy sympathizers rising again."

"And I should also point out, Mr. President," Haggerty said, "that the Catholic Church, led by Cushing in Boston and Spellman in New York, will certainly denounce the visit. Cardinal Spellman, who I know is a close friend of yours, will most likely lead the charge to cancel the visit."

"Keep in mind," the secretary of state added, "that the Catholic Church has suffered terribly at the hands of the Communists in Russia and Eastern Europe. I recall in 1957 you relaxed the immigration laws and allowed over one hundred thousand Hungarians to emigrate here. Some resettled in Minnesota, Wisconsin, and Illinois, but most of them stayed in New York and New England, and most of these people have lost family in the revolt or have relatives in Hungary's prisons."

Herter, now on his feet, aided by two metal crutches that allowed him mobility over his crippling arthritis, moved across the room while addressing the president: "No need to remind you about Cardinal Mindszenty . . . he's been in exile at our Legation in Budapest and residing there for nearly three years. So no matter how we cast the visit to this country by Chairman Khrushchev, Cardinal Spellman and his Church will denounce us for bringing Mindszenty's jailers here for a State visit. And right behind Spellman will be Cardinal Cushing. And, Mr. President, let me assure you that Senator Kennedy will side with Cushing on this matter, especially since he is considering his Party's nomination."

"It's a helluva bleak picture," the president stated.

"Not necessarily so, Mr. President," Haggerty said. "There's a way we can soften the political fallout and turn the visit to an advantage. You campaigned on the promise that you would wage peace whenever and wherever possible. How better to do that than by sitting down here—in this very office—with this country's leading enemy. None of your predecessors were ever willing to do it."

"Mr. President, that's a valid point," the secretary of state added. "We have an opportunity here to do something very ambitious and unique. It will be historical—two former Generals of World War II joining in a Summit Conference."

"That's an interesting way to put it, Chris," Eisenhower said.

"Mr. President," Herter said, "you know from your meeting with Khrushchev at Geneva in 1955, as well as from the vice president's trip to the Soviet Union, that it will take many meetings between the leader of this country and their's before there is an element of trust that will allow us to proceed on any agenda for peace and disarmament."

"What both of you are saying to me is that we are in for some rough treatment by the Party, the press, and Church leaders, as well as from the Hill. And, although neither of you mentioned it, from our allies."

"That about sums it up, sir," Herter said. "He's coming and we're going to catch a good deal of flack. But to turn our backs on this great opportunity for advancing the cause of peace would be a terrible mistake."

"I agree, let's do it. Let's go public with it, the sooner the better," the president said firmly. "Jim, on 3 August I want you to inform the press that we are inviting the Chairman of the USSR to the United States in September for a two-week visit, and that the details of the visit are now being worked on by our two countries. And, gentlemen, let's pray that we've made the right decision."

CHAPTER 4

"My dear husband," Hanna said as she brushed the dirt off her multi-colored, ankle length dress, "I never should have let you talk me into walking down to the village. See now, we must walk all the way up this dusty road."

"Don't let the dust stop you from seeing the beauty of Vermont," Laszlo said. "Look over to your left—the town appears snuggled in the palms of the Green and Taconic Mountains with the three thousand-foot peaks of Ball and Red Mountains standing as sentinels to the peaceful village."

"Laszlo, you're such the poet. You and Robert Frost would have had a lot in common. He used to live nearby and came to Arlington often, I'm told."

"See, Hanna, the Battenkill river. If you observe carefully you can almost see the trout leaping up through the water to snatch a bug. Why those fishermen standing in the river can't catch anything, I'll never know, especially now in the middle of the summer."

"You're as dreamy as those Allen brothers that people around here talk about, Laszlo, and just as daring."

"And look who's talking about being a dreamer. Hanna, when we got off the boat in New York City you found a book about Norman Rockwell and you had us all come here to his hometown. That was crazy, no?"

"Do you regret it?"

"Well, no. But he didn't live on a mountain, two thousand feet up a dusty road that we can't even get down in winter, now did he?"

"No, you're right. He lived and painted along the Battenkill, and he didn't raise pheasants, and he didn't want to be isolated and left alone like we do. And let's keep moving—Janos will be needing you to help with the pheasants. Incidentally, how many do we have now?"

"At last count nine thousand. You know, Hanna, it seems only natural that we would be raising poultry here in America. When you and I first met, in Miskok, you saw me and Papa raising pheasants and chickens. My God, that seems to have been so long ago."

"We're fortunate that we have the farm in spite of the fact that it is up the mountain," Hanna said, taking a stronger hold of her husband's hand and silently admiring the tall and handsome man she married earlier in another time and in another place. "It's been nearly three years since the revolt, and who would have expected us to be here? I, for sure, never did."

"We should be grateful. And I am, I truly am," Laszlo said softly, putting his arm around Hanna's shoulder. "I didn't realize that from here you can hear the pheasants, Hanna."

"Squeeze me tight, dear," Hanna said softly. "I never want you to let go of me. Right now I just want to be with you."

"Did I ever tell you, Hanna, that your hair is so brown and lush? Especially now with the morning sun reflecting upon it. Let's sit under these pines and soak up the beauty of this morning."

Hanna placed her arm around her husband's narrow waist, feeling his muscles react to her touch and pulled him closer to her and whispered softly to him, "Yes, my dear, you've told me many times and I love you for it—but no, I'm afraid if we sit by the pine trees we'll never get up—Janos is waiting."

* * *

At the Pelm Pheasant Farm, the penned-in birds, thousands of them of all different types—from Chinese ringnecks to jumbo ringnecks, to white pheasants and, to a lesser degree, Afghan Whitewing—chirped and pecked from daybreak to night fall.

Almost all of the birds were in their eighth and ninth week, having been hatched in April and May. Because of their size and feathering, the birds were no longer in need of heat lamps for warmth. Instead, day and night, they were to be found in the outdoor pens.

"How was the village, Laszlo?" Janos said as he carried two pails of feed to the pen.

"It was fine," Laszlo said, unlatching the gate for his brother-in-law. "We walked down and back. Forgive me for not being here to help you with the chores."

"It was good that you and my sister had some time to yourselves, Laszlo," the short, stocky Hungarian said as he began to empty his pails into the feeders.

"The jumbo hens are starting to peck at each other," Laszlo said, watching the birds through the wire mesh fence. "If we are to avoid a rash of cannibalism among them we must start to debeak them today."

"We must also locate a supplier of feed that can provide us with a vaccine for the new birds," Janos said, "otherwise we will be subject to the threat of coccidiosis. We were lucky that in this older batch we avoided any illness, but we cannot ignore the recent warning we got from Fish and Game that all of our new birds must have three weeks of the vaccine in their food."

"Coccidiosis can be avoided if we keep our cages clean and dry, together with using bleach when we clean the cages," Laszlo said, observing his brother-in-law scatter the balance of the feed pellets around the pen and compensating for the loss of his fingers by holding the five-gallon pail under his arm.

Actually cannibalism and parasites were far from the mind of the pensive-looking Laszlo. These problems could be costly and time consuming but, nevertheless, dealt with, controllable, and, with attention and care, avoided.

What Laszlo could not deal with or forget was the murder of his father three years ago at Hungary's Felsopeteny prison at the hands of the Communists. He pressed his head up against the wire mesh fence. His large fingers tightened their grip on the strands; all along he paid no attention to Janos's continuing banter about feed and illness. The events of three years before were not going to be forgotten by him. The others may be putting all of what took place behind them, but he couldn't—nor did he want to.

"Laszlo, what is it? What seems to be bothering you? Coming up the hill you were so cheerful," Hanna said as she approached the two men carrying a decanter of red wine. "Stop and quench your thirst and maybe the wine will bring back the smile you had before. Janos, come out here and drink."

"Hanna, your timing is always so impeccable. I just feel so helpless when I think about our people back home. Sometimes I feel that we all have become so content, we are doing nothing. The 'movement' is all but dead and America has done so little." Sipping the wine he said, "I know we probably should be grateful to the Americans and, in particular, President Eisenhower, for rescuing us and the thousands of our brothers and sisters from Khrushchev and his butchers. But in my heart I cannot help but feel contempt for General Eisenhower and his World War Two colleagues for not listening to Churchill who wanted the Allies to push eastward into Eastern Europe after the fall of Italy. Had they done so, the Germans would have been defeated in eastern Europe by the Americans and British and not by the Russians, who never left the countries they captured."

"Laszlo, Laszlo, my dear husband, that was over fifteen years ago; you must rid yourself of this bitterness. Neither you nor I can change what has happened. We must learn to love and accept our new home here in America, and pray that Uncle Joseph will some day be able to walk freely from the American Legation in Budapest."

Clasping the wine glass with both hands and staring at the ground, Laszlo said, "Hanna, I mean no disrespect, but you go ahead and pray. Prayers to me mean nothing and do nothing for me or for Hungary. God has abandoned us as well as Uncle Joseph."

"You must not speak like that, Laszlo. God has guided us here and we are safe," Janos said angrily, looking up at the man he respected more than any other.

"Oh, we're safe all right," Laszlo said with disgust, the muscles on his dark face constricting. "But Uncle Joseph is not free. He spent eight years in the communist prison at Felsopeteny, and we gave him his freedom during the revolution only to have to tell him that he was in imminent danger of being captured. Yes, I can thank the Americans for giving our Cardinal, our uncle, asylum in their Legation, but I still curse God for what has happened to my father and uncle."

With her arms now around her husband, Hanna said softly, "Don't curse our Lord, Laszlo. It's the Communists and Khrushchev you should curse. I will never ask you to forget what happened. We have begun our lives again and must not allow hatred to continuously chain us down. Did I tell you that I read a small article in the paper yesterday that the State Department and the Vatican were meeting in New York with the Russian deputy premier Kozlov to try to work out a plan for Uncle Joseph's release? The article said that Mama Pelm went to see her brother last week on her eighty-third birthday, but the Soviets only gave her permission for a one hour visit."

Laszlo replied angrily, "You see, Hanna, why I feel the way I do. Those bastards give her just one hour to see her brother. Christ, she must have traveled twelve hours just to get to Budapest and back to her home—and she gets one hour to see the Cardinal of Hungary! Nothing will come of that visit in New York between the Americans and the Russians. It is all show. By this time you would have thought that the Americans would have smartened up when it comes to dealing with them."

"Laszlo is right, Hanna," Janos said, "Americans are naive. The Vatican is powerless to do anything when they require the cooperation of the Soviets. For that matter, so is the United States, especially since there is no public support for this cause."

"So then what?" Laszlo said sarcastically. "We just sit here in this beautiful place and feed the birds? There must be something we can do. Just some little thing to draw attention to what is being done to Uncle Joseph."

"If we can only get the newspapers and television to see what is really happening and have them tell it to the American people," Janos said. "But how can we four do that? And who would listen?"

"Brother, I agree with you," Hanna said. "And you've given me an idea. It is the newspapers that we must approach. Did you see all the attention that little colored girl got when she was not allowed to go to a white school in Mississippi, or was it in Arkansas? Even the president got involved. He sent down the Army to make sure the all white school took her in. But what's important is that it had been in the newspapers and on television everyday."

"Well, maybe I should go to New York and shoot Kozlov," Laszlo said, "that will get everyone's attention."

"Be serious, Laszlo," Hanna said firmly. "No one wants you to go off and kill the deputy premier. You two must go back to work before you finish off all the wine and get too drunk to care for the pheasants.

CHAPTER 5

As the twenty-four man platoon stood at attention on the concrete parade walk at Eighth and I on a hazy, late-July morning, Lieutenant Fergurson, dressed in his khaki uniform, walked over to the platoon from the bachelor officers' quarters. For a brief moment he wondered whether he was up to leading the men he was about to meet for the first time, knowing all too well that they were not ordinary Marine grunts but two dozen hand-picked Marines that made up the Marine Corps' Silent Drill Team.

Fergurson returned the platoon sergeant's salute and said, "Gunny, I would like to address the men, so have them stand at ease."

Gunnery Sergeant Norman Kellerman turned toward his platoon smartly and shouted, "Platoon . . . at ease."

"Men, my name is Lieutenant Michael Fergurson, and I've been appointed your platoon leader, replacing Captain Marcham who left yesterday for FMF-Atlantic. I've spent a good deal of time over the weekend with Sergeant Kellerman, who brought me up to speed on the platoon's training program, inspection readiness, and ceremonial preparedness, and I must say that from what I've seen and have heard about all of you, a great job was done by my predecessor."

Before continuing Fergurson thought as he tightened his grip on his swagger stick, "Are they staring at me? Does a First Lieutenant always feel this way in the first meeting with his troops? How do they see me? God, I only wish that I had more self-confidence."

He continued, "Because you've been at Camp David for the last two weeks, your Silent Drill routines may be a bit rusty, and with the Evening Parade only five days away, practice will be the order of the day. Just so you know, the Commandant's guest during the parade who will be taking the salute during pass in review is Vice President Nixon. Our platoon will do the silent drill, so we don't have much time to get squared away. Also I didn't want to wait until late in the week to tell you, but the C.O. has ordered the Third Platoon back to Camp David this weekend to reinforce the First Platoon. Some of you may have made plans and they'll have to be changed."

"Sir, permission to speak to the Lieutenant!" shouted Lance Corporal Phillips from the rear rank of the platoon.

"Go ahead, Corporal."

"How long will this visit be, since we've just got back from there on Friday?"

"My guess is only for the weekend, Corporal. However we may be asked to relieve the First because they're scheduled to go on tour next week."

"When do we leave, sir?" came another question.

"The bus will be outside the main gate at 2300 hours on Friday, which will not give us much time considering the fact that the parade is over at 2200 hours.

"If there're no further questions, I will turn you over to Sergeant Kellerman and, in the meantime, I will do my best to get to know each and every one of you soon. Sergeant . . . ."

Kellerman, who picked and trained each member of the drill team, above all wanted his men to make a good impression on their new boss. And, after the weekend bringing Fergurson up to speed, the Sergeant believed that he was going to have a much closer relationship with this platoon leader than he had had with Captain Marcham, an officer for whom he had respect, but, in two years, was never close to. "Platoon—attention. Dress—right—dress."

Walking over to the first man of the first squad and peering down the front rank, and observing that each man was properly aligned to the one on either side, Kellerman, a Korean combat veteran who had the face of a man closer to his forties than late twenties, moved quickly to the rear-rank and repeated his observation.

Standing six paces in front of the middle squad of the platoon's three eight-man squads, he hollered, "Ready—front!" As if one, twenty-four left arms dropped to their sides.

Fergurson took several steps backwards. He wondered what initial impressions his men had of him. He wished he had spoken with more firmness and conviction in his voice. Nevertheless he felt that the ice was broken; they now had met one another.

From a distance the men appeared that they were clones, all except the four colored Marines, one of whom was in each of the first two squads and the others in the third. The fact that Negroes were stationed at Eighth and I was as much a surprise to Fergurson as his own transfer to the Marine Barracks, and he made a note to ask Sergeant Kellerman more about it.

"Okay, we'll go through the full drill routine for the Lieutenant, so let's shape up, look smart, and no screw ups or you've had it," barked the rugged and tanned Sergeant whose shoulders and waist gave him the look of a Washington Redskins fullback. "Forward—march!" he shouted, and at once the first rank of twelve moved off the concrete walk onto the lush green parade field that made up the inner sanctum of the barracks. Simultaneously with the step-off came a resounding smack as twelve left hands enclosed in finger-tight white gloves came up and grasped the middle of the M-1 rifles each Marine was now raising with his right hand. With the first rank two steps away, the second rank moved off and repeated the movement of arms done by the first rank.

The twenty-four Marines were now moving as if one to the center of the parade field. With the platoon commencing its routine, Kellerman joined Fergurson and they moved to the center of the parade field to take up a position that would be in the proximity of where Vice President Nixon would be viewing the parade on Friday evening. They observed with stone faces as the drill team moved their rifles to the right shoulder and executed a left face proceeding southward down the parade ground. For nine minutes neither man said a word; they watched in silence as the platoon carried out its precision and perfectly timed maneuvers.

Fergurson did not see his men reverse march and proceed in the opposite direction. Instead, his eyes were fixed on the barracks' two ceremonial cannons at the southerly end of the parade field.

"Sir, anything wrong?" the sergeant asked.

"No, not at all, Sergeant. It's just that an unusual sensation has come over me. However we had best get on with seeing if the men are ready for Friday. What are they doing now, Gunny?" Fergurson inquired.

"They're breaking off from the column and will reform into six groups of four, and then go through a rifle swapping routine, with all six groups doing the routine simultaneously."

"Kellerman, I've always wondered how they can perform as one, with no commands, scattered all over the field, tossing rifles in the air and to each other and yet rejoin in a single file."

Without taking his cold blue eyes off the group of four nearest him, Kellerman said, "Each routine is broken down and practiced separately until it's gotten perfect. When that occurs, it's added to the previous ones that have been done right. And, if you look closely at each man's face, you'll see that his lips are moving ever so slightly and, if you stood right next to him, you could hear him counting, with no count ever going over eight. That way, when the next routine begins, it is back to one. Just like dancers, I've been told."

"How long did it take them to learn it?"

"Oh, about three months, and from the time they were given the command, forward march, they started the count and when they finish, the whole thing takes ten or eleven minutes—they'll have had one hundred twenty or so separate count sequences," Kellerman explained, observing the platoon form one line of twenty-four directly in front of him.

"That is a sharp routine, Sergeant, and I'm impressed with the way they executed it. Will you dismiss the platoon and have them fall out at 1200 hours in Uniform Able; we have a MATS detail at 1400 hours at National. Oh, by the way, Sergeant, what is a MATS detail?"

"They should have told you, sir, but the Marines of Eighth and I make up a part of what is known as the Military District of Washington and we are called upon, together with units from the other branches of the services, to take part in ceremonies honoring the arrival and departure of dignitaries at Washington National and at Andrews Air Base. Most heads of state and other dignitaries are ferried into and out of Washington by the Military Air Transport Service. Can I ask who we are seeing in or out, sir? Is this the bigwig that the scuttlebutt is all about?"

"It's Deputy Premier Kozlov of the Soviet Union. He's arriving in Washington from New York. As for the rumor that is going around regarding a big detail—I heard it will be someone important, but who, I can't really tell you."

* * *

30

The second floor, enlisted Marines' living quarters, was a thirty foot wide, sixty-foot long room with a series of six double racks of bunks on either side of a six-foot wide aisle. A foot locker sat at the head of each bunk, and between each bunk stood a seven-foot high double-door wall locker containing all of the possessions of the members of the drill team platoon except for their rifles, which were neatly arranged in a rifle rack at the rear of the squadbay.

"Pass the brown polish, Arnold," Corporal Phillips shouted to his nearby bunk mate.

"Don't use it all up," Arnold replied, sitting on top of his foot locker wearing only shorts and T-shirt. He was holding a dress shoe in his left hand and using his right index finger, wrapped in a T-shirt, to make circles on the toe of the shoe. "I ain't got much left."

"When my D.I. said I was going to a 'spit and polish' outfit, I had no idea that I'd be spending my whole life at it," Phillips moaned, dipping his finger into the water contained in the cover of the Kiwi shoe polish can.

"You know," Arnold said, "we must spend two hours a day doing our shoes, brass, rifle slings, and caps and on top of that another four hours practicing the drill! Phillips, as much as I hate guard duty at Camp David, and especially the 4 to 8 watch in the morning, it sure is better than this chicken-shit stuff."

"Well, don't sweat it too much," Phillips said, "because I've got it on good authority that we're going to Camp David for a month."

"Do you know what for?"

"If you would clean your ears out once in a while you might be able to hear the scuttlebutt. Right now the word is that the King of England is coming over to the United States to visit with the 'Old Man.'"

"You know, Phillips, that you got to make lance corporal and I'm still a private just goes to show you how dumb the brass are around here."

"What do you mean?"

"Phillips, did it ever dawn on you that there ain't no King of England and that they haven't had no King for years?"

"So, I heard it wrong. So who do you think is coming? It's gotta be someone big otherwise why are we going to the mountain for a month?"

"My ears might be full of wax but I heard it is that little fat man from Russia. You know who I mean—Khrush . . . Khrushman or something like that. Hey guys, do you know that England now has a King—he was crowned by our own Lance Corporal Phillips."

"Shut up, you maggot!" Phillips snapped, pitching the remaining water in the Kiwi can at Arnold.

"Yeah," Arnold said. "I heard that the little fat guy who's the head guy of Russia is coming to Washington and Camp David in September, and the Secret Service wants a well-trained platoon to guard him and the 'Old Man.' So, if that's the case, why am I doing all this spit and polish bullshit?" His shoes now took on an almost mirror-reflective appearance.

* * *

"I see nothing is different here. They always pick on each other," Fergurson said as he and Kellerman stood outside the squadbay overhearing Arnold and Phillips.

"They just get hold of a rumor and work it over. It's their way of relaxing, sir," Kellerman said peering into the room, "which you should do, sir. You appeared tense outside—the men will be ready, don't you worry."

"It's not that, Sergeant, I'm sure they'll do just fine. You see, my older brother, Kevin Fergurson, was stationed here in the early fifties. Like you, he was a platoon sergeant of the First. His letters to us never described how beautiful a place this is. He did tell us that he was living next door to the Commandant of the Marine Corps and that his post, founded by Thomas Jefferson, was the oldest in the Marine Corps. But, you know, Sergeant, I was still in high school when Kevin was here and I got the impression that he was on some big base the size of Quantico, not a post that's only two blocks long and in the shadow of the Capitol building. Also Kev never told us about this drill."

"Well, I can see why, sir. This routine was added only a few years ago when the barracks started the Friday Evening Parade. I didn't realize you had a brother—and a sergeant—in the Marines, Lieutenant."

"Well, I don't talk about it much. Kevin meant a lot to me and it's probably because of him that I'm a Marine today. In his letters he always spoke so highly of his Marines, their training, motivation, and loyalty toward each other. From those letters, I wanted to enlist right out of high school. Instead he encouraged me to go to college and if I really wanted

32

to be a Marine to come in as an officer, so I joined the Platoon Leader's Class Program in college."

"Your brother must be a sergeant major by now, sir. Where's he stationed?"

"Oh, I should have told you. Kevin was with the First Battalion Seventh Marines during the withdrawal from the Chosin Reservoir and was killed while rescuing three of his wounded men."

"Oh, I'm sorry to hear that, sir."

"It was a long time ago. Commandant Shepherd personally gave our mom his Navy Cross medal."

"He must of been some hero, sir, to get the country's second highest medal for valor. You just have to be proud as hell, I'm sure."

"We are, Sergeant, and this assignment here at Eighth and I takes on special meaning for me. I now have the same feeling I had when I came here with my platoon in '56. And when our platoon goes out to Arlington Cemetery for burial details, for awhile, I'm sure, it is going to be difficult, so keep an eye on me, will you? Kevin is buried there."

"Count on it, sir. You'll be okay, and I certainly appreciate your telling me about your brother. If he were alive, he'd feel the same about you."

"Thanks, Sergeant. I'm not only proud to be with you and these men, it's an honor for me."

CHAPTER 6

President Eisenhower got up from his desk and walked over to the fireplace and said, "Bob, do you believe what Kozlov said regarding when Khrushchev wants to come?"

The immaculately tailored under secretary of state, Robert Murphy, watched his boss adjust the picture frame above the mantle and said, "I do, sir. He said its the August heat here in Washington."

"You wonder," the president asked, "why the White House staff was in such a hurry to hang this painting after all? And for God's sake, why here?"

Not wishing to become involved with the president's objection to the decorating, Murphy continued, "Kozlov said Khrushchev accepts your July 29 letter but that he doubted whether Washington at this time of year would agree with him and wishes to spend ten days here in mid-September."

The president, examining the painting titled *Spring Comes to the Farm,* muttered, "and the Butcher of Hungary comes to America. The reference to *The Butcher of Hungary* was in a New York paper's editorial yesterday. Did you hear what Bill Buckley is advocating? He wants to dump a red dye into the Hudson River to dramatize the cruelty and barbarism of the Russians."

The lanky assistant secretary was now on his feet and replied, "Buckley is only playing to the audience, sir. He'll never do that."

"Don't be surprised if he does; he's just nuts enough to do it."

Overhearing the president's comment as he entered the room, Jim Haggerty said, "Well, you did tell us, Mr. President, that the press would be frying us for the visit, and if it's not page one news everyday since you announced the visit last week, it's certainly close to it. And, of course, the Conservative press is reporting that we're playing up to the Liberals in Congress in order to placate them for our next round of nominations."

Turning toward Haggerty, the president said angrily, "That is pure and utter rubbish. If the press thinks for one minute that I or this administration will be crawling on our bellies up to the Hill in order to get my nominees through, that's pure trash, and I don't want to hear it." His face and bald head had now taken on the hue of the plush red carpet.

Haggerty watched his boss's complexion change and wished he had said nothing.

"Gentlemen, I'm not going to allow the Congress to use this visit by Khrushchev as a forum for posturing for some future gain. I've had it with that group."

"Mr. President," Murphy said, "Chris Herter and I feel that you're on the offensive with this visit. The press and, for that matter, the Congress has had not one germ of an idea on how to deal with the Soviets. Let's not allow any of them to get in your way."

"It's just that I don't trust that bunch on the Hill," the president said as he leaned on the back of the sofa. "Only two months ago we suffered our greatest loss when the Senate failed to confirm Lew Strauss for Secretary of Commerce. His confirmation defeat placed the democratic process at a low ebb in my book. A process that at times I wondered, as many of my predecessors often had, shouldn't it be our job to protect the American people from democracy."

The perennially red-faced Haggerty joined in and said, "They probably feel the same way, sir."

"Thanks a lot, Jim. I wondered if I weren't being paid back by the Senate for my immovable stance last year in not withdrawing the nomination of Claire Booth Luce for Ambassador."

Haggerty and Murphy knew exactly to what the president was referring but, not to get him anymore excited it was decided, almost by telepathy, to change the subject. Haggerty said, "Mr. Nixon's office has told us, sir, that he is anxious to see you when he gets back home."

"When will that be, Jim?" the president asked, appearing to have left behind the details of the previous discussions.

"The vice president lands at Andrews at noon tomorrow, sir, and we've already notified his staff that you would like to have him spend Saturday at Camp David with you and the secretary of state."

"Good!" the president responded. "Dick has done a terrific job on his visit to Moscow; his confrontations at the Kitchen Exhibitions with Khrushchev will go down in history. His knowledge in dealing with the

Soviet leader will be invaluable to us in planning for next month's visit. Will he be able to fly up to Camp David on Friday, Jim?"

"I don't believe so, Mr. President. His staff has told me that he's the honored guest at the Marine Barracks' Evening Parade on Friday. However he's expected to join you for breakfast Saturday morning."

"Well, if he's never seen the Marines' show, he'll certainly enjoy it. I did last year; very impressive and moving. Bob, bring me up to date on next week's trip to Europe?"

"We now have all three heads of state lined up to meet you starting one week from Thursday, Mr. President."

"You know, Bob, that I'm well aware of the deep concern that our European colleagues have regarding my scheduling a private summit with Mr. Khrushchev. And they're aware of the price Europe paid from previous summits held by America's wartime leader with the Soviets."

"They're not enthusiastically embracing your decision, neither publicly nor privately. To have Mr. Khrushchev visit the United States while so many European issues are still unresolved at the diplomatic level is risky. Also they have grave concerns because they believe you're not versed in foreign policy diplomacy and would be especially handicapped without Foster Dulles."

The president's face grew angrier as he snapped, "I've got more goddamned experience in dealing with heads of state than they all have together."

"I agree, sir, but I never expected Harold MacMillen to be so blunt in his criticism of the visit. Just where does he get off saying it is naive and stupid? And, for that matter, even DeGaulle feels we are acting in haste and should wait six months before meeting with Khrushchev. Mr. President, State feels that your going to Europe will be sufficient to reassure the Allies."

While the conversation had been going on, James Rowley, Chief of the White House Secret Service Detail, came into the Oval Office and stood as he always does to the left of the president's desk.

The square-jawed, rugged looking agent appeared more like a stevedore than an aide to the president. During his sixteen years as a Secret Service Agent, he had always done his homework in making sure the Secret Service White House Detail knew all there was to know about the place and the people the president would be encountering. However

Rowley had little patience for the people from State and even less when they interfered in his area.

Acknowledging his entrance with a nod, the president said, "Gentlemen, I've asked Jim to join us because he needs to hear our plans, and we need to hear and evaluate his concerns."

"Jim, don't be bashful," the president said. "I know there's something bothering you. If I'm not mistaken, it's the upcoming trip to Europe, isn't that it?"

"Not at all, sir," Rowley replied, "that part of your itinerary is in good shape. We have good dealings and arrangements with Scotland Yard and the French Sûreté, and in Bonn we have our own military police for crowd control. My concern, Mr. President, and I can speak for Chief Baughman also, is with the forthcoming visit by Mr. Khrushchev. The announcement of the visit has stirred up every right-wing organization in the country, not to mention those outside the States. He is not a very popular 'fella,' Mr. President, and much of the time that he'll be here the two of you will be together, day and night."

"Oh! You're overreacting, Jim," Haggerty said.

"Yeah, when was the last time the president had a guest here in Washington who heads up this country's enemy list?" Rowley snapped, his voice flat, his glance hostile.

Murphy lifted his giraffe-like body up from the over-stuffed chair and said, "It appears we are about to have to listen to an undocumented, unfounded, and premature security agency's reaction to the visit."

"Bob's got a point," Haggerty interrupted as he looked over the lip of his coffee cup.

Rowley moved his large frame closer to Murphy and, with his eyes taking on a menacing stare, said, "Mr. Murphy, when it comes to security, just butt out, if you please. In these matters, I'm in charge, not you or your people. And Jim, that goes for you too, I don't need advice on security from a reporter."

"Jesus," the president said, "how am I to deal with Khrushchev on world peace when I can't keep the peace with you three? Is this the way the Irish behave when they're together or is it just you three? Let's get on with what's worrying you, Jim."

"I'm sorry, gentlemen. It's been a hectic week," Rowley said as he walked back to his boss's desk.

"Jim," the president said, "no one wishes to minimize the logistics that are being heaped upon you and your men regarding the chairman's visit, but you must keep in mind that the results of this visit could have a strong impact on the future of peace."

"I don't doubt that for a minute, sir. I guess what really bothers me, Mr. President, is the fact that part of the visit will be held at Camp David."

"So much the better," Eisenhower said, "the place is as secure as Fort Knox and can be made more secure by adding additional Marines and agents. Isn't that so?"

"To a degree yes, it can be, sir. But our real concern is that we'll be sharing the security details as well as the other physical security precautions of Camp David with the KGB. Up to now we've been stalling the Soviet liaison officer in charge of the visit from obtaining the details of Camp David's layout, even to the point of turning down his request to visit the place."

"That must not be," the under secretary of state snapped. "You must give them your full cooperation, Jim. These people are suspicious enough and for us to be withholding our cooperation puts us in a terribly bad light and could have serious ramifications with the Soviets."

"I know that," Rowley said sarcastically.

"You should also know that yesterday Ambassador Thompson cabled from Moscow registering the KGB's complaint over the lack of cooperation they're receiving from us on the security precautions."

"I'm not the least bit concerned about giving the Soviets a tour of Camp David," the president interjected. "Jim, you'll want nothing less when I go to Khrushchev's Villa in November. However what does worry me is the comment you made earlier about radical groups and their potential for causing trouble. Can you be more specific?"

"The CIA and Hoover's people have provided us with intelligence reports that pinpoint a dozen or more groups that can be the source of trouble, Mr. President."

"Do we have any idea what these groups might be up to and what sort of disruptions they may have in mind?"

"Not yet; we're not worried about placard-holding demonstrators either here or at the U.N. Our concern with these groups is with a small core with roots in eastern Europe, in countries such as Lithuania, Latvia, Poland, and Hungary. They hold bitter resentment toward the Soviets in general and with Mr. Khrushchev specifically," Rowley said.

"I know what Jim is referring to, Mr. President," Murphy said, "State also follows the goings on of these groups. However we don't believe they poise any threat. They're vocal and demonstrative, but that's all. At the heart of their cause, of course, is the return to a free-Europe. They believe this Administration did not lift a finger in preventing the Soviets from going into Hungary three years ago."

Eisenhower got up from his desk and in an almost inaudible and halting voice said, "Bob, you more than anyone else should know, because you were there in Quebec—not in 1945 but in 1943—where the post-war plans for Europe were being drawn up. When the plans were presented to me I rejected them outright and wanted the Soviets stopped on the other side of Prague. But what were we to do for Hungary in '56? Start World War Three! We had no army nearby to get into that landlocked country, and NATO was useless. It would have been comparable to getting into Tibet. We did the best we could in a bad situation, and when it was over we brought thousands of their refugees into this country."

"And that is just my point, sir," Rowley interjected. "Within that large a group there can be those who still seek revenge, and this visit by Khrushchev could well set them off. We saw a little of this group's work when you were in New York last month. You remember, Mr. President, outside the Soviet Exhibition."

"Jim, I was there as well with Kozlov," Murphy said argumentatively, "and I would agree that they were a vociferous group, but that's all."

Rowley said, "What you saw, Bob, was the more mild-mannered groups representing the Assembly of Captive Nations. You didn't have contact with some of the more violent members of that group. My men and the New York City cops did. And it is that faction that keeps us up nights. We just don't have the resources to check out each one of them. And, for all we know, somewhere out there is a madman full of revenge and hate who feels he can get even and, by doing so, make a double score. You see, Mr. President, I have grave trepidations over the fact that both you and Mr. Khrushchev will be together."

"I appreciate your concern and I believe Jim and Bob do as well," the president said. "I'll have the Bureau give you all the help you need. In the meantime, I want full cooperation given to the Soviet security people. And, furthermore, I look forward to having you with me in Europe next week. Do you realize that this will be the first trip made by a president in a jet aircraft?"

CHAPTER 7

The Pelm farm was drenched in sunlight on this early August day. Laszlo felt good that he and Janos were getting caught up in their chores—especially putting on the pheasant shields. Getting them on early would insure a healthy crop come the fall. A warm feeling came over him as he worked alongside his brother-in-law. They were free and this was their farm, their birds.

Janos and Laszlo could put the shield on a bird in less then ten seconds with a minimum of discomfort to the pheasant. A time-consuming and tedious job but, nevertheless, most critical in raising pheasants.

Laszlo could sense from the banging and the erratic leg movements of the pheasant, its body jumping inside the cone, the short but sharp yell, together with the minute droplet of blood that indeed the pheasant was enduring some degree of pain. Laszlo knew that it was far less than the pain each bird could inflict on another through pecking.

"Mr. Smyth called this morning and said he'd be here the second week of September to pick up between a thousand and fifteen hundred jumbo hens," Janos said to his brother-in-law, who was moving feverishly placing the small plastic peeper on the struggling pheasant's nose.

As he watched Janos catch each bird with a fish net affixed to a four-foot pole, Laszlo said, "I hope we'll be ready for him, Janos, but all I can say from watching you is that it is amazing how quick you are in catching the birds. It still must be difficult without your fingers, and I wonder if much of what we do will ever get automated. There's so much labor involved."

"You must have been talking with Mr. Hoyt at the Wayside Country Store," Janos said, "because he brought up the same thing about dairy farming on Sunday after Mass."

"Laszlo—Janos—come quickly!" Hanna called from the porch of the farmhouse.

"What is it?—What is the matter?" Laszlo shouted back.

"Please, just drop what you're doing and come here and see this," she said holding a newspaper over her head.

Janos and Laszlo rushed out of the pheasant pens slamming shut the gate behind them and ran up the marble walk incline that led to the back porch of the house.

"What are you so excited about, Hanna," Laszlo asked out of breath. "What is it?"

Shaken, Hanna passed the newspaper to her husband and said, "Read this and you can see for yourself."

His arms around his sister and sweat pouring off his forehead, Janos asked, "What is it? What does it say?"

Trance-like, Laszlo said, "I don't believe it; tell me it can't be," and crumpled the paper within his hands.

"Laszlo, read me what it says," Janos repeated.

Laszlo uncrumpled the newspaper and, using both hands, smoothed out the page and in a halting voice started to read the news item:

James Haggerty, President Eisenhower's press secretary, announced today that the president has extended an invitation to Chairman Nikita Khrushchev of the Soviet Union to visit the United States next month. The Soviet Leader, through U.S. Ambassador Thompson, has accepted the invitation. The visit, the first by any Soviet Head of State, will be for ten days starting with the Premier's arrival on September 15 at Andrews Air Force Base in Washington. Mr. Khrushchev will stay at the Blair House directly across from the White House where he and the president will conduct talks during the first and second day of the visit, after which the Soviet leader, accompanied by Ambassador Lodge, will visit a steel mill and machine factory in Pittsburgh, a farm in Iowa, an IBM plant in California, as well as a movie studio in Hollywood. After Mr. Khrushchev's six-day tour of the country, he and the president will fly to Camp David on September 24 to spend the weekend discussing an agenda of issues that has been prepared jointly by our two governments.

Sweat dropped from Laszlo's face onto the pages of the out-stretched newspaper. "How in God's name could President Eisenhower do this to us?" Laszlo whispered. "He knows that Khrushchev was behind the nightmare in Budapest."

Moving toward her husband and placing her hands on his broad shoulders in an attempt to comfort him, Hanna said, "What can we do? The four of us are just a small voice in the wilderness. It seems like the more time that goes by since the revolution, the more the world is willing to believe that it never happened. Janos, you are older and wiser than all of us. What can we do? How is this happening to us after all these years? Has the world truly forgotten 1956?"

Janos, his round face partially concealed with dirt and never one to say much, was dismayed to see tears from his brother-in-law, his trusted friend, and leader. This was a man he had lived with for nine days and nights during the revolution. Laszlo was someone he could never be, a person who led others in attacking tanks with rocks and Molotov cocktails. "The world must be made to realize that it did happen, it did happen," Janos repeated.

"How do we enlighten the world to what we witnessed?" Hanna said, pulling away from her husband and lifting her apron up to his face. "Who would listen?" she asked. "Last month refugees from Hungary and even from Poland followed Premier Kozlov to every place he went. Don't you remember the thousands who were outside the Communist Exhibitions in New York? They even went so far as to jeer at President Eisenhower for having come to New York to be with the Russian."

Janos said, "Maybe they should not have protested in front of the president. He could have been embarrassed, resented it, and is now getting even with us."

Hanna sat down alongside Laszlo and held both of his hands and said, "No! No! Mr. Eisenhower is not spiteful and would never set up this visit just to get back at a few thousand protesters. No, I don't believe it."

Nina had heard Hanna's cry and had joined the others on the porch, appearing every bit the peasant woman as she was in her homeland. The stocky woman, wearing an oversized, pastel-colored dress and with unkempt hair, said, "I say the president knew what took place. He had to know."

"Know what, Nina?" Janos asked his wife.

"Everyone knew that Prime Minister Nagy had gotten the Russians to agree to take their armies out of Hungary. Europe and America knew that Nagy was looking for closer ties with them and this enraged Khrushchev. Don't be an idiot, Hanna, they all knew what happened. And they were aware of how Khrushchev deceived Nagy and Cardinal Mindszenty. That Russian swine is no fool. Eisenhower and the leaders of Europe are the fools. To think that Khrushchev wants peace when he tricked us so badly—does President Eisenhower think he won't do it to him?"

"Nina, you're bitter," Hanna said, clutching her hands. "Maybe this visit can help us? Maybe we can get the president to assist us to get Uncle Joseph and Mama Pelm out of Hungary."

Laszlo, who had just sat quietly and reflectively while the women spoke, used his large and muscular hands to raise himself from the porch step, turned to his wife and said, "Hanna, why do you think so foolishly? They would never let Uncle Joseph out. He was involved in all the meetings and negotiations. They hunted him down for days. And, if it wasn't for Janos and me hiding him in dark alleys and sleeping under bridges night after night, he never would have gotten to the American Legation at all."

"My dear, I know that, we all know that," Hanna said. "But why give up hope? That was nearly three years ago; changes are taking place, and we can't ignore them."

"Hanna, I love you dearly," Laszlo said, shaking the mud from his baggy, flannel shirt, "but I agree with Nina. I, for one, will not let time or events erase what has taken place, no matter how much change occurs. Don't ever ask me to forget. When we were making our way to freedom across Yugoslavia, they took my father to Felsopeteny Prison and shot him. That you don't forget, neither do you forgive them. I don't care what your faith tells you."

Janos said, "Your bitterness, Laszlo, is eating away at you. I told you this before, even before we knew that Khrushchev was coming here. Maybe we don't have to feel that we are alone. America has a large Hungarian and Polish community in New York, Chicago, and Philadelphia. These groups could be helpful. The president is up for re-election shortly and will want to get these people to vote for him, no?"

"No, Janos," Laszlo said, "Mr. Eisenhower does not worry about being elected. He can only be president twice and he's not going to be president anymore."

"Everyone, please listen," Hanna pleaded as she walked to the center of the porch. "We keep blaming the president. If you were in church last month you would have heard the priest read the president's Captive Nation's Proclamation."

"Proclaiming what, Hanna," Nina said sarcastically, "that the Soviets have taken full control of half the world? Was that it?"

"No, Nina, not at all," Hanna snapped. "The president and Congress approved that each year, the third week of July, will always be a week of prayer for the people held behind the Iron Curtain."

Janos said, "Good, Hanna, good. You see, Laszlo, this just didn't happen by itself. The Assembly of Captive Nations worked long and hard to get the government to pass the Proclamation. And we should work with them, they can do more than we can."

As he paced back and forth on the porch, Laszlo said, "Let's not be so naive. Something forceful must be done and done soon, not just words in a proclamation. We four are going to make it happen. Our people in this country must have new leadership, a new cause to go after."

"Laszlo, we must give the Assembly a chance," Hanna pleaded. "They're just now beginning to proclaim, to call attention. No one's forgotten."

"The free world has totally forgotten what happened to Prime Minister Nagy," Laszlo said angrily. "Khrushchev gave him safe passage to Yugoslavia but had him executed after that trumped-up trial." His voice was strained and made his listeners uneasy as they watched him. "We must never allow the memory of General Pal Maleter to be forgotten, not only his role in the revolt but for the deception and trickery the bastards did. When will the Americans stop bending to the Communists? Eisenhower has done it to us again as he did in 1945 . . . ."

"Laszlo, you keep saying how bad President Eisenhower has been," Hanna said, as she slowly walked toward the kitchen door. "I'm getting nowhere by talking to you. I'm going to make lunch and maybe you'll feel better. Nina, would you help me, and we'll let them get back to work."

"Laszlo," Janos said quietly, "we must get back to putting the peepers on; we still have fifty or sixty more to do. We could lose ten or fifteen by morning from pecking if we don't finish."

The two men stepped down from the porch and walked in silence toward the pens some fifty yards away. Laszlo pondered how in only a few minutes his whole life had been changed. Minutes before he was enjoying his work with Janos, but his reaction to the newspaper had altered that world forever. He felt that it was useless to continue talking about what must be done.

"They can't hear us now, Janos," Laszlo whispered. "I'm going to do something, Janos, and I'm going to do it alone. You must promise me that you won't tell Nina or Hanna. Yes?"

"Laszlo, what are you talking about? You sound secretive and you frighten me when you talk that way."

"I don't have much time, Janos, but I know I can count on you. I just don't want the women to be upset and to worry. And you can take care of the birds by yourself. Don't you agree?"

"Laszlo, what do you mean I can take care of the birds? I need you. Mr. Smyth will be here soon."

"My dear friend, have you ever looked up at these mountains? They are like huge arms reaching out and hugging the farm, protecting all of us. And if you look closely, Janos, you can see the trees at the summit begin to change their color from the dark, lush summer green to orange, red, and yellow. But it is now time that I slip away from their embrace."

Less educated and bewildered, Janos said nothing but moved slowly and quietly into the pens. He bent over and picked up his pole net. He began to chase after the birds. He swung wildly and aimlessly at the scurrying pheasants. All along he wondered, "What in God's name is Laszlo going to do—slip away to where?"

48

CHAPTER 8

Vice President Nixon said to Commandant Pate, "I have nothing but praise, General, for the way these units carried out the parade." They stood at the center walk at Eighth and I returning the salute as the last platoon marched in front of them.

"Thank you, sir," Pate said.

"It's good to be back home after a week in the Soviet Union, and what a stirring reception this is," Mr. Nixon said as he put his hat back on. "I have seen many military ceremonies, General, but the music, the drill team's precision marching, the lighting, everything you get to witness here is a rethinking of how much we owe to our young people in the military. Pat and I ask that you pass on to your officers and men our thanks for a splendid evening. John Philip Sousa would be proud of his Marines."

"I certainly will pass on those words, Mr. Vice President," General Pate said, "and our thanks to you and Mrs. Nixon for being our guests tonight. I'm sure you both must be exhausted."

* * *

"All right, we fall-out in ten minutes, so move it," Sergeant Kellerman shouted to his platoon as they hurriedly got out of their Dress Blues and into their green field dress and black boots.

"Ten minutes . . . no shit!" Arnold said as he popped open his blue tunic.

Kellerman moved up and down the aisle of the squadbay, tapping his swagger stick on the ends of each rack and said, "Make sure you've got at least two weeks' supply of skivees and socks as well as utilities. We could be on the Hill for a month, so I don't want to hear any bitching that anyone forgot something."

The quick change from ceremonial dressed Marines to battle-dressed ones took all of the allotted time but not a minute more. Kellerman shut off the lights in the squadbay as Corporal Phillips, the last man out, rushed by him.

Assembling in front of their building's parking lot on this moonless night were the twenty-four Marines who, only an hour before, had been demonstrating their drill maneuvers for Vice President Nixon. Each man was watching over his sea bag and clutching his M-1 rifle, silently waiting for the Marine Corps bus to roll through the main gate so they could board and get some sleep during the three-hour ride to Camp David.

The fifty passenger, green GMC bus with the word "Marines" painted in white on both sides rolled quietly through downtown Washington's Pennsylvania Avenue, passed the Treasury Building and White House, its driver maneuvering it with precision through the quiet streets that were now free of their daytime hustle.

At precisely 2245 hours, it had picked up its cargo at the Barracks, and at 2300 hours, the platoon was asleep, except for Fergurson and Kellerman.

Staring out the window at the sprawling Bethesda Naval Medical Center, Fergurson began to reflect on the events of the night and how proud his immigrant parents would have been had they seen their son leading his platoon before the Vice President. In his mind he began drafting his next letter home: "Mom, you just can't imagine the majesty of the parade. It's been three hours since I gave my platoon their initial and only command . . . and I'm still having goose bumps. The way they stepped off, turned, exchanged rifles, with their glistening chrome bayonets fixed on the end, has to be one of the finest ten minute pieces of choreographic movements performed anywhere. The manner by which the spotlights from up in the ramparts are used to search out and illuminate, at exactly the right moment, the Marine who had just twirled his rifle in the air, the bugler playing taps or the drum major in his scarlet and gold jacket bringing his mace up to lead off the Marine band was thrilling and not without suspense. I guess that's what it is that holds you, the mystery, the anticipation, the precision of all the different forms working as one. You and Pop just have to come here and see it for yourselves."

Fergurson turned his head to see if Kellerman, who was sitting next to him up front in the bus, had fallen off to sleep.

"No, I know what you're thinking. I'm not asleep yet, sir," Kellerman said, seeing the Lieutenant glance at him. "But you better get some shut eye; it'll be awhile before we get to Camp David."

"How can you possibly sleep?"

"What'd you mean, sir? It's easy."

"Sergeant, we've just put on one of the most splendid and riveting drill performances imaginable, and before Vice President Nixon, and now we're on our way to Camp David. How can you go to sleep?"

"You'll get used to it, sir. Takes a while."

"I hope not, at least not soon," Fergurson said with a sense of anticipation in his voice, and his wide-opened eyes now focused on the bus's windshield.

"Forgive me, sir, but you look like a kid going on his first date."

"Tell me about Camp David," Fergurson said to his sleepy Sergeant. "I got some information the other night, but not much on the layout."

Kellerman pushed himself up in the seat and said, "I can see that you're not one bit interested in getting any sack time, and as long as you're not, I won't get any."

"I'm sorry, Sergeant. It's just that I'm full of anticipation. Can you blame me?"

"No, I guess not, sir. I can tell you a little about the place, but we have to speak softly; the driver may not have full clearance. The Camp's at nineteen hundred foot elevation, the highest point on Mt. Catoctin. It's about a hundred fifty acres in size, and it's part of the State Park. We've got to go through the Park road to get to it. It's not very big at all. My first time there I was surprised at just how simple the place was, and still is, considering who uses it."

"That doesn't surprise me," Fergurson said. "President Roosevelt wanted it that way when he first came here in April of '42. He told his Secret Service Chief, Mike Reilly, that if he spent more than ten grand to fix it up, he didn't want it. But that's back when it was called Shangri-La."

Kellerman turned toward Fergurson and said, "Where did that name come from? I've always thought of it as Camp David—you know, after President Eisenhower's grandson."

"No, Roosevelt got the name from James Hilton's book *Lost Horizon,* and Eisenhower felt the name was too rich for him. So in '53 he renamed it after his father."

"How do you know this, Lieutenant?"

"The other night I went to the library and did some research on the place. It appears that back in the early days of World War II, the Secret Service told Roosevelt he could no longer go sailing the Chesapeake, because the German subs were off the coast. And so the Secret Service had to find a place for the president to scoot off to on weekends . . . and, I might add, in the event that Washington came under attack."

"But why way the hell up here? Why not someplace closer to D.C.?" Kellerman asked, becoming interested in the Lieutenant's knowledge.

"Actually, this was the closest. There were a couple of places in Virginia, but too far and too expensive. This place was secluded, high up, and within a two-hour drive. They didn't say anything about how high or that it was in a State park."

"Did you discover how it was that Eighth and I got to become involved?"

"I didn't see a whole lot on that. Secret Service Agent Reilly wanted Marines. A hundred and fifty were sent there. They lived in tents and had a dozen patrol dogs as well."

"That's a hell of a lot more than we go with now . . . and dogs!"

"And you know something else—the Marines then were about thirty-five to forty years old, not seventeen and eighteen year olds like we've got in the back here—which reminds me, let me see how they're doing."

The lighted shade tree boulevard of Bethesda quickly gave way to open countryside as the bus made its way up Route 240 towards Frederick. The blackness of the late hour was momentarily interrupted by porch lamps on a farm house or an all-night filling station. As the bus maneuvered around the curves, its headlights illuminated farm tractors and wagons at rest for the night, waiting for another day's work.

"There isn't one of them awake; they're all crapped out," Fergurson whispered, gently slipping back into his seat.

"They know all too well that it'll be up and at it at the break of dawn," Kellerman said. "So they grab their shut eye anytime and anyplace."

"Why is it that the Negro Marines don't ever separate? I've noticed that they stay close to one another—here, the mess hall, parade field, practice . . . ."

"I guess it makes them feel more secure. There's no question that they're accepted—Christ, they're tops when it comes to marching."

"I've been meaning to ask you; when did Negro Marines begin to be stationed at Eighth and I? When I came here from Basic School during the summer of '56, I didn't see any colored Marines."

Keeping his voice low, Kellerman said, "Rumor has it that when Prince Philip of England was at the Barracks to see a parade back in the fall of '57, he asked the Commandant why there weren't colored Marines in the ranks. After that visit, our four Negro Marines were sent up from Parris Island. And so, those guys back there, Lieutenant, are the first Negroes ever to be stationed here in over a hundred and fifty years."

"How have they fitted in?"

"They do well, just as good as the white guys. But, like you've just said, they stay close to each other. I don't know if you're aware of this, but the four of them will have to stay on the bus in Frederick when we go for chow."

"No, I'm not. Why's that?"

"We're below the Mason-Dixon line, sir. That doesn't mean shit to them, but it does to people down here, and these food places don't take the coloreds in, whether they're Marines heading to Camp David to guard the president or not. Also the same thing happens when we put the Drill on in the South. The Negroes are replaced with four whites from the First or Second platoon. We can't perform in public below Virginia with a mixed group."

"I can't believe that this type of segregation is still in existence," Fergurson said with contempt. "It's intolerable; just a hundred miles south of New York and these conditions exist! They must feel awful, knowing they could be asked to put their lives on the line but they can't go into a diner for a sandwich."

"That's the way it is, and has been, ever since they came aboard."

"When Captain Marchem was in charge, what did he do?"

"He did shit, sir. He accepted it and had the guys bring food back on board for them."

"How about the First and Second?"

"We're the only platoon who's got Negroes and, sir, you should know that Captain Marchem was raised in the South, so he just took it for granted."

"Pure rubbish, I can assure you, Sergeant. Things will be different! For one, we're not stopping at any restaurant that only feeds some of my men. If that means we go right through to Camp David, so be it!"

"By the time we get to the Hill, sir, the men will be pretty hungry."

"I'm aware of that, and that's why we'll get the mess hall opened, and I don't give a rat's ass if it is 0200 hours—it will be opened up for my platoon!"

Frederick, Maryland, came and went. The driver was ordered by Fergurson not to stop. The bus continued on, making its way up the narrow and twisting Route 15 toward the Village of Thurmont. Kellerman had a good feeling; his young platoon leader was his kind of officer.

The bus worked its way through Thurmont's main street and on to the State Park's circuitous mountain road that led to the Camp David access road.

* * *

At the doorway of the Camp David gatehouse and silhouetted by the small overhead lamp was a large-framed man dressed in a grey suit and yellow polka dot tie. Standing inside was a Marine sentry. The civilian was holding a cigarette and, in his left hand, a small radio. Secret Service Agent James Rowley had stood at this gatehouse spot many times before, and he had made it a point to always be at the Camp's main gate when President Eisenhower was aboard.

"Get the men on their feet, Sergeant," commanded Fergurson to his sleepy-eyed Sergeant.

"Where the hell are we, sir?" inquired the groggy Sergeant.

"Camp David."

CHAPTER 9

The white, clapboard Marine squad bay at Camp David was encircled by fifty-foot hemlocks and pine trees, a trail of white smoke exiting its stone-faced chimney. The building's Franklin woodstove was providing warmth to the sleeping Marines of the Third Platoon.

At 0620 on Saturday, the peace and quiet that prevailed was shattered by Sergeant Kellerman. He pushed open the squad bay door and shouted, "Condition Orange! Condition Orange! First and Second squads to the pad! Move it, move it!"

"What the hell is going on, Sarge?" yawned Corporal Phillips. "Shit, we just got in the rack a couple hours ago."

"What is it, Sergeant?" Lieutenant Fergurson said, running over to the squad bay door and pulling up his trousers at the same time.

"Sir, Marine One has just radioed in that they're fifteen minutes out and have the Vice President on board."

"Jesus! What the hell am I supposed to do? I haven't even toured the place yet!"

"Lieutenant," Kellerman said, "just stick close to me and the men. Let's go! Let's go! Now!" the Sergeant ordered the three squads of Marines who were tripping into their fatigues.

"Sarge," PFC Arnold asked groggily, "got time to clean up?"

"You can brush your teeth and wipe your ass later, but now listen up so you know whose doing what. Third squad, you're in reserve, so stand by here in the area. Second squad, you're on the perimeter. First, the fire rescue team. Any questions?" Not waiting for any, he said, "Let's go."

As the squads passed by him at the door, Kellerman handed each man three eight-round clips of ammunition. Once outside Fergurson watched as Kellerman counted heads. Taking his lead from his NCO, he joined Kellerman at the front of the formation as they moved on a run down the winding footpath, through the intersection to the path that led to the president's cabin. Two minutes later, they were at the Camp's main road. They crossed near the main gatehouse where a Marine sentry was standing with a Secret Service agent. The Marines took up their positions at the Camp's helicopter landing area located several hundred feet beyond the gatehouse.

"Where will the chopper land, Sergeant?" Fergurson asked. "And what are the men's orders?"

Sergeant Kellerman, watching his men, responded: "The 'bird' will land just behind second base, sir. It'll kick up a good bit of dust even after the men have laid water on the infield. You see, this landing area is also used by the Camp as a softball field."

As the squads moved out onto the ballfield, Fergurson watched the First squad pick up portable fire extinguishers and pull out a three-inch fire hose connected to a stanchion near the dugout. Off in the distance, near the far side of the outfield, he could see the Second squad take up sentry positions between the edge of the outfield and the inner chainlink fence, at all times facing away from the field and standing at the ready two hundred feet from each other.

"Eagle Nest, this is Marine One." The pilot's garbled voice came over the ground amplifier located next to where Fergurson and Kellerman were standing. "Request permission to land. Over."

"Marine One, this is Eagle Nest. Permission granted. Wind velocity ten knots, west/northwest. Over."

"Roger, Eagle Nest. We're coming in. Over and out."

"Who's in communications with the pilot, Sergeant?" Fergurson inquired. "And where's the helicopter?"

"Army Warrant Officer Staly, sir. He's in the dugout near first base. The 'bird' is just below the hill, not far from the Camp's west gate. The pilot keeps it below the tree line on the west slope until he gets clearance to land. That's because the helicopter becomes a target for anyone with a rocket launcher or a high-powered rifle who just might be waiting in the woods."

"Has that ever happened?" Fergurson asked as he scanned the tree line in search of Marine One.

"No, thank God. Here comes the 'Old Man,' sir. He just loves to drive a Jeep when he's up here," Kellerman said.

The gray Jeep created a trail of dust as it shot down the dirt road leading from the Camp's main road. Its driver was the President of the

United States. Sitting next to him was his Secretary of State, Christian Herter, and in the rear of the Jeep holding on were James Rowley of the Secret Service and Commander Nicholson, the Camp's Commander.

"Sergeant, hit me to let me know I'm really here!" Fergurson whispered excitedly. "Jesus, the president is a hundred feet from us!"

"You'll get used to it, sir," Kellerman said wryly, "it gets to be routine after a while." As the Jeep roared by them they came to attention and rendered a snappy salute.

The president, wearing a white sweater, brown slacks, and a golf cap, returned the salute and brought the Navy Jeep to a jerky halt with Rowley and Nicholson doing all they could so as not to wind up in his lap.

Standing at ease while the president and his party got out of the Jeep, Kellerman leaned over to Fergurson and said, "Here she comes."

All sound was drowned out by the roar of the revolving blade and single engine of Marine One as it rose above the trees from the direction of right field.

The helicopter loomed large as it came in to land. Painted white on top and green on bottom, the VH-34D Sikorsky was the latest in vertical takeoff aircraft. With large white letters spelling out the word "Marines" painted on both sides and in smaller letters the number "147191," the aircraft was one of two that was part of HMX-1, the Marine unit stationed in Quantico.

Instantly after the chopper was safely on the field, Corporal Phillips placed his fire extinguisher on the ground and ran to the helicopter's side door, using his left arm to shield his eyes from the blowing dust. With the blade of the chopper rotating at a slow idle, Phillips slid back the door and set the steps and looked up at the vice president who was anxiously waiting to get off the aircraft.

"Welcome home, Dick," the president called as the vice president descended the steps to the field.

"It's good to be back, Mr. President," Nixon said as both men moved over to the Jeep. "Governor, how are you this morning?" Nixon greeted the Secretary of State, who still preferred to be called by the title of his former office.

"Just fine, sir. The president and I are anxious to hear about your trip. I'm sure you must have a lot to tell us about Mr. Khrushchev."

"Sorry, Dick, that you had to get up here so soon after your coming home," Eisenhower said. "I hope Pat forgives me, but I leave for Europe in a couple of days and your briefing will be invaluable to my discussions with our allies."

"Perfectly all right, sir," Nixon said, climbing into the Jeep with the president at the wheel.

"And now let's get you some breakfast, Dick, providing, of course, I don't put this contraption into a ditch."

The president led the Jeep caravan with Commander Nicholson's Jeep following closely, carrying Rowley and two other agents.

As the Jeeps roared away, creating a dust storm in their trail, Kellerman said, "What we do now, sir, is to post a two-man guard around the chopper for as long as it's here."

Bewildered and appearing lost, Fergurson said, "Go ahead, Sergeant. At the speed in which things are happening, I would like that tour right after chow."

"Corporal Phillips," Kellerman barked, "have the squads secure and set up the guard detail for the 'bird.' I'll be taking the Lieutenant on a tour, and we'll be back in the area by 1100 hours."

* * *

"Well, you've certainly had a great deal of work done at Aspen since I was here last year, Mr. President," Nixon said.

"Yes. I had the Navy bring the place up to more modern accommodations. At the same time we have kept the rustic nature of the house and the cabins."

"Mr. President, breakfast is on the terrace," James Rowley said. "Can I help you, Mr. Secretary?" he asked the secretary of state, who seemed to be having trouble adjusting his crutches as he rose up from the sofa.

"No, I'll be fine, Jim. But thanks," the secretary said, moving slowly toward the living room's sliding doors that opened onto the stone decked terrace fifteen feet above the three-hole putting green.

The morning sun lit up the terrace that surrounded the back of Aspen Lodge and provided a feeling of warmth to offset the cool mountain air and morning dampness.

The Filipino staff had set the wrought iron table for breakfast. At the table covered with a white table cloth and five place settings, the four men waited to sit down until the secretary of state was made comfortable.

The president said, "Sit here, Dick, and tell us what is it that we can expect of Khrushchev. What were your impressions of him?"

Adjusting the white napkin on his lap, Nixon said, "It did not take me long to see why this man destroyed Bulganin. Khrushchev can be tenacious and cajoling almost in the same discussion if not in the same breath. He does not cling to ideology but, clearly, to power. Frankly, Mr. President, he gives you the impression that he envisions his country to be stronger than we are and was quick to remind me that since he came into office more of the third-world countries are moving to accept the hand of socialism."

Herter placed his cup into its saucer and said, "He sounds like a pure demagogue."

"On the contrary, Chris. He's no raving demagogue; he is well versed on the issues. He makes his points well and he can be convincing, especially when he twists certain facts about a particular issue to suit his own cause. Incidentally Khrushchev has absolutely no second thoughts or shows any remorse with regard to the events that took place in Hungary. Matter of fact, when I approached him on this during our so-called kitchen debate, he charged right back and told me it was an internal affair and not ours to worry about."

Interrupting, Eisenhower said, "Well, that's no different than the way he behaved in Geneva, but he appears to have gained more self-confidence—or arrogance."

"Please excuse my language," Nixon said as he nibbled on his toasted bread, "but he can clearly piss you off. He reminded me of how he did not interfere when we sent troops to Little Rock two years ago so some Negro children could go to an all-white school. I told him I failed to see how that situation stacks up against the invasion of Hungary. Nevertheless this is the type of antagonist we're faced with."

The secretary of state said, "Well, in a way we do have a bit of time. You might not be aware of his itinerary, Dick, but when Khrushchev comes here, he'll be leaving for a six-day tour of the States."

"Well, that does give us some time to prepare," Nixon said. "By the way, Jim, has the press lightened up at all?"

"Not much has changed since you left, sir," Haggerty said. "There has been no let up by the right-wing press in their condemnation of the invitation. And, by the same token, the liberal press prints every single comment muttered, no matter from whence it comes, and it just galls me to see this type of reporting. Take the *New York Times* as an example. They reported that our Allies said that 'we have a sterile and unimaginative foreign policy'."

Grinning, the president said, "Well, of all people, Jim, you, a former correspondent for the *Trib,* should not be so thin-skinned when it comes to reading what is said in print by our allies. We all know that they're playing up to their own constituencies, as we do."

"Nevertheless," Haggerty said, "I'm concerned with a story in the *Times* about a letter from MacMillian. The Prime Minister believes the French, Germans, and his country are not being asked for their advice or allowed to share their concerns. In other words, they can't 'touch the wheel' was the way the PM put it."

Finishing his breakfast, Herter said, "More the reason for the president to visit the Allies. We're sure that once we share with them what it is we hope to accomplish with the Khrushchev visit they'll have far less concern."

The breakfast meeting discussion continued for another hour as the Filipino waiters saw that there was no interruption to the flow of coffee. All were held captivated by Nixon's summary of his encounter with Khrushchev at the kitchen display in the Moscow Exhibition Hall. Eisenhower was seen as being especially pleased with his vice president's visit, and said, "I need your advice in connection with my forthcoming trip, not to mention Khrushchev's visit as well. And what I would like to do is to have you join me for lunch at the farm so we can continue. Why don't you all plan to drive down with me? I understand Mamie will be there and later we can lunch together. So enjoy the rest of the morning going for a walk. As you can see, the trees up here are changing color and it sure is a magnificent sight, one not to be missed. In the meantime, I'll get on with signing these bills. The wheels of government must not stop. There's a domestic side to this job as well as a foreign one."

Mike Rowley did not miss a word that was said at the breakfast table, nor did the president miss seeing the concern on his bodyguard's face as the Secret Service agent approached the table, almost on cue, to help Mr. Herter from his chair.

Having stood several yards from the table and hearing all that was said, Rowley felt that these men had their own agenda and in no way were concerned about security. He wondered if Haggerty had read Dana Schmidt's column in the same *New York Times* describing how security officials were squarely facing the danger of an attempt to assassinate Khrushchev.

* * *

Laszlo, his hands gripping the wheel of his car, looked to his right and saw the sign "Thurmont's Auto and Truck Repairs." He swung his car into the station and pulled alongside the gas pumps. He got out of his car and walked over to the office. The white-haired man dressed in striped overalls was drinking a cup of coffee. Laszlo said, "Good morning, can you give me three dollars of gas?"

The old man nodded, picked up his oil rag, and went out to Laszlo's car. Laszlo looked around the office and saw a box marked "For Tourists." He picked up a flyer from the box and read the notice.

The word "Thurmont" in German means "Gateway to the Mountains." Thurmont village is nestled at the foot of the Catoctin range of the Blue Ridge Mountains. The quaint village played a leading role in the Revolutionary War and also during the Civil War. From its vast deposits of iron ore came the armor used in both wars. The town's proximity to Washington, D.C., and Baltimore provided the town with a new economy for its three thousand inhabitants. In April of 1942, its importance took on a new meaning when it became the bedroom and feeding station for hundreds of news people from around the world.

Laszlo folded the sheet of paper and stuffed it in his shirt pocket. He joined the old man at the pumps. "Do you always have this many people in the village?" Laszlo asked the white-haired attendant who was filling his car with gasoline.

"Not always," the old man replied. "Papers say the president is on the mountain for the weekend." He turned and replaced the hose back in its cradle. "I see from your car tags that you are from out of state—Vermont, is it?"

"Yes, I'm a farmer and I'm here to look into starting a farm in this valley." Not wanting to seem unsociable, Laszlo continued, "From what I've seen so far, you have many dairy farms and the soil is far less rocky than that in Vermont."

"Well, for years me and my family milked many a cow, got out of it a few years ago—no money, too many hours, no help, and too much red tape."

Not wanting to hear the old man ramble on about dairy farming, Laszlo asked, "Oh, so it's when the president is here that the population swells, is that so?"

"Yep, and you should of been here around daybreak; all kinds of noise from those helicopters. Radio said a little while ago that Nixon went up to visit with the president. So, with both of them big shots on the mountain, that just brings out all the people and these press guys and their newsreels."

Laszlo found the old man's remarks beneficial. With the president at Camp David, the Village of Thurmont becomes inundated with press personnel, most of whom are strangers to the local people. What could be a better source of cover for him next month when an even greater number of press people, especially foreign journalists, would be infiltrating the area?

His three hundred mile journey from Vermont to Thurmont had been tiring. His thoughts had been partially occupied with nursing his six-year-old Chevrolet Coupe along the way, but most of the time he kept asking himself if he had been too impetuous. Should he have stayed at the farm and thought out what he was going to do when he got to Thurmont? What was it that he wanted to know? The long and monotonous drive south down the New Jersey Turnpike and then west across what seemed to be an endless road—the Pennsylvania Turnpike—had indeed provided him with the solitude that he had needed. Early in the morning, almost at daybreak, as he crossed into Northern Maryland, his plan began to crystalize. He had formulated in his mind a series of goals he would want to accomplish on this initial visit to Thurmont.

However Laszlo's concern regarding the automobile's ability to endure the journey had not erased the memory of his departure. He felt that the reasons he had given Janos for leaving fell on deaf ears. However he had hoped that when Janos told the girls he would be convincing. Laszlo was off to Pennsylvania to see if additional buyers could be found for their pheasants and in doing so he would be away for a while.

* * *

"We can take that tour of the Camp anytime you're ready, sir," Sergeant Kellerman said to Fergurson, who was sitting at his desk in the officer's quarters studying a topographical map of Camp David.

"Before I came in, Sergeant, I received word that the president, Mr. Nixon, and the rest of the president's guests have just cleared the main gate and are driving down to Gettysburg."

"Lieutenant, so you know, the two mile road from here down the mountain to Thurmont crosses several mountain streams, and whenever the president or his family comes up or leaves Camp David by car, we send out a detail in advance."

"What does the detail do?" Fergurson asked, pushing the maps to one side.

"They inspect the bridges near each stream crossing for explosives. We then post a sentry in the woods within eyesight of the bridge to maintain cover until the president has crossed. Matter of fact, I can show the bridges to you on this map—here, here, and the other two."

"Looks like they go almost down to the ranger station," Fergurson said.

"Almost, sir. The station is a quarter mile on down the road from the last bridge."

"Well then before we go on the tour let's make sure all the bridge guards have been picked up. For that matter, we can requisition a truck and you and I will do the pick up. That way I can get a better idea of the security measures and also look over the terrain."

* * *

The gas station attendant said, "Here they come now, mister, and you better look quick because when they come through town they don't stop for nothing; there ain't no speed limit as far as they're concerned."

"Who's coming? I don't see a thing," Laszlo said as he placed his change in his pocket.

"Look up there—the six or seven black cars," the old man said, pointing toward the mountains. "They're going by Crestview and down to Main, and I bet they'll turn left on Main to Route Fifteen."

"Look's like a wedding, and you're right, they're moving fast," Laszlo said.

"Yep, just like I said."

"I wonder who's in the cars," Laszlo asked as the caravan came screeching onto the State highway a hundred feet from the Socony-Mobil station where he and the old man were.

"Why the president, mister!" the old man shouted. "He's in the big Lincoln, the second car back. The first car is full of those security guards and don't ask who's all in those other cars. Must be some big doings going on up at Gettysburg."

"Why do you say that?" Laszlo asked as he peered over the roof of his car.

"The president has a farm about ten miles north of here and that's where he sometimes goes on weekends."

Laszlo's hands clutched the top of the car door for support; his forehead was wet with sweat. He felt his legs trembling, and his mouth had gone completely dry.

"Are you all right, mister? Didn't you see him wave to us? He always does."

"I'm fine," Laszlo said, regaining his composure. The experience had left him weak in the knees. "I saw him wave to us. I guess it's just that I've never seen the president in person before, and being so close."

Still looking at the road where the presidential party had passed, he recalled having once before experienced a similar physical sensation. It had been when he, Hanna, Janos, and Nina were being questioned at the Yugoslavian border during their escape from Hungary. The feeling that the border guard was going to have them return to Budapest for the proper exit papers was gut-wrenching to him. Only by the intervention of a compassionate sergeant were they allowed to cross into Yugoslavia.

Feeling better, Laszlo asked, "Where is the Army? Does he always get this close to the people?"

"What Army?" the old man asked. "Sometimes even closer."

"I imagined there would be many soldiers around him at all times."

"Are you kiddin', mister? Ike, if he had it his way, wouldn't even have those FBI guys you saw. Hell, when he had the British Prime

Minister here last year on the way back from the farm they both got out of the car and walked around the park over there."

"I just didn't think there would be so few guards, I just had this impression."

"That's more the case in D.C. There he's got a lot of security people, but not out here. People leave him alone; they know he comes up here to escape all that, you see."

"I do."

"Now up at the Camp it's different. There you've got guards, not Army, but Marines. A whole bunch and last night another bus load of them came up from Washington. We were still open when they rolled in."

Laszlo did not want to arouse suspicion; it was time to go. What the old man had told him in a few minutes would have taken days to find out. What an unusual country America is, he thought. How open the people are. What he had just witnessed was not an apparition, it was real—the challenge was how he was going to use it. He now added Gettysburg to his list.

CHAPTER 10

"Where does this dirt road lead to, Sergeant?" Lieutenant Fergurson asked as they stood in front of the log cabin gatehouse at the main entry to Camp David a few hundred feet from the State park's main road.

"A quarter mile down that road you'll be at Aspen Lodge," Kellerman said. "When the president is 'on board,' travel on the road is restricted."

"I'll want to go down there later."

"Here comes post number fourteen up the fence line path," Kellerman said, watching the lieutenant stoke his pipe. "He's got orders to come to within a hundred feet of where we're at, make contact with the main gate sentry, wait a minute, and then walk back along the interior fence to post number thirteen. I didn't realize that you smoked, sir."

"Only a pipe, and only when I'm by myself or taking a walk, a form of relaxation that I picked up in college," Fergurson said, attempting to get his pipe lit as he stood with his back to the breeze.

"Lieutenant, what's the scuttlebutt that Khrushchev might be coming here soon? Any truth to it?"

"I swear, Sergeant, the men have a more fine-tuned intelligence system going than O.N.I. and, as is often the case then not, their scuttlebutt is more accurate."

"You know as well as I do, sir, all you have to do is stand outside the squadbay when they're polishing their shoes and brass and listen and you'll be brought up to date on everything that's happening and going to happen."

"September fifteenth—that's the day he'll be here and the First will be meeting him and his party during a MATS arrival at Andrews, and guess what? We'll be up here with him. He and the president will be having negotiations right here at Aspen for three days."

"So the men are right after all. I should have known it. I knew there was more behind what you said about us relieving the First up here for a month."

"I wanted to let you know then, but was ordered to keep it quiet until we were here. When Khrushchev is here our men will be walking their posts along with a member of the KGB."

"Why the KGB, Lieutenant?"

With smoke rising from his pipe, Fergurson replied, "The KGB is the equivalent of our FBI, Secret Service, and CIA all rolled up in one—better known as the Soviet Secret Police in Charge of State Security. Sergeant, let's leave the truck here. I'd like to walk the perimeter fence and become familiar with the guard positions."

* * *

The emotion Laszlo had experienced an hour before of having seen the president was all but gone. He had parked his car and decided to walk over to Walnut Street. It was farther than the attendant had told him. None of the late-morning strollers seemed to pay much attention to the stranger in town other than to bid him good morning. It was unnerving, but not unlike the way the locals are in Vermont. He was reminded of what the old man had said to him, that for years now, heads of state have come through town to visit the president at Camp David. Their presence in town attracted news and security people, out of town curiosity seekers, but very little interest from the locals.

"Could you tell me where I might find 129A Walnut, sir?" Laszlo asked the postman who was stuffing his leather satchel with mail and packages from a metal drop off box on the corner of Alley and East Main.

"Yes, just go two blocks down Main and turn left. You'll go past Lombard and Benjamin, and Walnut is the next street. By the way, 129A is on your left about halfway down the street. It's Mrs. Gropp's house."

Within minutes Laszlo was at his destination. The postman's instructions had been correct. He saw the number 129A just below the black mailbox. He looked over the white clapboard house with its wraparound porch and neat beds of mums growing next to the porch lattice work.

He unlatched the small white picket fence gate and walked up the several steps to the front door and, not finding a door bell, knocked gently on the screen door and in a half shout said, "Good morning—anyone home?"

"Please come in," said the short, red-cheeked lady with her silver hair tied in a bun as she unlatched the screen door and pushed it open for Laszlo. "I see from the newspaper you're holding that you saw my ad for letting the house, yes?"

"You're correct. Are you Mrs. Gropp? My name is Henry Bender," Laszlo said, looking around the entrance hall and noting how clean and tidy the place was. "It smells delicious in here! It must be a strudel you're baking."

"Yes. I'm Mrs. Gropp, the landlady, and no, not strudel, it's my favorite German crumb cake that you smell. I just took it out of the oven. Can I offer you a piece with some fresh coffee I made only a half hour ago?"

"That would be wonderful. I parked my car on Altemont Avenue, near the cemetery and walked here. For some reason I thought your house was in the direction of the senior school."

"A lot of people make the same mistake. I should make a better ad. Are you Dutch, Mr. Bender?" Mrs. Gropp asked. "Forgive me, but I noticed your accent."

"No, German. Bendermeister was my name in Germany. My father shortened our name when we came to the United States ten years ago from our village near Hamburg."

"That's a wonderful name," Mrs. Gropp said. "Your father should have left it alone—too many German people change their names. So many from the old country have done it here. So what brings you to Thurmont? Are you touring the area?" she asked as she poured the coffee into the cups she had set out on the oak kitchen table.

"No, we're dairy farmers in Dutchess County, but we only lease the land. That's upstate in New York, if you've never been there. Papa wants me to spend time here to look at farms that might be up for sale," he said, choosing his words carefully and at the same time keeping his lie simple.

"Oh yes, my late husband and I visited Mr. Roosevelt's home in Hyde Park there in 1949. Many German people live there too."

"I noticed a great deal of German names in the cemetery when I walked through. Are there many Germans still living here?" he asked, congratulating himself on parking his car, with its Vermont license plates, far enough away from the house.

"Yes, there're people here in town who can trace their families all the way back to the 1760's. Mr. Bender are you married? Do you have children?"

"Yes, my wife Hanna is still in Ver—ah, New York," Laszlo replied. "We have no children, but my brother will join me in a few weeks. My father is too old to travel and he doesn't want to leave the cows. He rarely ever goes away from the farm."

"Typical German farmer, I'd say," Mrs. Gropp said, wiping her face with her red plaid apron. "All through this valley and on up to Harrisburg you'll find farms and orchards with mostly German-Americans."

He had not eaten in hours and gratefully accepted Mrs. Gropp's crumb cake. Holding a sliver of it in his hand, he said, "Mrs. Gropp, the paper said the house is available for the month of September but didn't say for how much or whether there would be other people here."

"I'm asking seventy-five dollars for the month, because the tourist season will be over next week. I normally get a hundred twenty-five dollars. I go away in September, down to Virginia to see my daughter. The house has only one tenant here in September. Are you interested in it for September?"

"Yes. How do I pay you? Do you want a deposit?" he asked.

"Why don't we take a tour first, see if you like the house. But finish your coffee and my crumb cake, Mr. Bender, and we'll worry about money later, yes?"

* * *

President Eisenhower had always enjoyed getting away to his Gettysburg farm. It was no different on this sunny Saturday afternoon. What was even more pleasing to him was to show his guests the farm. He purposely asked his vice president to join him on his walk. "Dick, I just can't tell you how much Mamie and I enjoy this farm, the first home we owned. We had lived in military- or university-supplied residences for close to forty years."

"Mr. President," Nixon said, "just looking around, I can see why you try and come here as much as you do. I hadn't thought about the fact that this was the first house you and Mamie owned."

"When I got back from NATO, we nearly chose the Hudson Valley as our home. Instead we're now back in the area where my ancestors arrived from Germany to become farmers. And later on my father left this valley as a little boy to go west with his relatives to Kansas. Another reason I enjoy this place so much is that a half mile down this driveway and across Route Fifteen is the very site where the Battle of Gettysburg took place."

They looked over the wide board, freshly painted fence at Eisenhower's small herd of Black Angus steers, Eisenhower suddenly turned to Nixon and said, "I felt after my 1955 meeting with Khrushchev in Geneva that he was amicable, but with a will of iron. Now I feel he's gotten harder to deal with."

"If not more so, sir."

"On what basis do you draw that conclusion?" the president asked frankly as they started to walk down the farm road toward Route Fifteen, shadowed by Agent Rowley and four other Secret Service agents. Behind them was Agent Deeter Flohr, driving the president's car ever so slowly.

Picking up a small limb that had fallen from the white pines that lined the driveway, the vice president made the limb into a walking stick, collected his thoughts, and said to the president: "This man is cunning, arrogant, and does not for one minute submit to the ideology of Marxism and Leninism but, instead, to the theory of power from which, in his opinion, all things flow. He is convinced that we in the West have concluded that he was within his right to crush the revolt in Hungary.

"Sweet Jesus, we're going to have some time with this bastard, aren't we," Eisenhower said. "Maybe what I should do is to call the whole thing off. Who the hell needs him here and having to put up with his arrogance?"

"No, sir. Don't even think about that; we'll just be playing into their hands."

"I know, I'm just mad, that's all," the president said. Staring at the pea-gravel stones in the driveway, he went on very somberly, "Dick, there's something I want you to know that I have deliberately kept from you up until now because if you had known about it, it could have had an influence on your findings during your trip to the USSR."

Surprised and waiting for a bomb to drop, Nixon said, "What is it, Mr. President?"

They stopped once again to gaze out at the Black Angus herd that had moved farther away from the fence, and the president said, "You recall that at the Geneva Convention in fifty-five I proposed to Bulganin that we should have mutual aerial inspections of our respective countries. As you know, he turned this idea down."

"I remember it well. You were awfully upset and wanted to do something right then and there," Nixon said.

"Well—we did. For some time now we have been conducting over-flights of Soviet territory by using a SR-60 or U-2 high reconnaissance plane that flies at seventy-five thousand feet. From that height the pilot can photograph the number on a car's license plate."

Surprised, the vice president said, "Do the Soviets have any idea that we're doing it? From where do these missions originate?"

"Since 1956, these flights have originated out of Adana, Turkey, enter the USSR near Peshawar, Pakistan, and they come out of Russia somewhere near Norway. There're only a handful of people who are aware of this, and I should tell you that even Chris Herter doesn't know. But, yes, I do believe that Khrushchev knows we are carrying on over-flights and will never acknowledge it because it would be too embarrassing to him and his military. Also he would be questioned as to why the Soviets do not have a similar aircraft and why they can't shoot ours out of the sky."

Eisenhower turned and looked at Nixon's face. He wondered from his expression if he was more shocked from the news of the U-2 or from not having been kept informed. He said, "We should be getting back to the house; the others are probably wondering what's going on."

Nixon turned around toward the house and said, "I'm troubled, Mr. President, as to why you want to continue the tremendously high risk that the over-flights pose, especially now, with Khrushchev acting so erratic and issuing his weekly ultimatums on Berlin?"

Solemnly the president said, "It's for that very reason, Dick, that I authorized the flights. We must know what the Soviets are up to. It's a different world we live in now that each of us has missiles that can be at their assigned targets within thirty minutes of launching. We're not in this alone. The British are acting as our joint venture partner."

"When did this all begin, sir? Does Congress know?" Nixon asked.

"It all started in fifty-three. The British were able to uncover the Soviet missile testing facility at Kapustin Tar. They used a retrofitted B-

57 Canberra, and you may recall how the Soviets got bent out of shape when they discovered the high flying air balloons.

"In 1954, we asked Lockheed to give us a plane that would fly above seventy-five thousand feet and have a range of four thousand miles. We reassigned thirty-five million dollars from the CIA budget and, in ninety days, we had our plane. Allen Dulles was in charge, and he has kept the Senate Defense Committee up-to-date on all plans as well as the results which, incidently, are more than we ever had hoped for. The clarity of the photographs, the intelligence material we're gathering, cannot be overstated enough. Although I'm somewhat concerned about discovery, General Twining has asked for more flights than the two we're now operating, one from Turkey and the other near Wiesbaden. This, I felt, was too risky, and it is only two per week that we now have in operation."

"Mr. President, what if, for some reason, the U-2 is brought down inside Soviet territory? Maybe for mechanical failure, weather related, or is shot down? What then? What kind of story do we give the Soviets concerning our intrusions into their air space?"

"We have thought of that, and the cover is that the U-2 is a NASA weather reconnaissance plane doing weather mapping and strayed off course. Also I've been consistently reassured by Dulles and Twining that it's impossible for the U-2 to be brought down by anti-aircraft or by missiles."

Nixon stopped walking just short of the flagstone path that led from the driveway to the house and said curtly, "The fact that I was not made aware of this project deeply concerns me. For that matter, what else is going on?"

"That's it. Dick, you spent a week with Khrushchev and can you honestly tell me that this man can be trusted after what you experienced in July and what the world witnessed in Hungary? I requested mutual aerial inspections. They were rejected, and this president will not sit by while they build missile bases or move large armies toward their Western neighbors."

"I can sincerely appreciate that, sir, but my concern is that we don't allow these over-flights to torpedo your meeting with Khrushchev."

"Dick, all of us connected with the U-2 have given this a great deal of thought—and it was unanimous—continue the flights. And you have done aerial spying for us, too, you know that?" the president said with a grin.

"No, I didn't. How was that?" Nixon asked.

"Oh! I thought Allen or his CIA boys might have told you before you left for Moscow. Allen had the lower front fuselage of Columbine II set up so that when you were flying over the USSR, a high resolution two hundred forty inch camera got rolling and was snapping photographs of the Soviet countryside.

"But the plane was piloted by a Soviet pilot at all times when we were over Soviet air space."

"Right, but when he turned on one of the air intake switches, he was turning the camera on. And, Dick, I saw some of the photographs, and they look swell. Welcome to the world of spies, Dick. Let's go and have some lunch."

* * *

Lieutenant Fergurson was finding the tour along the Camp's interior fence line revealing and Sergeant Kellerman's on-going monologue instructional as they continued walking from one sentry post to another.

"In case you haven't been counting, sir, there're fourteen guard positions along the three miles of interior fence and each sentry is responsible for approximately a thousand linear feet of area. At each post is a telephone box that allows the sentry to be in touch with the guardhouse. You saw the guardhouse this morning halfway between the squad bay and Aspen, near Laurel Lodge."

"I seem to have lost my bearing for a minute, but I know where we are now."

"This interior fence is eight feet high with ten strands of razor sharp barbed wire on top. On the other side of that fifty-foot clearing is the exterior fence. In between is called the 'kill zone.' The clearing is watched by two roving Jeep patrols that come from opposite directions and travel completely around the Camp but never on a pre-set schedule."

"Don't mean to interrupt, but tomorrow I would like to take a run over that road."

"I'll set it up, sir.

Fergurson led the way up the path toward the next post and said, "Well, at least we don't have to tend to guard dogs as Roosevelt's Marines did."

Kellerman, a few steps behind and carefully watching each of his steps along the rock-covered path, said, "One thing that hasn't changed a bit are the weapons. Each of the fourteen walking posts carry M-1 rifles or a BAR, and, in some cases, the Thompson submachine guns, as well as the .45 caliber side arms. Each of the Jeep patrols has a mounted, .30 caliber machine gun."

"I didn't see any automatic weapons this morning at the helicopter pad," the lieutenant said.

"You wouldn't there, Lieutenant. They're issued when the guys go on fence guard duty. The weapons are checked in and out at the guardhouse."

"Where does that road go to, Sergeant?" Fergurson asked, pointing to a dirt road that came up to two large swinging gates.

"That goes to the garbage disposal area about a quarter of a mile down the road. There's a steep drop and that's where we 'deep six' the garbage."

"Seems to me that is a pretty large opening under the gates. Why hasn't that been covered over with barbed wire?"

"Can't say, sir. No one ever seemed to have noticed it before. The Officer of the Day and the Sergeant of the Guard personally come out and check posts at least once during each four-hour watch."

Fergurson, now bent at the knees, studied the opening more carefully and said, "From all of the gullies and swales I noticed as we came through the woods, there's considerable run-off of rain water from inside the Camp."

"Who goes there?" was the command from the woods that took both the sergeant and the lieutenant by surprise, with Fergurson rising and looking at the direction of the command.

"Lieutenant Fergurson and Sergeant Kellerman, Third Platoon," was the Sergeant's reply to the still unseen sentry.

"Step forward and be recognized, with your hands out in front of you," the sentry said, still concealed behind a large walnut tree that was next to a five-foot high rock outcropping.

Moving closer they came to within thirty feet of the rock when the voice snapped, "Recognized! Good morning, sir. PFC Mullins, post number six, sir. All's well."

"Good job, Mullins. Neither the Sergeant nor I heard you come up on us. Carry on, Mullins."

"Aye, aye, sir," Mullins replied, making his way down the well-trodden path alongside the fence toward post number seven. "The men are alert, Sergeant, and take their assignments seriously."

"They certainly do, sir. They're checked a lot, not only by us but also by the Secret Service. Those guys sometimes play games on us and at times it gets serious."

"What do you mean?"

"Well, the Secret Service will check posts and get challenged just as we were. Our guys don't know all of them, so the Secret Service will show their identification. There have been times that where their photo is supposed to be, there'll be a picture of Donald Duck or Mickey Mouse. I regret to say, we have let them through. And, when the skipper hears that we let Donald Duck into Camp David, all shit breaks loose."

"I can imagine. But let's not allow those Disney characters to penetrate security on our watch."

As they headed to post number five, Kellerman said, "Guard duty is a lonely job, sir. The glamour of guarding the president and the other big shots wears off quickly. You'll see it happen yourself. Being out here on the fence line at 0300, walking into a thirty-knot wind with two feet of snow under your boots and a ten below temperature, can be a bitch."

"I've never thought of it under those conditions, Sergeant," Fergurson said, recalling his brother's letters and remembering that Kevin never mentioned Camp David, or was it Shangri-La then? It must have been that, because Truman was president back then.

"Take Mullins for example," Kellerman said. "He's not a coffee drinker, but we bring coffee to all of the guard positions twice during each tour. Mullins still takes the coffee but uses it to dip his fingers in so they stay warm. I'm not complaining, but these guys have the same cold weather gear that we used in Korea. We keep hearing we're going to get the same stuff the Air Force uses up at the D.E.W. line, but it never happens."

"It's not easy to imagine, walking post in the dead of winter, Sergeant, when we have a day like today. But I'll follow up on the cold weather gear, I promise."

"I know, sir, but believe me, it can be bad. When Corporal Phillips was a PFC he nearly got busted for stripping the interior wood trim out of Walnut Lodge which is right next to Aspen and using it for kindling to keep warm. That was in the 1957-58 winter. That was a really bad one; food came in by helicopter drops because the road up the mountain was closed for a week."

"God, was it that bad?" Fergurson said.

"The thing we watch out for, sir, is that the guys never sit down on post. If they do, they'll be asleep in a minute and that can happen at anytime or in any weather."

"I can see now, Sergeant, why the Secret Service wants us Marines here and no one else. And, between the two of us, we'll be out here day and night with the men. I don't want any of these men, not for a minute, to think that we're in a nice warm rack while they're out here freezing their asses off."

"Well, along the same line, Lieutenant, the Secret Service agents are known to come at our guys by jumping out of the trees along the fence path. We had some close calls a couple of times when our people let a round go at them saying, 'I shoot first and challenge later.'

"However, that chicken shit has stopped ever since Brewer broke an agent's jaw last year with the butt of an M-1."

As the two Marines continued walking along the fence line path, Fergurson was only paying half attention to Kellerman's bitching about how the Secret Service agents behave. His mind was on the gaping holes that were created under the fence by rain run-off and what he should do about it. He quietly asked himself why no one else ever noticed them, or was he just being overly concerned? He thought he very well might be. There was the second fence, the exterior fence on the other side of the kill zone. Nonetheless he was going to bring it to Commander Nicholson's attention when he and Kellerman finished the tour. As long as those holes existed, the fence was useless.

CHAPTER 11

"How far to Gettysburg?" Laszlo asked the clerk at the Emmitsburg General Store, glancing down at the story on the front page of the *Emmitsburg Times: "Ike and Nixon to confer at Camp David today before president leaves for four-day visit with European Allies."*

The shopkeeper replied, "Just go through town and stay on Fifteen. You go right into Gettysburg. It's about ten miles north. You know you are on Fifteen when you go by the Mount, which will be on your left. Traffic will be slow going through Gettysburg; big doings there today with the president and all that."

"Thanks for your help," Laszlo said. "I'll pay you for the newspaper."

Laszlo thought that the shopkeeper could easily have been Barbara at the Wayside Country Store in West Arlington—friendly, talkative, and just full of information, whether you solicited it or not.

As he drove his Chevrolet away from the small store, he was pleased with himself and the progress he had made. He had found out many things about the president's movements that would prove useful. Mrs. Gropp's house was just what he wanted, although getting away from the charming but nosy old lady was almost impossible. He had never thought that she would stop talking, stop asking questions about him and his family. His eating her crumb cake was not enough; she insisted he stay for lunch. But, short of being rude, he managed to excuse himself and was now driving north, opposite the Mount.

The clerk had told Laszlo that the Mount was the locals' way of referring to Mount Saint Mary's College, that it was the oldest independent Catholic college in America, and it also was one of the oldest and largest training facilities for Catholic priests in the United States.

Tucked into the gently rising hills at the northern end of the Catoctin Mountain range was the College campus.

Laszlo found what caught his attention as he drove slowly northward past the College was not so much the beautiful campus awash in the noon-day sun but the sign on the road noting that "Next left to the Grotto of Our Lady of Lourdes-National Shrine." He knew that the world-famous shrine of the Patron Saint of crippled people was in France, and he remembered the many inspiring stories told to him by his Uncle Joseph about the Shrine's many miracles and cures.

What blind faith people must have, he thought. How foolish they were to go to these places for cures. There're no cures, no miracles—no God. For if there was a God, he and his family would not have been forced to leave their home in Hungary. The Khrushchevs of this world would not exist nor the Hitlers before them. "And, if there is a God, what does He want? Why is He putting me through this?"

Suddenly he swerved his car onto the right shoulder and brought it to stop with the engine still running. He lowered his forehead onto the steering wheel and wept. The Chevy's passenger door was within inches of the briar bushes, and the northbound traffic raced by Laszlo's door within a foot or two. But being confined in the car was temporary for Laszlo; all he needed to do was to go forward and get back on the road. Escaping from his thoughts was not as simple—even if he had a way in which to escape. Over and over again he asked himself, "Why has God forsaken me?" Or did he abandon God? Why was it that Hanna had so much faith and he didn't? It wasn't that way only a few years ago when Uncle Joseph asked him to become a priest. "What changed me? And where have my hope and faith gone? There might be a way to escape, it might be back at the shrine," he thought. "I'll go there on my way back."

* * *

"Good afternoon, General," Sergeant Kellerman said, bringing up a sharp salute. "A beautiful day to be about, sir."

"I couldn't agree with you more, Sergeant," said General Snyder, returning the Sergeant's salute.

"Your new boss, Sergeant?"

"Yes, sir," Kellerman said. "This here is Lieutenant Fergurson, the Third Platoon's new leader."

"Pleased to meet you, Lieutenant. You're taking over a swell platoon."

Fergurson said, "Thank you, sir."

"One thing about Camp David, Lieutenant, is that we try to avoid most military formalities, and usually after spending all week at the White House, where I feel it's like living in the lobby of the Willard Hotel or, for that matter, Union Station, we just try to relax when we come here. Thanks in large part to you Marines we, and especially the president, can do it in peace.

"Carry on Sergeant. Nice meeting you, Lieutenant; good luck with your command."

"Thank you, sir," Fergurson said, as both he and Kellerman saluted the General who was now walking toward Laurel Lodge.

"Who in hell was that, Sergeant?" Fergurson said. "How do you know him anyway?"

"That's General Howard Snyder, the president's personal doctor. He's a two-star Army general from Walter Reed Hospital and is always close to the president, and always around the general are a bunch of Army guys with oxygen and other emergency equipment. General Snyder walks around the Camp quite a bit. You'll see a lot of him up here; he's a swell guy and more often than not wears civvies."

"Are there any more generals or admirals just strolling around about which I should know?" Fergurson asked.

"No, he's it, at least for now. The way I understand it is that ever since recovering from his heart attack in fifty-five, President Eisenhower is required to have a medical doctor close by at all times. The general is an old traveling companion and friend."

Fergurson and Kellerman, now having completed their fence line tour, took a short-cut through the woods. A quarter mile from the squad bay area, Fergurson stopped and said: "What's inside that brown structure, Sergeant? It looks like a farm silo."

"We call it the sparkshouse, Lieutenant, but it really is the Camp's communication center and is manned day and night by the White House Army Signal Agency. Like us, when the president is here, they bring more people up from Fort Mead. The building also contains one of the entrances to the Camp's tunnels. I've been through all of them, and some lead directly to the Camp's living quarters. It is quite a honeycomb, and we use the tunnels in bad weather to get around to each building."

"I see some of our people going in now, Sergeant."

"When the president is up here, sir, our people become runners and bring incoming communications to Aspen. That's one of the reasons you got that super, super clearance, Lieutenant. We all have one."

* * *

Mrs. Ann Whitman, working at her small, antique, maple desk at the Eisenhower's farm, was in her sixth year as the president's private secretary. Ohio-born and a graduate of Antioch College, the fifty-one-year old woman was as close as anyone to the president. Her office in the White House was just outside the Oval Office and more elegantly appointed than her office at Gettysburg or Camp David. Despite all of the trappings of the White House, the place she most liked to work was here at Gettysburg where her office was a converted boot room just off the spacious living room.

"Ann, would you have Jim Rowley come in?" Ike said.

"Mr. Rowley will be here momentarily, Mr. President. He is seeing Mr. Nixon and the others off. Mr. President, will you be joining Mr. Herter for dinner tonight at Camp David?"

"Yes, Ann. Tell him I'll be up there around six and maybe we can watch a Western together."

Pushing open the screen porch door that led directly into Ann Whitman's office, Rowley, dressed in his familiar tan raincoat despite the fact that rain had not been forecast, said, "I understand the boss wants me?"

Overhearing his Secret Service chief, Eisenhower said, "Jim, come in and rest your feet. It's been a long day for you and it's only three o'clock. I hope you were able to grab something to eat between all of the goings on here."

"One thing I learned years ago, Mr. President, and that was to make sure you have a full breakfast because supper could be fifteen hours away."

"Jim, you know what I recently found out?"

"What's that, sir?" Rowley asked, waiting for a missile to come at him as he sat in an overstuffed arm chair in the president's wood paneled study.

"That both of us have the same birthday, October fourteenth. But what I do not know is why you're not joining me on next week's trip to Europe?"

"I'm not an alarmist, Mr. President, and I believe you know that. But this visit by Mr. Khrushchev and his group continues to worry me no end. And, for that reason, I want to stay here and work out the security measures—and we still don't know where and what Mr. Khrushchev wants to visit. We've nailed down with his advance people that he wants to take in the West Coast and see Disneyland as well as an IBM facility out there."

The president loosened the zipper on his windbreaker and said, "Jim, I learned a long time ago that when you put people in charge, delegate, let them do their job. So you go ahead and do what you feel is right. But I wish you were coming."

"Thank you, sir. Now, if I could only get your friend Cardinal Spellman to let up a bit, I'd sleep better. You know he's got a newspaper, *The Catholic News,* and ever since this trip was announced he has blasted Khrushchev's visit in his column. And, in doing so, has asked that all the faithful send off letters to protest the trip. There're a lot of nuts who all of a sudden have discovered letter writing, and if they would just let up. Sir, maybe you could get the Cardinal to say something more constructive, more positive."

"When the good Cardinal joined me on a tour of Korea during Christmas of fifty-two, Jim, right after I was elected, we made a pact. If he did not tell me how to run the country, I would, in turn, not tell him how to run his Church. You notice he's not asked me to cancel the visit; you see what I mean?"

"Well, I can see why you haven't made much of it, sir."

"Spellman is not so bad, Jim. You just have to get to know him. He has a wonderful sense of humor. On our way home from Korea he told me that Adam and Eve were Irish. Now Jim, as an Irishman, did you know that? And, as Spellman tells it, when a breeze came up and blew their figleafs away, Adam looked at Eve and shouted, 'O'Hare' and she then looked at him and exclaimed, 'O'Toole.' "

Rowley shook his large head and forced a smile on his face. He was glad to see his boss in good spirits. He hadn't joked in some time. Rowley got up from his chair and slowly made his way to the door. He knew it was the time of day for the president to take a nap. "The boss is probably right, I should delegate more," he thought. "Where the hell is Matt Hogan? Why isn't he here yet?"

* * *

The burly Pennsylvania State Trooper said to Laszlo, "What's your problem, buddy? Can't you hear? Move your car—this area is restricted today."

Looking up at the trooper straddling his Harley Davidson motorcycle with its two red lights flashing intermittently, Laszlo said, "I only want to see the monuments and take some pictures."

"Any time but now, mister. The vice president is on his way out and we want the area cleared. So move it along."

Laszlo glanced across the road and saw several black Fords with their engines idling and two to three men standing near each of them, looking up the chipstone-covered driveway, and he realized immediately that this was the president's farm.

Obeying the trooper's command, Laszlo turned his car around and proceeded south on Fifteen toward Mrs. Gropp's house in Thurmont. The late hour of the day had made him change his plans about visiting the Grotto of Our Lady of Lourdes—instead he would put off a visitation until tomorrow. Meanwhile he would stop at a general store to pick up a map of the area.

On the drive south, he congratulated himself once again on how he handled the situation with the trooper, who he felt never noticed the Vermont license plates. He slowed as he saw a wayside stop ahead.

"How can I help you, sir?" was the cheerful greeting he received as he entered the store. "Vermont, I see from your car. Always wanted to go there, especially when they make that maple sugar. We always sell loads of it to tourists."

"Yes, I'm from Vermont. Dairy farmer, looking over the area for possible farming," Laszlo replied, still astonished at the friendliness expressed by all that he met. "But what I would like is a map of the area, if you have one to sell."

"You bet I have maps, all kinds. Road maps, maps of the battlefield at Gettysburg, maps on the area's parks and lakes—got those in topographic detail as well but that will cost you more, you know. Picked a heck of a weekend to come look at farms. The highway has been crawling with those government people all day—President and Nixon are up at the farm. God! It was only a short while ago that a bunch of them went speeding south. Any time they go at seventy to eighty miles an hour, you can bet that it's the president or some other "big-wig." There've been times they even stopped in for soda and cigarettes, you know."

"May I see the topographic map?" Laszlo said, reaching out his hand and hoping that the shopkeeper would soon become tired of talking. Satisfied with the map, Laszlo paid the shopkeeper and continued back to Thurmont.

The ten-mile return trip had gone quickly. His seeing the president and the ability to get a map in such detail as the one he was now studying on his bed gave him a sense of exhilaration and expectation. A euphoria was overtaking him. Even more when he had arrived back at the house he found he would be alone. Mrs. Gropp's note explained that she had gone to Baltimore to shop and would be back late.

His room was on the first floor behind the parlor. Its low ceiling looked down at a double bed, and the walls papered over with floral scenes gave the feeling that the room was a bit confining, if not small. However Laszlo was pleased nonetheless. He had moved the lamp on the night stand closer to the bed.

"Why is this area over here marked 'Restricted, U.S. Government property'?" Laszlo asked out loud.

"Let me see where you are. Oh! That's Camp David, the president's retreat up on Mount Catoctin," Mrs. Gropp said to the startled Hungarian. "No one is allowed near there—the sentries would spot you a mile away. The closest you can get is by driving up the park road, right here, and it'll take you to the Camp's entry road, here. But that's as far as you'll get before you'll be ordered to turn back."

"I didn't hear you come in, Mrs. Gropp," Laszlo stuttered, getting up off the bed and hurriedly folding his map. At the same time, he wondered how he was going to explain to her his interest in Camp David. Did she know what he was doing? Does her knowing impact his plans? He just didn't know, not yet.

"My friend down the street took me out in her car, that's why you didn't hear me drive up—have you had supper yet, Mr. Bender?"

"No, I haven't, Mrs. Gropp. But I'm fine. You don't have to worry about me. I'll just go out."

"Nonsense, I've got some leftover pot roast and mashed potatoes. It won't take but a minute to warm it up for you. Oh, by the way, don't look for good farmland up on Mt. Catoctin. That's all park land except for the place where Mr. Eisenhower goes. I'll call you in a few minutes when I have dinner ready."

"Thank you, Mrs. Gropp. You're very kind." When she closed the door behind her, he told himself that her interruption was harmless. His studying the map and Camp David was, perhaps, no different than what any other visitor to the area would do. But unlike other guests, he had discovered a route to the Camp. It was, moments ago, laid out right in front of him on the bedspread.

Laszlo was anxious to call home to let them know his good news. But, for the time being, it would be wiser to say nothing. Instead he would call them tomorrow. He now felt that he knew his route up to the outside fence of Camp David; tomorrow he would find out how he was going to get into the presidential retreat. In the meantime he was going to exercise more caution. Had he been found out by the old lady, he would have had to act in a way he didn't want to.

CHAPTER 12

"Tell me, Hanna, what did he have to say? What is he doing? Will he be back soon?" an excited Janos asked his sister, who had just placed the receiver back on the telephone cradle.

"He's well and misses us all," she replied, staring at the black telephone. "Oh! And he said he saw and waved to President Eisenhower on Saturday, and the president waved back at him. He has rented a house in Thurmont from an elderly German widow. He said he'll be home in a few days and is wondering how you're doing with the pheasants." She paused and then said, "Janos, something is not right. I know it. Why is Laszlo in Thurmont? Why is he renting a house, for God's sake? He said it was in Maryland. You know something, Janos, don't you?"

"Sister, I only know he went there to see if there was a farm that would buy our pheasants, that's all," Janos said.

She stared at him. "Janos, you're not telling us the truth. You know what Laszlo is doing and you haven't told me or Nina. Laszlo would not go running off to a place in Maryland and rent a house. You said the other night it was Pennsylvania, no?"

Pressed, Janos said, "Well, Maryland is near Pennsylvania, but don't worry. Laszlo knows what he's doing."

"But why rent a house, for what purpose? We don't have money to do that. I don't know why you won't tell me, Janos, so I'll wait for Laszlo to come home. I have this feeling he did not go away to sell pheasants. I pray he won't do something that will get him in trouble. Call in Nina and come inside and let's have some goulash and bread."

Nina had left her chores in response to Janos's summons. Quietly she entered the kitchen and walked over to the sink and washed her hands. Nina's disheveled appearance was her way of projecting her feelings. Since her rescue nearly three years ago, Nina had abandoned any effort to appear feminine. Janos's pleas to change were ignored. If Italian widows wore black as their manifestation of the loss of their husbands, she had adapted her own design—and no one was going to change her.

Janos and Hanna had already sat down at the table. They were tolerant of Nina's bitterness. They also knew that, unlike themselves, she suffered in silence. Her oftentimes sullen and stoic expression was her way of carrying her grief for the loss of her family.

Nina had always felt she was an outsider when it came to discussing politics or, for that matter, even the uprising. Her role then was that of being a messenger. She had escaped being witness to the initial onslaught of Russian tanks, having been in Baja on the Danube one hundred seventy-five miles south of Budapest. On that eventful night in early November, on her way back to Budapest to join Janos and the others, she had been detained at Kabosca. She had received word that her mother and father, while crossing the Lancid Bridge to the twelfth century Matthias Church, were killed by machine gun fire.

The warm and lived-in atmosphere of Hanna's kitchen was lost on them; they sat silently eating their meal, until Hanna spoke.

"Oh Nina, what I would do to just to be back in Budapest. First I'd drown myself in the spa on Jozef Street, after which I would walk over to the National Museum and spend the day."

Nina paid no attention to Hanna. She stared at her dish. Trancelike she lifted the food with her fork.

"Don't you miss the folk festivals, the food, and dancing, Nina? This will be our third year of not being there, and I miss it immensely!"

Janos sensed that his sister wanted the silence to end, so he joined in and said, "Please pass me some paprika, Hanna. If Khrushchev were to die, God willing, maybe we could put someone like Imre Nagy back in power and then you could go back to enjoy the things you yearn for . . . ."

"It would seem all but impossible to get rid of Khrushchev and, if it was to happen, how would it happen?" Hanna asked.

"If asked, I'd do it," Nina said abruptly. "I would do it without reservation, and I have no remorse in saying so. All I need is Laszlo to show me how to get close to him."

"We all feel like you do, Nina."

"You don't know how I feel, Hanna, nor do you, Janos," Nina said angrily. "How can you? Only Laszlo knows how I feel, how I think.

He's not looking for a buyer for the pheasants, Hanna. Don't be so naive. He's looking for something much different."

"What do you mean?" Hanna said.

"You sensed it yourself, Hanna. Your reaction when you got through talking to him must have told you something."

"Nina, if you know, tell me. What's he looking for? Why's he there?"

"He's looking for revenge and what he can do about it, that's what he's doing," Nina said. "And don't worry, he's done nothing now. Khrushchev is not here yet."

* * *

Mrs. Gropp left her house early the next morning, but not until she had served her guest a hearty country breakfast. She had made no further mention about seeing Laszlo the night before pouring over the topographic maps of the Catoctin State Park. And for that, Laszlo was thankful. He was also grateful to see that Mrs. Gropp had made a large pot of coffee—he felt that he was going to need it. Sleep had not come until the early hours of the morning. His rethinking of events of the previous day had continuously flashed across his mind. But it was the question of where God stood in his plans that had weighed upon him through darkness and dawn. He could deal with the wrath from his family, but he was uncertain if he could deal with His. Was he to reconcile himself with God before he began his mission, he kept wondering.

* * *

The quarter mile path from the grotto's parking area to the Shrine was lined with brick pavers bordered by ten-foot high privet hedges. The tops of the hedges cantilevered toward the middle of the walk as if forming a tunnel up to the Shrine. From decades of constant visitors walking over them, only the center of the brick path was free of the grassy moss that grew on the sides of the path.

There were only three visitors to the Shrine on this damp and chilly morning. Two were dressed in the black habits of the Sisters of Charity. Laszlo wore a thin windbreaker, flannel shirt, and gray slacks. He was kneeling at an oak alter rail that separated the public viewing area from

89

the statue of the Blessed Virgin. The four-foot statue stood on a marble pedestal under a concaved stone roof that appeared like the entrance to a cave and was surrounded by hundreds of flickering candles encased in small red jars.

Laszlo raised his head and looked up at the marble scroll stretched out above the statue and read its inscription:

"Agnus dei qui tollis peccata mundi miserere nobis"

"Lamb of God who takes the sins of the world have mercy on us."

Laszlo knelt at the rail and said aloud, "I do not ask You to have mercy on me, God, but if You can hear me, I ask You through the Blessed Virgin to have mercy on my family. Do not forsake them the way You abandoned our people. They have not sinned as I have. They have not left You as I have, and You must not desert them."

Laszlo raised himself from the kneeler, and out of habit he dipped the fingers of his right hand into the font that contained holy water but did not bless himself. Instead he wiped his hand on his jacket.

"She stands there so beautifully and majestically, Our Lady. Don't you agree, sir?" said the lady dressed in the black habit.

"Yes, yes she does," Laszlo replied, startled by the nun and her companion. "Very much like the one in France, sister."

"Were you at Lourdes? Were you cured, my son?" the nun said excitedly. "I hear a visit to the Grotto of Lourdes in France is breathtaking and just being there can be the highlight of one's faith."

Laszlo said, "No, I was not there to be cured, but to visit with my uncle who is a priest. Just after the War he wanted me to accompany him on the journey."

"You're not from around here, are you?" asked the nun's companion, who appeared to be much younger. "Your accent sounds slavic. Is that so?"

Wishing he had not been so polite and had just walked away, Laszlo said, "No, sister, I'm originally from Germany. I now live along the Hudson River about a hundred miles north of New York City on a farm my father owns." Keeping his cover consistent, he continued, "I'm staying in the area where I'm making inquiries into available farmland for sale, and I happened to see the sign for the Grotto."

"Your eyes tell me that there is deep sadness and trouble in your heart," the nun said. "I hope our Lady can bring you comfort as she has done for so many."

"I didn't realize that it showed that much, sister," Laszlo said. "You're very observant and compassionate, just like our sisters in Germany."

"Not much can be hidden that one's eyes do not reveal, and your eyes tell a great deal."

"I'll remember that, and thank you for caring, sister."

"Please forgive us," the younger woman said. "I'm Sister Mary Teresa and this is Sister Paula. You must think we're prying into your affairs—but it is so rare that we get out from the convent, and we so much want to meet others. We're sorry if we disturbed you."

"You haven't disturbed me, sister. Just where is your house?"

"I'm sure you must have gone past our place, we are near Gettysburg—Elizabeth Seton College. It's a four-year, liberal arts college for girls."

"I see that no one is in attendance here at this college. Why's that?" Laszlo asked.

"There won't be anyone here until freshmen orientation and that's about two weeks from now. The Mount brings in their students the same week we do. So while the students are still on summer vacation, you have the place to yourself, except for us busy-bodies."

The nuns' last comment was critical to Laszlo. It now became apparent that he could embark on his journey up the mountain and not be conspicuous.

"Sisters, I must leave you now. I planned on taking a hike in the woods and walking over to the falls before it gets dark. These mountains remind me so much of my grandparents' farm in Bavaria where I grew up. It was good to talk to you. Goodbye."

"Yes, my son, we enjoyed meeting you. Please go in peace, and God bless you," the nun said as she watched Laszlo place his knapsack on his back and start to walk up the well-worn path that led from the statue into the dense forest.

Laszlo quickened his steps. He moved deeper into the forest, up the leaf and pine needle covered path. But the burden he had brought to the Shrine was still with him. He felt he had made no reconciliation with God. That would have to wait for another time, at another place.

* * *

"One more level, Lieutenant, and we'll be there," Kellerman said as they descended into the underground shelter. "There're five flights down to the tunnel when you enter at the sparkshouse. What we're going to see, sir, at this end are a couple of open rooms, much like our squad bays, but without windows. This part of the complex can house up to fifty of us for about three weeks, if we have to go under."

"Where do you get air, food, and water for three weeks, Sergeant?" Fergurson asked as they walked down the well-lit, seven-foot high, five-foot wide concrete tunnel. "How far does the tunnel . . . ."

"Little Eagle, Little Eagle. Do you read? Over," came the voice on Kellerman's walkie-talkie.

"This's Little Eagle, read you Eagle Nest. Over," Kellerman said.

"We've got a Condition Yellow in the tunnel at Alpha six, over."

"Nature of condition, Eagle Nest? Over."

"Unauthorized entry. Being detained by Schaffer. Over."

"Is unauthorized individual armed? Over."

"Negative. Over."

"Eagle Nest, Little Eagle and me are at Delta One so tell Schaffer we'll be there in one minute. Have 'em take no action, only detain. Over."

"Roger, Little Eagle. Over and out."

"Let's go, Lieutenant," Kellerman said, placing the radio back in its holster. "It's not far, but there're a lot of turns."

"Who do you think it is, Sergeant? And how did he get in? And what the hell is Alpha Six and Delta One?"

"I don't know, but we'll soon find out, sir. I'll explain the codes later, we've got to move before Schaffer gets trigger happy."

They raced down the tunnel making several right angle turns where at the entrance to each turn large, heavy metal doors hung from three-inch wheels instead of from hinges.

"Why so many turns?" Fergurson asked as they headed for Alpha Six.

As he picked up the pace, Kellerman said, "These turns are to prevent a zig labeled bomb from creating a fire storm that would carry a fire from one end of the tunnel near Aspen all the way to the opposite end."

Surprised at Kellerman's physical condition and doing all he could to keep up with him, Fergurson said, "I feel like I'm inside a big "M" turned on its side."

"There they are, in the presidential section," Kellerman said with his right hand opening the flap of his holster and almost within the same motion drawing out his .45. "What do we got, Schaffer?" Kellerman asked, panting. "Who's this guy? How'd he get in?"

"I don't know, Sarge," Schaffer said. "He won't say a thing, says he'll only speak to Mr. Haggerty."

"Oh, is that so. Well," Kellerman said, cocking his .45 and aiming it at the intruder's head. "Mister, you tell me and the Lieutenant who the fuck you are or I'll put a round straight through your hairless head."

"Henderson, William Henderson is my name," the short, slightly-built man said, acknowledging that the sergeant was more menacing than the sentry.

"Well, that's more like it, Mr. Henderson. Who are you and what the hell are you doing here?" Kellerman asked firmly, letting the hammer on his .45 slowly go back to its safety position.

"Why do you want to see James Haggerty, Mr. Henderson?" Fergurson said with more restraint than Kellerman. "How did you get in here?"

"I'm a reporter, Lieutenant, and I got my White House press pass from Mr. Haggerty's office. Here, I'll show it to you . . . ."

"Easy mister, not so fast," Kellerman said resolutely. "Schaffer, reach in there and pull it out. Let's see if it says you are who you say you are, Mr. Henderson," Kellerman said, handing the wallet over to Fergurson.

Fergurson pulled out several cards, looked them over and said, "White House press credential, *New York Herald Tribune,* White House Correspondent. Looks legit, Sergeant."

"Now that we know who you are, why are you in here and, for that matter, inside Camp David?" Kellerman asked.

"Mr. Haggerty gave me a private briefing on the president's meeting with Mr. Nixon," Mr. Henderson said. "Once we finished, Mr. Haggerty left to go to Gettysburg—he was to attend Church today with the president—and told me to let myself out."

"So why didn't you go out the main gate? Why the fuck did you wander down here?" Kellerman barked.

"Look, Sergeant, I don't appreciate your profanity or your belligerence, for that matter," Henderson said, looking at the lieutenant for compassion. None was returned.

Kellerman moved himself to within inches of Henderson's face and said, "No, you look, Mr. Reporter, if that's what you do. You're in deep shit being down here. Now just tell us how you got in."

"I was walking from Aspen back to the Main Gate and I needed to relieve myself. Not wanting to go back into the president's lodge, I saw what appeared to be an outhouse. So I went in. But instead of a toilet, there was a heavy steel cover, something like a ship's hatch. I opened it and saw a ladder so I went down it and found myself in the tunnel. Next thing I knew was this sentry stopping me. And that's the God's honest truth, Lieutenant."

Fergurson motioned Kellerman to him and whispered, "What do we do with him, Sergeant? Story appears reasonable to me. How about it?"

"Schaffer, who else is on watch with you," Kellerman asked.

"Wilson—here he is now, Sarge," Schaffer said.

"Okay, then," Kellerman said. "Schaffer, you take this guy to the main gate and turn him over to the Secret Service. Tell the agent at the gate what you just heard and when you're through, call in to the guardhouse and get back here. Wilson, you take over Schaffer's area."

"What will happen to him?" Fergurson asked, watching PFC Schaffer lead the reporter down the tunnel.

"Usually they'll pull his White House pass. But this guy knows Haggerty, so who knows, sir. Anyone's guess. But I'm sure he's in for the hassle of his life for the next few hours."

"You were pretty hard on him, Sarge. You scared the daylights out of him," Fergurson said. "Would you have shot him if he didn't tell you his name?"

"Probably not. But most people never had a cocked .45 pointed at their head. It can be frightening, and that's all I wanted to do, sir. Hope you didn't mind."

"Not at all. You got the job done, and very well, I might add. Oh, by the way, Wilson, how did you get in here?" Fergurson asked. "And what are your orders?"

"I came in from Charlie Six, sir."

Kellerman interrupted by saying, "Sir, you're probably wondering what's all this gibberish. The Camp area is divided into six quadrants, with each quadrant assigned a letter. Within each quad there're between two and five outside entry-exit points, each given a number identification, and each appearing to look like outhouses just like Henderson thought."

Wilson, with his rifle slung over his shoulder added, "My orders are to enter one Alpha section and leave the tunnel from another Alpha section, covering ten entry points during my four-hour watch, sir. I'm to look out for and report to the Corporal of the Guard any fire, water leaks, light outages, unusual machinery noises, and any person I see in the tunnel or rooms."

"How do you report?" Fergurson asked.

"I use the wall phones, sir. They're located every two hundred feet. If the phone don't work, I smash the glass on the full-alert buzzer, and there's one at the end of each section."

"Who else is down here with you?" Fergurson said, wiping the sweat from his forehead.

"Schaffer was, sir. PFC Schaffer—he would be doing the same thing, but we come in from different directions."

"I bet that on a cold February night, this is the best guard post up here, Wilson."

"That's right, sir. But Sergeant Kellerman doesn't let us spend too much time down here. You see, sir, we call in to the Corporal of the Guard when we enter and do the same when we leave. The whole tour takes fifteen minutes."

"I saw those entry points when we were topside, but I never thought they were anything other than outhouses," Fergurson said. "And that's what seems to have confused Henderson."

Wilson said, "And he was right, sir. Inside there's an iron hatch and under the hatch is a ladder enclosed by a semi-circular guardrail.

"Carry on, Wilson. Well done and very interesting, Sergeant," Fergurson said, appearing anxious to get topside. "I want to pay another visit to the fence line, Sergeant. Especially where the road leads off to the garbage area."

"Aye, aye, sir. Let's head down this tunnel. It'll take us to "Baker Three," which is not far from the back gate."

* * *

Laszlo looked at his watch and figured it was almost four hours since he had left the two nuns back at the Grotto. By his calculations he felt that he was within one mile of the north side of Camp David. The map was proving to be invaluable.

Despite spending his whole life growing up near mountains and deep forests, he knew that he could have easily overshot the Camp's perimeter by a couple miles. However his map disclosed everything he needed to cover; the five miles of woods, streams, and ledges between the Grotto and Camp David. Two of the most distinguishable landmarks were now between his present location and the outside fence that showed on the map as "UNITED STATES GOVERNMENT RESERVATION—RESTRICTED."

Cunningham Falls was his next landmark, and he knew he was close to it by the sound of the water and seeing the mist. The forest contained many hardwood trees, and Laszlo noticed it did not have the abundance of pines and spruces that made up large parts of the Green Mountain Forests. However, once he got up to the twelve-hundred foot elevation, the maples, oaks, and birches were shedding their supple green and were beginning to develop the same hues as found on Ball Mountain in Arlington.

* * *

Exiting through the heavy metal hatch at "Baker Three," Fergurson immediately felt the cool air against his wet shirt. His forty-five minute adventure in the tunnel complex was enough to make him want to end his tour and return to the BOQ and shower down, but he knew that the warm September breeze would have him dry soon.

"We should call in, sir, and let Corporal Phillips know where we're going."

"Let's do it, Sergeant."

"Eagle Nest, this is Little Eagle. Do you read? Over."

"Who made up those call signs, Sergeant?" Fergurson said, watching him fold the antennae on his two-way radio after Kellerman finished his transmission.

"They've been with us since I first came here, sir. I guess you might call it tradition. The 'Old Man' is the president and 'Big Eagle' is the Eighth and I Commanding Officer. On patrol or guard duty, the platoon leader doing Officer-of-the-Day duty is referred to as 'Little Eagle.' "

"Okay, I understand, Sergeant. And 'Deep-Six' must be the garbage dump I would have to guess. Right?"

96

"Yes, sir. And that's where we're off to, with your permission."

"Lead the way, Sergeant."

As they walked away from the outhouse facade known as Baker Three, Fergurson wondered where men like Kellerman come from. Where did he acquire his leadership qualities? He didn't attend any leadership school. Is it purely innate? His aggression in the tunnel toward Henderson came on instantly and was instinctive. Would he have done the same? Would it have had the same affect? No, he concluded. No way would he have been as convincing or as quick as Kellerman had been. Earlier in his career, maybe. It made him feel low. As they moved on to the back road, he told himself that this assignment would be his final one. But before that happens, he was going to restore his self-confidence and the courage it takes to demonstrate it.

* * *

Laszlo raised himself over what he hoped was the last ledge. He heard the sound of a motor car approaching. Without a moment's hesitation, he dropped below the ledge and hid in a crevice between two boulders. Wondering why a vehicle would be out here in the forest, he took the chance to find out and slowly climbed back over the ledge. To his surprise, he saw a Willy's Jeep with Navy markings carrying two Marines heading toward him on what appeared to be a logging road. Studying the road to be taken by the Jeep, Laszlo realized that the road was inside a high chain link fence topped by strands of barbed wire. Suddenly he was gripped by the same feeling he had had on Saturday when the president's motorcade had passed. His mouth went dry, perspiration coming off his forehead. He was now at the perimeter of Camp David. Remaining concealed Laszlo could hear the Jeep slowing down while the driver maneuvered through a series of gullies made by directing the surface water running from the interior across the road toward the outer fence.

The Jeep came to a stop seventy feet from where he was hiding, and for an instant he felt that his mission would be over in seconds. He wondered how fate could deal him this setback only to overhear the Marines talking as they got out of their Jeep.

The taller of the two said, "You know, I don't know why, when the Navy bulldozed this lame excuse for a road, they never put in culvert piping from one side to the other. Look at this shit. Every time it rains these ruts start to become trenches. I don't know why they don't pave this road."

"Are you kidding? They're too cheap."

"We better keep moving, but let's get this log the hell out of here before we wind up with a broken jaw."

Laszlo did not dare look out from his position but could hear the two Marines bitch and moan as they lifted the long, heavy log and rolled it down the embankment where it was stopped by the exterior fence.

"Joe," the taller Marine shouted, "did you see that move—over there?"

Laszlo froze. He pushed his back into the front of the boulder. He drew his legs up to his stomach, wrapped his arms around his knees. He did not have his knapsack on. It was on the ground—a few feet from him. They must have seen it and him too. He could feel his heart racing up against his thighs. "Should I get up and run back down the hill?" he wondered. "For sure I'd be spotted. If caught, I'll tell . . . ."

"Get the bag, Joe. Christ, there're four of them . . . big ones . . . they'll bring us eight bucks at the Thurmont Snake Farm."

Laszlo was unable to see the Marines scoop the four snakes into the burlap bag. Using the business end of his rifle, the taller Marine coiled the snakes, one at a time, and hopped them into the bag that was held open by his buddy.

"If they were rattlers," Joe could be heard saying, "we would get twice as much. These copperheads don't bring us much."

"Joe, eight bucks is three days' pay and that's a lot of beer, so let's tie the bag and get the hell out of here."

With the sentries and the bagged snakes back in the Jeep and heading down the road, Laszlo peered out to see them depart. "They must be half crazy," he thought, "collecting snakes." However, his observational skills were not lost on noticing that mounted on the back seat of the Jeep was a light machine gun framed between two spotlights.

Laszlo knew he had taken a desperate chance. He could have been stopped, but instead he had gained valuable information. It wasn't just one fence barrier that he would have to overcome, but two, and between the two fences was a type of kill zone all too familiar to him and used at German Stalags in World War Two and by the Soviets at border locations. The roving patrol was going to be a problem, especially with the lights, but unless one walked right into the Jeep while it was stopped, its approach could be heard well in advance.

Placing the topographic map upon a small ledge on the boulder and staying alert for the possibility of being surprised by copperheads or rattlesnakes, Laszlo tried to mark where he thought he was and calculated that he was about one mile from where the north fence line met the Camp's east line.

Studying the small squared area marked on the map as "RESTRICTED," he knew that he would have to move more toward the west side of the Camp in order to get farther away from the Park's highway, which led to the Camp's main entry road. Before he moved on, he decided to snap some pictures of the fence and the terrain so he could show Janos what he would not be seeing when they came back because it would be dark.

* * *

"If you want to test fire your forty-five, Lieutenant, this is the place to do it," the sergeant said, surveying the hoards of garbage dumped over the side of the mountain. "You see those rats? We often come here and pick them off. It's wild when you bring down the B.A.R.; six or eight round bursts just raises all kinds of hell with the little buggers."

"No, that's okay, Sergeant. I'm sure the sound will carry all the way back to Aspen Lodge. This place looks a mess. Is this what they do with the Camp's garbage? Throw it over the hill?"

"Have been for years, sir. Nowhere else to put it. Navy doesn't want it burned, can't bury it, too much rock. We don't want a garbage truck coming on board."

"Why don't we haul it down the mountain to Thurmont? They must have an incinerator or something?"

"I can't tell you, sir. Never thought of that. I guess it has to do with security. You know, not wanting the civilians to know what we are eating or reading."

"If there're weak spots in the Camp's perimeter security, Sergeant, this area, together with those two holes under the fence gate, are it. Plus, of course, those culverts. Well, we can't do anything about it now, but I hope the Navy follows up on my concerns."

"Been telling them that ever since I've been here, sir, and nothing happens."

"Well, I'll get action now. Let's head back . . . who the hell is that?"

"Where, sir?"

"There! Over there near that cluster of pines!"

Bewildered, Kellerman said, "I just don't fucking believe this. In one day, two reporters. It can't be," Kellerman said.

"Might not be a reporter. Be careful."

As he and Fergurson drew their automatics and, in the same motion, slid back the receivers, Kellerman said, "Halt! Who goes there?" the sergeant commanded. "Get out from behind the tree and show yourself. Now!"

Thirty yards away, Laszlo slowly stepped out from behind the tall pine tree where he could be seen.

"What ever that is in your hand, mister, drop it," shouted Kellerman.

Responding to Kellerman's command, Laszlo gently placed his .35mm Zeiss camera on the ground.

"The pack, also, mister—on the ground with it."

"Who else is with you, mister?" Fergurson asked sternly.

"No one, sir. Just me. I'm only taking a hike and some photographs. I meant no harm," Laszlo said innocently, garnering all the sincerity he could.

"Now, put your hands above your head and for your sake don't move a muscle. You hear me, mister?" the sergeant said, slowly approaching Laszlo.

"Cover me, Lieutenant. I want to see if this guy is armed. Lean against the tree and spread your legs," Kellerman ordered.

As he watched, Kellerman ran his hands up one side of Laszlo's body and down the other, Fergurson was thinking, "Who is this man? Why is he in this location? And what nationality is his accent?"

"He's clean, sir."

"Find out what's in the pack, Sergeant," the Lieutenant said, keeping his pistol trained on the foreigner.

Kellerman opened the two snaps and pulled out several items and said, "Just a map of the park, remains of a sandwich, thermos, and a compass. No I.D. Now, turn around, mister. What's your name?"

"Bender—Henry Bender. I live in the village just below here. I come for walks up through the Park all the time to photograph the leaves as they begin to turn in color."

"Do you know that you have come into a restricted zone? U.S. Government Property, Mr. Bender," Fergurson asked sternly.

Repentantly Laszlo said, "I know that Camp David is restricted—we all know that in the village, but I tell you that I didn't think I was this close."

"Why not, if you've come up through the woods before?" Kellerman injected.

"Because I normally don't wander too far off the mountain roads but, as you can see, the colors are more changed on the west and north side of the mountain than anywhere else," Laszlo said, proud of himself for thinking up a logical explanation of why he was here and, at the same time, sensing he was regaining his composure.

"What do you do for a living in Thurmont, Mr. Bender?" Fergurson asked. "Why are you up here on your hike during the work week?"

"I'm a dairy mechanic, sir. I work at nights at Mueller's Dairy Farm just a few miles north of the village on the way to Emmitsburg."

"Do you have any identification, Mr. Bender? Anything that would say who you are?" Kellerman asked.

"No, not with me, but I do have papers in my car. I parked it near Cunningham Falls. We can go over and get it."

"No, that won't be necessary," Kellerman said, with Fergurson now looking puzzled by the word "papers" used by the stranger.

"Mr. Bender, how long have you lived in Thurmont? And, I want to make a note of your address," the Lieutenant said. "I've lived on Walnut Street, 129A, for three years, sir. I came here from Hamburg."

Fergurson came to the conclusion that Laszlo was not a threat and that his explanation appeared reasonable. He said, "Mr. Bender, I'm going to let you go. But I never want you up in this area again. Otherwise you'll be subject to arrest for trespassing on U.S. Government Property. However I'm going to have to confiscate your camera. It'll be returned to you within a couple weeks, and you can pick it up at the Thurmont police station."

Gingerly placing the sophisticated camera into its leather carrying case, Laszlo handed the apparatus to Kellerman, who slung the camera over his shoulder.

"Mr. Bender, you may go back the way you came" Fergurson said to Laszlo, who was now picking up his knapsack and looking relieved that he was not going to be taken into custody.

As they watched the retreating Hungarian work his way down the ill-marked path and into the forest until he disappeared from sight, the two Marines uncocked their sidearms and returned them to their holsters.

"What do you make of that, Lieutenant?"

"I don't really know, Sergeant. It seems innocent enough. Normal, I suppose. Much different situation than the one a few hours ago, but one we should write up in any event. And for some reason, which I cannot explain or fathom, I keep asking myself, "Why is this German, with a camera, up here at the fence?" And, Sergeant, for a fraction of a second I felt Bender and I had met somewhere before. But, for the life of me, I can't remember where it was or when. Or, for that matter, under what circumstances."

"You're letting your imagination get the best of you, sir."

"Perhaps."

"We've had these types of characters before, mostly hunters who wander too close."

"You're probably right. Let's go home."

Laszlo did not do as Fergurson had ordered. He did not take the path back to the grotto. Instead he ran through the dense woods, went under the fence where the Marines had found the snakes, and bisected the trails. He stumbled as he tried to slow his rapid descent, using his knapsack to shield his face.

Branches whipped at his head and thorn bushes pricked at his hands. He moved faster to distance himself from Camp David. He reached a clearing and collapsed in the high grass exhausted. As he lay there looking up at the sky he asked if the Marine lieutenant had recognized him and, if so, had his short-lived mission come to an end? And, worse, would he make it back to Vermont or would he be arrested when he went to Mrs. Gropp's house?

CHAPTER 13

Turning his key and pushing the front door open to Mrs. Gropp's house, Laszlo saw a note addressed to him on the small plant stand next to the hall clock.

> *Will be gone until October 10. Hope you and your family have a nice stay in Thurmont. I liked meeting you and wish you well in locating a suitable farm. I won't see you when I get back, so enjoy the house. I've left you a strudel in the oven and some biscuits in the bread box.*
>
> *Mrs. Gropp*

Laszlo was relieved to know that he would now be alone in the house. His mind was still racing. The confrontation with the Marines was just too close. He continued to wonder if the officer recognized him. "Could I be wrong? Maybe it was not the same person; that was a long time ago. The scene on the beach was chaotic. This man is thinner, older looking. He met hundreds of us that day and we never saw him again on the ship. If he remembered me he would have said so."

"Stop this!" he shouted aloud. "I'll drive myself crazy," he thought. "I must get control."

Sitting at the kitchen table and gazing at Mrs. Gropp's note, he pondered his next move. After several minutes of staring, he concluded that it was his calmness when under stress that allowed him to be here. And now was not the time or place to abandon that. Instead an alternative plan must be developed. A plan that would not have him and Janos facing the Marines. A plan that would have a place where he would not be conspicuous and could get to. The farm in Gettysburg had no Marines, no soldiers. And it was right off the road—but how would he get to see it up close? There was no cover, only open fields.

"No, no, not the farm," he thought. "What did the old man say about the high school—yes, yes, that's it . . . the high school in Gettysburg. The president will hold his news conference there along with Khrushchev.

"I'll leave for Vermont and go by the high school and see if this should be the place. I shouldn't stay here anyway for the next few days just in case that Marine officer decides to pay me a visit."

With his arms stretched out and grasping the edge of the stainless steel sink, Laszlo asked aloud, "Why has fate put the Lieutenant and me together again?"

* * *

James Rowley stood on the corner of Fifteenth and Pennsylvania Avenue waiting for the traffic signal to turn. His trenchcoat and his ever-present Stetson protected him from the rain. The oncoming cars came to a halt in response to the red signal. He stepped off the curb and wove his way through the traffic to the U.S. Treasury Building.

The traffic and rain did not interfere with his thoughts of the meeting he was about to have. As he slowly walked by the wrought iron fence that surrounded the multi-colonnaded Treasury Building, he decided he would not go into the building by the employee entrance. Instead, he would enter by the visitor's entrance, using the extra time to put his case together for his meeting with his boss, U.E. Baughman, Chief of the U.S. Secret Service.

He proceeded down the marble corridor that led to the building's center hall and main entrance. He paid no attention to the Treasury employees who were hustling in both directions or to the guards that stood in front of the many doors. Doors that, he knew, led to the currency vaults or bond vaults two floors below. He did not want his thoughts to get away from his meeting. They did anyway, as he recalled how only fifteen years before he had escorted President Roosevelt down this hall as he rushed the crippled president to his bomb shelter deep below Pennsylvania Avenue.

He brought his thoughts back to protecting another president and how he was going to persuade his boss regarding the concerns he had about the Khrushchev visit. Rowley also knew that Baughman would not have a whole lot of time for him to get his points across.

Four floors above the vault was the office of the chief, United States Secret Service, U.E. Baughman, who was responsible for all sixteen field offices of the Secret Service (the White House office was number sixteen). Going after those who would dilute the value of America's currency by dumping fake copies of it into circulation was what occupied the chief most of his time. Baughman cleared his calendar on September 13, 1959, to see his friend and Chief of White House Detail, James Rowley.

Dressed in a blue Brooks Brothers pin-striped suit with wide lapels, the wiry and thin-faced chief said, "Come in and sit, Jim. I bet you'll relax now that the president is back on U. S. soil. Don't let me forget to send a personal thanks and 'job well done' to Matt Hogan—he orchestrated the security well considering the fact he had to deal with the French, Germans, and the Brits. The secretary heard from the 'boss' yesterday and he said the president was pleased with the way things went, and he also said the boss missed you."

Rowley accepted Baughman's comments with a slight nod of his large head. "I'll pass on your comments to Matt, Chief. I've got him up at Gettysburg checking out some last details over at the high school and at the farm. We know Khrushchev and the old man will be at the high school, but so far there's no plan for him to go to the farm."

"Jim, you wanted to see me, and when Barbara said it was important I didn't need to hear any more. What's up?"

Looking at his boss, who appeared to be more like a bank executive than the nation's second top cop, Rowley said, "Chief, I don't like this visit by Khrushchev. I have bad feelings about it. I can't present to you any facts to support my feelings other than pure gut reaction and I know I must sound like a broken record."

"Look Jim, you're staying behind and not making the European trip because you wanted to work on security preparations for the visit, so what's happened in the last eight days to make you feel this way? What have you found out?"

"That's just it, Chief. I've nothing to substantiate my feelings, not one shred of anything to go on. Myself and the other field offices are working closely to implement the security plan we devised last month and, on paper and by 'walk-throughs'—it is a good plan."

"So what's the hang-up? That's all anyone else in your position could do short of pulling rank and ordering the president to cancel the visit. And you're not suggesting that—or are you, Jim?"

"Chief, I would like nothing better than to leave here, cross the street, and tell the boss the visit is off. But I can't do that. And just look at what we're undertaking when Khrushchev comes here. Washington, Iowa, Los Angeles, San Jose, Pittsburgh, and, oh yes, Camp David."

"Out of the question, Jim. The whole world will be watching. State tells me there'll be over a thousand reporters here from all over the world. And for that reason we must show them that we are as we say—an open society, and don't you forget that Khrushchev will be taking every advantage of that privilege, to its max."

"That's exactly my point, Chief. By Khrushchev wanting all that exposure he, in turn, puts the Old Man at risk. And, before you remind me, I know that we've never had an attempt made here on a foreign head of state. But that gives me little comfort with this guy."

"Why's that?"

"Because he is hated, and by so many refugees who resettled here," Rowley said. "And some of them believe strongly that their causes are justifiable—remember across the street? The shoot-out two blocks from where we're sitting, the near-successful attempt at the Blair House to assassinate Truman by those two Puerto Rican nationalists was just too damn close."

"Jim, you can't use that to justify your feelings. So what else is bothering you?"

"Fire," Rowley said, "both at the White House and at Blair. If the White House is the District's number one fire trap, then certainly Blair is a close second. The worst thing they did at Blair when they obtained the adjoining houses was to knock out the walls and turn the place into a hodgepodge mansion with no fire walls between the three buildings. This bothered their KGB guy Andropov as well."

Baughman said, "This can be overcome by having more men in the halls, especially at night, as fire watchers. You know, Jim, just like the military does in barracks. It seems to me that the greatest threat will be when both the boss and the premier are together. You agree?"

"Absolutely!"

"And when would that be—when are they together, I mean?"

"At Andrews during the arrival both will be side by side and riding in an open car over the fifteen miles from the base into D.C. There'll be a meeting at the White House on Friday afternoon and a dinner that night."

"Jim, the open car from Andrews—is that necessary? Fifteen miles. Let's see if the boss will allow the top to be up."

"He won't go for it, Chief, or at least we have been told that Khrushchev wants it that way. Wants to 'wave at the Americans,' is what State has told us. There're some speeches on the day after at the Executive Office Building, and the Soviets are holding a dinner that night at Blair. Also, the boss and Khrushchev will be together the following weekend here at the White House. Then Marine One will bring them to Camp David. Andropov and his KGB guys feel very uneasy about having Khrushchev go to Camp David."

"What's their concern, Jim?"

"The first is that the two of them will be lifting off in a helicopter in the middle of the city, next to apartment houses and office buildings—well within range of a hand-held rocket launcher, a bazooka-type weapon. I believe I was able to calm their fears by letting them know that we have people on the roofs of all the buildings as well as street observers checking the windows. And, when you really come right down to it, it is only the houses on Seventeenth Street that pose any threat, not a government building."

"And the second?"

"It's in the mountains, isolated. Khrushchev will be out of communication range with his military, you know. All of the concerns we security people have."

"How was it resolved?"

"I told the KGB that of all the places Khrushchev will be during his ten-day visit, there's no place as safe and secured as Camp David, and that we will put at his disposal the facilities of the White House Army Signal Agency."

"Did they buy it," Baughman asked.

"They did."

"I don't know what else to suggest, Jim. You seem to be on top of it. It is complex and it's going to be a tense ten days."

"I'll say. So I gather, Chief, that you're not convinced."

Baughman's secretary did not wait for a response to her knock on the door. She came into the room. There was sheer panic in her eyes. She was trembling and did all she could to say, "Mr. Rowley, the White House AIC is on the telephone. They've got two intruders inside . . . ."

Rowley leapt from his chair in front of Baughman's desk and snapped, "Chief, hit the speaker button!"

Anticipating Rowley's order, Baughman had turned his chair toward the credenza and pushed the telephone button putting Special Agent-in-Charge, John Stewart in communication with Rowley and himself.

"What do you have, John?" Rowley shouted toward the enamel speaker box that Baughman had placed on the desk.

"Two men broke away from the 11 A.M. visitor line and took off toward the House."

"Where's the Old Man? Is he still at EOB?" Rowley asked.

"He's still there. We got him covered well, Chief. He's safe and we . . . ."

Interrupting Stewart, Rowley said, "Where're the intruders now? Are they armed?"

"They're around the west side, sir. Each one took off in opposite directions, one around back, the other the front. No arms seen, but they were carrying posters of some sort rolled up under . . . . We got them, Chief. Just coming in—Gallagher's on the radio—no weapons."

"Who the hell are they?" Rowley shouted.

"Appear to be foreigners, sir. They don't speak English."

Baughman turned the speaker box toward himself and said to Stewart, "Any idea of their intentions, John?"

"Gallagher said, Chief, that they wanted to make a statement of some sort—they had two white sheets rolled up on a sawed-off rake handle."

"What kind of a statement, John?" Rowley asked.

"Gotta move, sir. The boss is on the move."

"What the hell," Rowley said in disgust. "Barbara, get Webster on the radio. Tell him to hold the president at EOB until we get these two under lock and key." Turning toward the speaker, Rowley said, "Stewart, have Gallagher and his men do a thorough search of the grounds. For all we know this could be a diversion of some kind."

Stewart spoke again, "The boss has agreed to hold, Chief. Written on the sheets was 'Long Live Hungary' in red letters."

"Get the two of them over to my office as quickly as you can. I'll be right there. Also get someone at State to come over and interpret for us." Rowley took a deep breath and sat down.

Baughman replaced the speaker phone back on the credenza and said, "Pretty daring—and stupid."

Rowley turned his head and stared out the window and said softly, "Just the beginning, sir. These jokers could have just as easily been armed."

* * *

On this Friday evening, Laszlo could hear drum rolls, bugle blasts, and cheers coming from the other side of the building. The signs and posters on the school fence announced that the Gettysburg High School football team was going to be deep in combat with the Frederick High School Panthers. He gathered from the ear-shattering noise Gettysburg was having some success. He hoped he would, too, as he entered the school building.

"If you're looking for those guys with the suits and hats, mister, they're down in the auditorium," the janitor said to Laszlo as he pushed his wide broom down the marble floor hallway.

"I was just looking for the men's room. If you could tell me where I might find it, please," Laszlo said.

"You know, there's one underneath the stadium," the janitor said. "But now that you're here, go back the other way. It's right next to the auditorium."

Laszlo expressed his thanks. He turned and headed in the opposite direction. As he did, he could hear the janitor mutter, "Foreigners, they're all the same." He paid it no heed. His thoughts were on the janitor's comment about the men in suits. He walked briskly down the dimly lit hall. The small wooden sign affixed to the wall had an arrow and underneath the word "auditorium." He turned and walked a short distance and saw two large doors. He pulled one and stepped inside.

"Can we help you, sir," Matt Hogan shouted from the auditorium's stage where he and two other men in business suits were standing.

"No, I was looking for the men's room and I heard voices," Laszlo said as he stood in the center aisle under the balcony overhang.

Walking up the aisle toward the intruder, Hogan said, "It's not in here, but you'll find it down the hall on your right."

"Thank you, sir. I'm sorry to have disturbed you," Laszlo said.

Laszlo retreated through the opened double doors to the hall, turned to his right, and headed for the men's room. As he heard the doors close, he thought that these men were not part of the faculty or, for that matter, associated with the high school.

CHAPTER 14

Fall arrived early in Vermont in 1959. The maples were shedding their lush summer green and acquiring a crimson red and corn-like yellow. The oaks were yielding their green for a collage of yellows, reds, and oranges.

Fall's early arrival was not a surprise to the area's old-timers. The severe winter of 1958-59, together with the dry spring and summer, was a precursor to the changing of the colors, depicted so well in the illustrations by former Arlington resident Norman Rockwell.

The season also brought out the entrepreneurial spirit of the local people. Little stands were set up along the state highway and were filled with jugs of cider, corn, and tomatoes; hand-crafted wooden objects; and multi-colored quilts. Nowhere was this more evident than on the Arlington Town Green on this sunny and warm Saturday morning.

"Janos, can't you go any faster?" Nina said. "Hanna wants the groceries for lunch."

"I'm doing the best I can. I've never seen so many people in Arlington before now," Janos said. "And I can see why. With the early change of seasons about to take place, the tourists have come to Arlington to bear witness to one of nature's most beautiful, if least understood, phenomenon."

Nina pleaded, "I'm not interested in nature, Janos. I want to be back at the farm before Laszlo wakes up. He looked exhausted when he came in last night, don't you agree?"

"Yes, and we should not have kept him up asking all those questions. We could have waited until this morning."

"Janos, let's not stop at the Green for the vegetables," Nina said. "Fisher farm will have them. The Town Green looks like a county fair."

* * *

Oblivious to all that was going on in the village below her mountain farm, Hanna was having her own celebration on this crystal clear morning. In the late hours of the night, her exhausted husband had come home. He had stayed up until almost dawn telling his family all that he had found out and accomplished during his two weeks away.

When he had begun to tell them what his mission was about, Hanna broke down in tears. Despite her husband's assurances that it would all work she, nevertheless, continued to weep.

It was only after hearing about each aspect of his mission, the renting of the house, his trip to Gettysburg, his visitation at the Shrine, and his near arrest in the woods near Camp David, that Hanna regained her composure and began to believe in what her husband was leading them into.

"Why don't you stay in bed and get some more sleep, Laszlo?" Hanna said as Laszlo appeared in the kitchen doorway wearing only shorts and an undershirt.

"No, no. I'm well rested now. There's much to be done, and we must all get together. There's a great deal to discuss."

As she dipped a fully feathered pheasant into near boiling water, Hanna said, "Lunch will be a celebration, Laszlo. We wanted to have a surprise for you but didn't know when you'd be arriving."

"If you keep staring at me, wife, you will ruin the skin of the bird by leaving her in the water too long."

"I know, my love. Fifty-two seconds, no more, no less."

"Where's Janos? And Nina? Are they out at the pens?" Laszlo said, removing his work shirt and dungarees from the kitchen door hook.

"They went into town for groceries and the newspaper. They should be back shortly; they left an hour ago."

"Well, while they're gone I'll get dressed and look at the pheasants. Janos said they've grown a lot and that we only lost a few dozen to pecking."

"While you are out there, Laszlo, be thinking of Nina. I'm worried about her. She harbors so much hatred and bitterness that I'm afraid that she might not be of any use to us," Hanna said, removing the feathers from the two scalded pheasant hens.

Tucking his red flannel shirt into the well-faded dungarees, Laszlo said, "That is exactly the attitude we will need, Hanna, if we want our mission to be a success. Our hatred for Khrushchev and for what he's done is precisely what is going to carry us through. Anything less and we will fail, and unless we all feel and believe as Nina does, we might as well stay home."

"Khrushchev is revolting to me," Hanna said, "I despise him, I loathe him and his associates. And yes, I hate him—as much as anyone here. But we mustn't allow ourselves to become so transfixed with our hatred that our judgment is impaired. And from what you said to us last night, Laszlo, we will need all our judgment and courage if we are to get at him."

"I know what you're saying and I too have noticed Nina's disposition and it does give me concern. It just needs to be channeled in the right direction. After lunch I'll talk to her, I promise," he said as he planted a kiss on his wife's neck while she finished removing the last of the birds' small feathers.

"Hanna, I can't tell you enough how I missed you. I've never been away from you this long," Laszlo whispered in her ear. "The birds can wait. They need to cool off anyway, but I don't think I can."

"My love, you cool off now, too. Nina and Janos will be back soon and I must get dinner ready."

"I never thought you would treat me like a pheasant, Hanna. It seems you just don't love me anymore," Laszlo said, running his fingers alongside the collar of his wife's blouse.

"Nonsense, dear, and you know it. If you keep this up you'll be as hot as this water. Tonight, my love, let's wait till tonight and then I'll show just how much I love you and missed you. So go out and tend to the birds and let me finish here."

"Show me a little bit now," Laszlo said as his hands moved down her flanks, stopping at her thin waist.

Hanna wanted to grab his wandering hands but couldn't. Her hands were covered with feathers. He wrapped his hands around the back pockets of her jeans and pulled her in tightly to him. Resisting was useless, she thought, and why should she? Laszlo lowered his unshaven face to hers and gently their lips came together. From the feeling she was getting through her apron, she knew he desired her now, but they had to wait. As she pulled her face away from his she whispered softly, "Later, my dear. I promise."

* * *

113

Janos's assessment was accurate, Laszlo thought to himself as he surveyed the fly-away pens; the pheasants had grown a great deal, especially the jumbo hens. After he entered the pen, he turned and locked the gate. He looked down the long, two-hundred foot runway and realized the beauty of what he and Janos were doing. The pheasants were in their fourteenth week and only a few weeks before maturity. Their magnificent beauty stood out, making them as grand a bird to view as any other, and probably as beautiful as the peacock. It was the cocks, more so than the hens, that were more noticeable and, of course, more beautiful. Their manner of strutting by the hens gave them an air of superiority, if not one of defiance.

Laszlo cleared a spot on top of the waterers and sat down. Looking at the birds he wondered what kind of world exists here, inside the pens. Judging from the missing back feathers, the violence the birds do to each other had not subsided, even as they matured. He was not surprised to see some birds deliberately peck at others who only moments before were content as they sat in small dugout holes.

"God," he thought, "they behave just like people. The hens just want to be left alone in peace to enjoy their last few weeks before they must be sacrificed for someone's dinner." But peace they would not have. The cocks, with their sharp and sturdy beaks jutting out between the scarlet red wattles followed by coal-black and snow-white rings on their necks and topped off by the beautiful colors that made up the rest of their body, including the golden brown hackle and blue saddle, were not about to let that happen.

In awe at what he was witnessing, Laszlo thought how little different life was in here compared to what he had experienced in Hungary. We are all hens and we must quickly move aside and let the cocks strut by. The members of the Party, the Communist Party, were not much different than these cocks who felt and acted as if they were the prima donnas and not the hens—not the people. With their long tail feathers cantilevering almost two feet, the cocks instinctively knew that only by intimidation and by violence could they rule. And so they did. And Laszlo was powerless to stop them. What went on in the pens was the natural law: survival. But in Budapest it was man's law and not nature's law that dictated who and how you were to live. And that could be interfered with—it should and it would be.

Laszlo retreated back to the house and wondered what would happen to the birds when he and the others left for Maryland. Soon he would have to inform the others that they would be going in three days. He wondered if Mr. Smyth could come sooner and take all of the pheasants, especially if he would be given a lower price to buy them. The money could be used to help with expenses, especially since after they made their escape there would be no coming back to Vermont. The others did not know that yet, and they would have to be told soon. At dinner he would tell them.

* * *

Its size and restricted nature made a tour of duty at Camp David confining. Many of the off-duty hours' amenities found on larger military bases were non-existent. However because of the cloistered nature of the Camp there was much more interpersonal activity, the kind one would find aboard ship or at a distant radar listening post. Fergurson took advantage of this and made it his job to get to know his men. The quasi-solitude of Camp David also provided him with the time to observe and obtain a deeper respect for Sergeant Kellerman.

"Norm, take the platoon, at least what's not on guard, and have them do some compass and map work at Look-Out Rock," Fergurson said. This was the first time that he had called Kellerman "Norm," and it was both out of respect and comradeship. "God only knows they get so little combat training by being in this unit that I fear what would happen if we were called up to Division for a combat role."

"That's not as far fetched as you might think, Lieutenant. It occurred last year when the Corps activated one-third of each East Coast command to move to Camp LeJeune and we joined the Sixth Marines and headed out to Lebanon."

"What they do here, in Washington, with the silent drill team is first class, no doubt about it, but we must not forget that our real mission is with the Fleet Marine Force. Meantime I'll try and meet with Commander Nicholson about the fence and see what he's been doing about it."

"I'll bet not much."

* * *

115

Fergurson knew relations between the Marine Corps and the Navy had always been, at best, lukewarm and, at worst, strained. The Marine Corps was a branch of the Navy and, since the days of Archibald Henderson, the Corps' first Commandant, all Marines to some degree had resented the Navy. Some would go so far as to call it paternalistic, with the Corps being the Navy's stepchild.

This historical relationship between the branches was not evident at Camp David. The present commander and his predecessors, dating back to 1942, recognized the critical role the Marines undertook and the many hardships they endured.

"Well, Lieutenant, have you seen all of the Camp? What do you think of it?" Commander Nicholson asked, seated at his desk cluttered with the many mementos he had garnered during his twenty years at sea and from his last assignment as Naval Attache to the U.S. Ambassador to Great Britain.

"Pretty much, sir," Fergurson said.

"Oh, by the way Lieutenant, please stand at ease. For that matter, relax and sit, if you wish."

"Thank you, sir. I'll stand if you don't mind. I'm more at ease this way, believe it or not," Fergurson said. "And from what I've seen so far, sir, it's quite a place—not what I had expected."

"Let me start by saying, Lieutenant, that I'm no stranger to the Corps—I took you guys in at Guadalcanel and picked you up at Iwo and with our ship's sixteen inch guns blasting the hell out of the hills above you at Inchon—yes, I know Marines, Lieutenant, and I very much look forward to knowing you and your men."

Fergurson was taken by surprise by the warm reception.

"Are you married, Lieutenant? Have a family?"

"No, sir. Never been married. Did have a girl while in college, but she did not want to wait the four years while I was in the Corps."

"Too bad, but just as well. The problem of being up here as the Camp Commander is that I can't have my family here. It's like being out at sea."

"So where're they now, Commander? Is that a picture of them?" Fergurson asked, having noticed a photograph on the Commander's credenza.

"They're staying in a rented house in Hagerstown just west of here. I get to see them at least a couple of nights a week plus weekends, so long as things are quiet here. Well, Lieutenant, you didn't come here just to hear about me. What can I do for you?"

"Its got to do with some security matters, Commander. Sergeant Kellerman and I toured the Camp last week and came upon several large openings between the fence and the deck out by Posts Six, Twelve, and Fourteen and also by the gate to the Deep-Six. These gaps seem to be caused by surface runoff that has created channels which now are wide and deep enough to render the fence ineffective in some places. With your permission, sir, my men will fix them, provided we can requisition some twelve inch corrugated iron pipe and some barbed wire."

"I appreciate the initiative, Lieutenant. I can get you the wire now; the pipe has to come up from the Washington Navy yard, and I'll get off a memo for that today."

Fergurson's lips tightened at hearing Nicholson's response. This was the second time he had mentioned the problem and still there was to be no action taken, only a memo. It was high time that he spoke up, he thought. Hell, he's responsible for security. "Begging the Commander's pardon, sir, but that could take weeks and the holes are wide open now. Why not go down to Thurmont and get the pipe ourselves—it's no big deal."

"Lieutenant, we don't do things that way. There're budgets, authorizations, procedures. You should know that by now," Nicholson said testily.

Fergurson felt he was beginning to try Nicholson's patience, but said anyway, "Commander, we're only talking about a half dozen ten-foot lengths of corrugated steel pipe. How much could it cost? I could go get it and have it installed in a day."

"Lieutenant, you're looking at several hundred dollars. It's not authorized by me or the Navy and they run this place. So let's do it my way. Okay? In the meantime, stuff the holes with the wire."

"If I had the money, I'd do it myself, sir."

"I bet you would. I have to leave soon, Lieutenant, so let's move on. Is there anything else?"

He then said: "Sir, I also feel that the Deep-Six area is a potential security threat, and I wondered why we just don't send our trash off the hill to the Thurmont dump?"

"Against Secret Service orders, Lieutenant. They don't want the locals poking through presidential garbage, either for souvenirs or intelligence.

However we do have a request in for next year's budget to fence in the dump and bring that road leading down to it within the secured area. But we'll just have to wait and see how appropriations go. Prior to my taking over, a considerable amount of money went into the Camp's tunnel and communications systems. Just before the president went to Europe, Captain Aurand, the president's Naval aide whom you'll meet next week, told me that for budget reasons the Old Man wants no more spending up here for this fiscal year. Instead let his successor get it through Congress."

"I appreciate the info, sir, and apologize if I seem to be a little pigheaded. By the way, Commander, did you see the report regarding the civilian we stopped in the woods last week?"

"Yes, I did and I mailed it to Washington yesterday. I'm glad you read him the riot act. Sounds like you scared the pants off him. In any event, with those kinds of matters, orders are to forward the report to the White House Secret Service detail for any follow up by them. Pass on to Kellerman "a job well done," Lieutenant. Hey, not to mention the stopping of that reporter—good work there, as well."

"By the way, sir, what ever happened to him after we turned him over to the Secret Service?"

"Oh, they questioned him for about an hour and got an affidavit that he wouldn't shoot his mouth off about what he saw."

"That's all? What about his pass?"

"They were going to lift it but the president's press secretary stepped in and rescued his butt. Seems like they're old friends. But I did hear that by and large he's a good guy and writes up the administration real well. Lieutenant, I'm due at Aspen for a meeting in a few minutes, so if I can be of help to you in any way, let me know. And I'll get on that pipe, I promise."

"Thank you, sir. There's something that continues to bother me."

Nicholson was startled at Fergurson's comment. He stopped walking towards the door, turned, and said: "What's that? And why not tell me as I head over to Aspen?"

Now that he had broached the subject, Fergurson wasn't sure where to begin. He was hoping Nicholson wasn't watching him rub his fingers along the brim of his cap. He said: "Oh, it's probably nothing. Kellerman thinks it's my imagination."

"Well, let's have it."

"It's that guy Bender, sir. You know, the fellow in the woods, the one in the report."

"What about him? He seemed from the report to be innocent enough, harmless if you asked me."

"Commander, I just can't get it out of my head that he and I met somewhere. When, and under what circumstances, just won't come to me."

"Well, maybe you bumped into him in town. The report said he lived in Thurmont."

"I've been up here ever since the platoon was reassigned. I haven't been off the hill other than to check and pick up the bridge guards."

"I don't have time to discuss it now, Lieutenant, but take some time and think about where it was you might have seen him. We'll talk later. In the meantime, go about it logically, Lieutenant, and what I mean is that he is a foreigner, German you stated. Well, have you been to Germany? Your service jacket notes that you were in the Med' and in Lebanon. Could you have run into him in Beirut?"

"I'll do that, sir. By the way, I didn't put this concern in my report; I just felt that it was too vague."

* * *

"No one cooks pheasant like you do, Hanna," Janos said, sucking the last juices from the leg of the well-cooked bird.

Laszlo leaned over and kissed his wife on her forehead and said, "Having been away for two weeks and eating out every night, I can only say, Hanna, that I never realized I married you for your cooking. You're just the best any man could ask for in a wife."

"You've been away too long. You never said that about my cooking before, Laszlo. Janos, maybe you should go away, and you would appreciate Nina. Isn't that right, Nina?"

"I think your brother loves me and doesn't have to go anywhere," said the pensive-looking Nina.

All the way back from Thurmont to Arlington, Laszlo wondered how and when he was going to tell them that they had to leave Vermont, the farm, the pheasants. He dreaded the moment. Lunch was festive. "They're in good spirits. Even Nina, up to a point." Boasting about what they would do to Khrushchev was all they had ever done since coming

119

to America. It had consumed so many discussions at dinner in the evenings. Talking about him and his cohorts had to end. The taking of actions must begin. Now was the time. There would be no going back. He began by saying, "Now that we all know how much we're missed, we must talk about our plans. Let me start by saying that we'll be leaving here in three days to go to Maryland. We don't have much time. Khrushchev will be arriving in America on Tuesday the fifteenth and we must be in the Thurmont house by then so as not to arouse suspicion. Also, and I don't really know how to say this—there's a good chance that we'll never return to the farm. So if you want to take any small things as remembrances, we can do that but we must not let on to anyone that we're not returning."

"Laszlo," Janos said, "I don't understand why we will not return here. You don't think we'll be caught."

"My plan is for us to escape and ultimately work our way back to Hungary. At the proper time we'll make contact with the Hungarian Refugee movement. They'll assist us out of the country. As you know, they have many safe houses that will give us shelter and new papers. The officials, in time, will figure out that it was us that executed Khrushchev. We must not fool ourselves. After we carry out our mission, there's going to be enormous repercussions here, in Hungary, and in Moscow. The governments will be under severe pressure to track us down. They'll come here, so that's why we must be prepared not to come back or even stay in the place I rented in Thurmont."

"Laszlo, what if we get captured—either one of us or all of us?" Janos asked meekly.

Laszlo looked at their solemn faces and said, "We have to plan and hope that will not happen. On the other hand, we must be ready for it. However I leave it up to each of you to decide what you would do. If I'm captured, I, for one, will take my own life so as not to betray any of you."

Hanna did not want them to dwell on Janos's question, so she asked, "Laszlo, why must we leave in three days if the president and Khrushchev will not be at Camp David until two weeks from now?"

"Because I want each of you to become familiar with Thurmont and the area, and you can only do that by being there and going over each step of the mission. But, more importantly, is that we must be able to do it at night. And that will require a good deal of practice."

Nina, who was clearing the dishes, was listening in silence.

Hanna, looking over her husband's shoulder at a map Laszlo had opened up on the table, said, "Won't we be conspicuous? Strangers walking around town and the woods each day for a week? We probably should do it in two groups."

"I agree, Hanna, that we should never move around as four. But, while we're there, much will be going on—it is very much like Arlington during foliage week, but ten times more people and cars."

"How do you know that, Laszlo?" Janos asked.

"Whenever the president is at Camp David, there are hundreds of reporters who flock to Thurmont waiting for some news story to come down from the mountains. With the Khrushchev visit, they expect almost a thousand reporters. So many, in fact, the press conferences held at the local high school gym are going to be held at the Gettysburg high school auditorium. And, don't you see, the president and Khrushchev will be at those press conferences. Also during the weekend two local colleges start their Fall terms and that brings in many students and their families. I saw a poster in the Thurmont General Store that showed that the annual Thurmont Harvest Festival will be held on Friday, September twenty-fifth to Sunday the twenty-seventh, which is perfect for us."

Janos said, "Hanna, we're blessed with a good sign already, with all that should be going on during our stay. No one should give us a second glance."

"You don't think the neighbors next to Mrs. Gropp's house will become suspicious of us?" Hanna asked.

"Mrs. Gropp told me that for the past twenty years she has been letting her house out every September. And she does it just like many people do here during the fall in order to make some money and to get away from the tourists. She probably has already told her neighbors about us. One family has already met me and are pleased that we are from Germany, because most of the town is German. No, my biggest worry is here—what happens if someone comes by before the twenty-fifth?"

Janos, his voice registering concern for the birds, asked, "Laszlo, how do we leave here in three days with nine thousand pheasants out there? Who will take care of them when we're away and, now that you told us that we won't be coming back—what are we to do with them?"

Laszlo said, "Before you came in for lunch, I called Mr. Smyth and gave him a proposal to buy out the flock. He said he would come out today and look at the birds. He didn't believe that they were heavy enough. You know just from looking at them, that we're about a quarter to half pound below his minimum requirements."

"If only we could have hatched them two weeks sooner," Janos remarked.

"I know, Janos, but we didn't and now we must make do," Laszlo said somewhat irritably. "We don't want to leave the birds unattended, and we also could use the money."

"We have thousands of dollars out there, Laszlo," Hanna said, "and we will need it all to get away. The money we have in the bank is not that much."

Janos asked, "Laszlo, just where will we be going after camp. . . ."

"Who's coming?" yelled Hanna, her nerves on edge.

"It's Mr. Smyth," Nina replied, looking out the window over the sink where she was washing the last of the luncheon dishes.

"Janos, let's go and meet him. I hope he's in a buying mood. We'll continue to go over our plans when he leaves."

* * *

Mr. Smyth held a jumbo hen in his hands and ran his fingers through its flight and back feathers and said, "I'm sorry to disappoint both of you, but I just can't buy the birds until you can overcome the mite infestation. Look here, you see these scratches on its back, those red lines, and you see those little black dots—those are mites and she is scratching like the blazes to get rid of them."

"I don't understand the harm in a few mites, Mr. Smyth," Janos said, noticeably shaken by the news.

"Janos, my stores and restaurants will not buy birds that have scratches in the skin. When they go to cook them, the skin will tear and not only will the pheasant appear unsightly, but it will cook unevenly."

As if pleading, Janos said, "This problem wasn't here a few days ago."

"This summer we had a major infestation of mites hitting the tomato growers, more so than in prior years, and all brought on because of the two weeks of heavy rain in July. Unless you can control this soon, the birds will loose their back feathers and could easily die from sunburn and, if we get frost and they get wet, they'll be exposed to pneumonia."

"What do you do to treat this, Mr. Smyth? How did we get them way up here?" Laszlo asked, unfazed and knowing that he would not be around to see the cure.

"The mites are in the air and are blown up here by the wind. As far as treating them, you must obtain a pesticide in powder form and spray each bird. Also you need to set up boxes in the pens and fill them with the pesticide so that when the hens sit down they will be dusting themselves. The cocks will not use the boxes, so you must hit them hard with the spraying. The other thing I warn you about is that although the pesticide is harmless to the birds, it can be deadly to humans. Therefore you must not spray on a windy day, and when you do spray, you must wear a mask at all times."

"Where can we get this pesticide, Mr. Smyth?" Janos asked.

"Whitman's Feed Store in North Bennington can get it for you. Also, boys, the reason your birds' weight is not up to what it should be is that the birds are using all of their energy to fight the blood sucking mites and, if not treated, in time they will become lethargic and become prey to the healthy birds, especially the cocks."

Janos appeared dejected; he felt humiliated that his birds were infected. Worse he had never heard of the parasite that was causing the problem. Looking over at Laszlo, who was running his hand through a hen's feathers, he asked, "What do you think we should do?"

Before Laszlo could respond, Smyth said, "I'll tell you what. If you get on this by tomorrow, I'll need seven days after you spray before I can buy any of them especially if they get slaughtered the day after I buy them. It will take that long for the pesticide to work its way out."

"If that's what it'll take to rid the birds of mites, Janos and I will do the spraying today."

"In any event, Laszlo, I'll be back here in a week to see how you're getting along."

Mr. Smyth walked back to his car, got in, and drove down the driveway, Janos and Laszlo waved goodbye to him for the last time.

CHAPTER 15

Between Monday and Friday, at eight-thirty in the morning, the gates to the White House South Portico colonnade are open to tourists. Visitors walk through the ground floor area up to the first floor where the State reception rooms are located. It was no different on this mid-September morning.

"You know, Matt," Rowley said to his second-in-command, "ever since the Biddles gave the White House their silver collection, the tourist traffic through the Gold Room makes it feel like a herd of cattle is over my head."

The twenty-eight-year-old former Fordham University football star said, "Well, Chief, just think what it would be like if the House were to be opened seven days a week. The uniform guys tell me there's a lot of bitching by the tourists who come on weekends, not realizing that the White House is only open for tours on weekday mornings."

Rowley, walking over to the coffee pot for his third refill, said, "Who can blame them? If I came all the way from Idaho to see the White House and it was closed, I'd be pissed."

"Jim, with all your influence with the boss, why isn't your office up on the living quarters' floor? By the way, if you're successful in having it placed there, see if you can have it a bit larger—this place reminds me of a cell in a fifteenth century Jesuit monastery."

"I don't think now would be the time to ask him about office requirements," Rowley said, holding up his outstretched arms. "For that matter, I hope I can survive the next ten days. If so I'll be extremely grateful for these humble surroundings."

Not trying to hide his grin, Hogan said, "By the way, I heard you had some excitement here while I was in Gettysburg. See what happens when I'm gone for a few days?"

"Don't be a wise guy," Rowley said. "It could've been serious."

"Just a couple of nuts, wouldn't you say?"

"Matt," Rowley said seriously, "those two intruders were not your average screwballs. They were desperate. They knew they could never have gotten away with it—and it's these kinds of individuals who keep me awake."

"Don't misunderstand me, Chief, I do take it seriously."

"So, enough said, let me bring you up-to-date on what is the latest with the schedule and personnel. Incidentally, there is no assurance that by noon this program won't change dramatically. Here, have a look." He handed the flip chart to Hogan.

Tuesday, September 15	1100 Hours	Khrushchev and party arrive Andrews Air Force base
	1230 Hours	Motorcade arrives 14th Street
	1245 Hours	Party arrives Blair House
	1330 Hours	Private luncheon, Blair House
	1530 Hours	Party arrives White House
	2000 Hours	State dinner
Wednesday, September 16		Washington
Thursday, September 17		Washington—New York
Friday, September 18		New York
Saturday, September 19		New York—Los Angeles
Sunday, September 20		Los Angeles—San Francisco
Monday, September 21		San Francisco
Tuesday, September 22		San Francisco—Des Moines
Wednesday, September 23		Des Moines—Pittsburgh
Thursday, September 24		Pittsburgh
Friday, September 25		Washington—Camp David
Saturday, September 26		Camp David
Sunday, September 27		Camp David—Washington—departs

"Well, I hope not too many people are in possession of this schedule, especially in this kind of detail, Chief. Jesus! You have that down to a gnat's ass."

"Are you kidding?" Rowley snapped. "Did you see this morning's *Washington Post* or the *New York Times*? They have this in print so the whole world can be made aware of what will be taking place. I pleaded with State to hold off on the details until the night before the president and the premier were to arrive in each city . . . ."

"What did they say?"

126

"That we're being too cautious and that Khrushchev's advance party want his travel plans publicized. Thank God for Hipsley, and even he was against such a detailed schedule being put out to the press."

"How's Hipsley getting into the act?" Hogan asked.

"Matt, I bet Khrushchev doesn't know Hips, but he will soon. Hips will be all over him," Rowley said, with a grin. "I can't wait for Khrushchev to see this six-foot, five-inch giant. He's not the Director of Physical Security at State because of some political appointment. He earned it. And Elmer Rodie Hipsley, as Khrushchev's personal guard, is not about to take any guff from State, the KGB, or, for that matter, from us. He's as tough as nails, Matt, and you're in for an experience—just wait and see."

"Wasn't he with Roosevelt and also one of us?"

"That's right. Hips and I go way back. Matter of fact, Hips was to Agent-in-Charge Mike Reilly what you're to me. Reilly and Hipsley were at Yalta together and he was at Warm Springs, Georgia, when President Roosevelt died. I believe he was in the Secret Service about fifteen years. God, he's probably close to fifty by now."

"Why did he leave?"

"More pay at State from what I gather. But let me just say that having Hips with Khrushchev does help us a lot. Also he's well known to Andropov. By the way, let me tell you who'll be here from the KGB, because it seems like they're bringing in their 'big guns' with Andropov moving down to fourth place."

"Can't say that I blame them, Chief."

"The three in-charge guys will be Burdin, Grubjakov, and Zakharov. Burdin, I believe you met briefly, Matt, in Geneva in fifty-five. The others I want you to get to know real well, along with Burdin, because when the boss goes to the Soviet Union in November, you'll be working closely with all three."

Rowley thought for a minute. Getting to know and work with the Soviets would be no easy task. Although he had the highest praise for his intelligent and aggressive second-in-command, he knew Burdin was the best the Soviets had.

"Matt, let me tell you a little about this guy Vladimir P. Burdin, who is ten years your senior. He's thirty-seven and it's remarkable that he holds the position of Chief Section A of the First Directorate of the KGB. He's skilled in languages, including flawless English, and is aggressive while at the same time the quintessential diplomat. And I'm told by the CIA that Burdin's role with Khrushchev is more than just being a bodyguard. Allen Dulles's people are of the opinion that one day this soft-spoken but smart agent will be the heir apparent to the very man he's protecting today."

"What about Zakharov, Chief?" Hogan asked. "You worked with him before, if I'm not mistaken."

"I know General Zakharov well. He's middle-aged and a major general, heads up the Soviet Internal Affairs Department. We worked together on the preparations for Nixon's trip to the Soviet Union. On the other hand, we know little about Vasily Grubyakov. The CIA did tell me that he is an accomplished spy and distinguished himself in pre-World War Turkey, is fluent in a number of languages, and dropped from sight after the War only to return two years ago as a diplomatic assistant to the Soviet Foreign Minister."

"I'll do my best to get to know them."

"Let's get back home for a minute, Matt. How did you find things at the Gettysburg High School? Can we secure it?" Rowley asked.

"It looks good. We'll have men on the stage directly behind the boss and Khrushchev, in the stage lamp girders as well as in the balcony. Only those with the plastic ID card will be let in, and we won't issue those until the morning of the press conference. Matter of fact, Chief, they'll need the card just to get into the parking area."

"Well, it looks like you're on top of it. I wish I could say the same," Rowley said.

"The school people are pretty loose up there, Chief. It seems like anyone can walk freely in and out. Hell, while the boys and I were checking out the auditorium some guy sauntered in looking for the head. Unbelievable!"

"I'm sure that's happened to you before, Matt."

"Yeah, it has, Chief, but this guy seemed different. Too smooth, too cool, if you know what I mean."

"What gave you that impression? Was he a local? Anything going on at the school?"

"A football game, but it was a long way from the men's room, I assure you. This guy was no local, he had a deep European accent—German, maybe."

"Hell, Matt," Rowley said impatiently, "the whole area is 'Little Germany.' That doesn't surprise me one bit."

"Chief, I would like to go over with you our file on this Hungarian priest, Tomas Padula, and also a memo that came in from Commander Nicholson at Camp David regarding some guy the Marines picked up near the back gate."

* * *

It was Monday morning in the Oval Office and President Eisenhower said, "You know, Chris, I'm anxious to have the next two weeks over with. I'm afraid to say what we're in for—the biggest propaganda exhibition this country has ever seen."

"Mr. President," Herter said, "Khrushchev certainly will use his trip across the country as a stage to herald that socialism is every bit as good as capitalism."

"And can he act the part, Chris? Just wait and see how he behaves when he goes to Pittsburgh and sees the strike at U.S. Steel. Were we able to substitute Chicago?"

"No, unable to get his people to agree to the change, and the way the secretary of labor describes it, the strike will be on when Khrushchev visits there a week from Wednesday."

"Jesus, he'll surely move to the offense over the strike and be patronizing to the workers, you watch. Incidently, Chris, while I think about it, what have you done for interpreters—both ours and theirs?"

"Mr. President, later today you are scheduled to meet Alex Akabovsky and Natalie Kushnir; both are with State. "I heard good things about Akabovsky. The vice president said he did a fine job this summer in Moscow and that when he and Khrushchev had the encounter in the 'kitchen' at the Exhibition Hall, Alex stayed right up to what was being said. However Miss Kushnir is less experienced but qualified. She is young; she's about twenty-five, born in the Soviet Union. She and her family were rescued from the Germans where they were held captive during the War. She has been with us for about one year and is a graduate of a New York City university. I believe, Mr. President, that you'll find them to be quick, intelligent, and expert in the dialect as well as the language."

"Well, I look forward to meeting them then. From this morning's *Times,* I see that Khrushchev is bringing with him Ambassador Troyanovsky's son as his interpreter. That does not surprise me; he's well respected and I worked with him before. It doesn't give us much time, Chris, for our interpreters to get to work with me. However I don't believe there'll be anything of substance discussed before Khrushchev leaves for New York. Nevertheless, I do want to work closely with Akabovsky and Kushnir over the next few days so that they're ready when we go to Camp David. And I would appreciate it if you would let Ann know so she can get me time each day to spend with them."

"I'll see to it, Mr. President."

* * *

Janos went out on to the porch, carrying two old suitcases and said, "Sometimes, Hanna, I just don't understand Laszlo. Here we are trying to get out of here and where does he go, but to buy the newspaper."

"Don't let it worry you, brother," Hanna said as she held the screen door open. "You know whatever Laszlo does he has a well thought out reason for doing. Look! Here he comes now."

Laszlo, running up the path out of breath said, "You won't believe what's here on the front page of the *New York Times* . . . ."

"Tell us!" Hanna said.

"On the front page is the day-by-day and hour-by-hour schedule of Khrushchev's visit. It's all here, every place he'll be going to," Laszlo said.

"Let's see it," Janos said.

Holding the newspaper up so they could see what he was describing, Laszlo said, "It never ceases to amaze me how open Americans are. And look! A week from Friday at six in the evening Khrushchev leaves with the president for Camp David. This gives us more time than I had thought. I was under the impression that Khrushchev and Eisenhower were going there sooner."

"Does that mean that we can stay here until next week?" Hanna asked, hoping to receive a yes from her husband.

"By no means—no. What it does for us is give us more time to practice for our mission."

Janos said, "The extra week here, Laszlo, will help us get rid of the mites, and you heard Mr. Smyth, he would be back late this week. A week would allow us to get the pheasants healthy."

Placing his arm around Janos, Laszlo said, "I know how attached you are to the pheasants, and how hard you've worked to get them to where they are, but you'll need the time in Maryland. We all will, if this mission is to be successful."

Overhearing the conversation from the kitchen, Nina joined in and said, "Laszlo is right. We need time to go over the plan. Our break-in will be at night if it is going to be at Camp David, and we know that hiking in the woods at night is not the same as doing it by daylight. And, if it takes place at the high school, we still have lots of preparation to do."

"Thank you, Nina. I believe I know how each of you feels about leaving this place. It has been our home for three years."

"Laszlo, you always seem to be right," Hanna said. "If we keep waiting to go, it will only be that much harder to leave. How was it that only you knew that Khrushchev and President Eisenhower were going to Camp David? What would we do if they did not schedule talks at Camp David, but, instead, someplace else—the White House?"

Laszlo said, "If the White House, there's nothing we could do—it's too obvious. You saw it on television. It is well guarded and all lit up at night. But it won't be there, I know. When I first heard about the Khrushchev visit, I read in the newspaper that the president wanted to hold major talks and do so away from Washington where he and Mr. Khrushchev would not be hounded by the press. So Camp David was suggested to the president."

While the others continued to talk on the porch, Janos quietly loaded the last of their baggage into the truck and car. With his head down and his eyes swollen with tears that would not flow out, he joined the others and said, "Before we leave we should say a prayer and ask our Lord to watch over us."

"Laszlo, you're our leader—would you offer a prayer?" Hanna said.

"Don't be foolish," Laszlo snapped.

"I'm not being foolish," Janos replied. "We'll need God's blessing."

"What we need is motivation and courage. Don't get me started on this religion stuff, not now!"

Hanna said, "All we're asking is for God to strengthen our will and motives and to . . . ."

Interrupting her and with anger in his voice, Laszlo said, "And why would God do that? If you need motivation for what we have to do, let me address them for you by reading a statement made by 'the Butcher' yesterday in Moscow to European reporters. It's here in the *New York Times*. It was the answer Khrushchev gave to a question about his country's invasion of Hungary and the feelings of the Americans toward what he had done:

> '*The Question of Hungary has stuck in some people's throats as a dead rat. The Americans feel it is unpleasant and yet he cannot spit it out.*'

We must go now."

* * *

"Six culverts have been dug out, Lieutenant," Kellerman said, watching Fergurson check the armament in the guardhouse. "All we need is the pipe and wire to complete the job. Any word from the Navy as to when we might be getting it?"

Fergurson did not answer. Instead he turned to Corporal Mullins and Private Phillips.

At the beginning of each day's guard rotations, usually at 0800 hours, the guard coming on for the next twenty-four hours was required to conduct an inventory of all the gear that the Sergeant-of-the-Guard and his watch would be assuming.

"You prepared to sign off on the inventory, Corporal Phillips?" Fergurson asked.

"Yes, sir. All equipment and arms are present and accounted for," the Corporal said.

"Carry on. Mullins, you are relieved as Sergeant-of-the-Guard. Now, to answer your question about the pipe, Sergeant. I was told by Commander Nicholson that we should have it within a week and that worries me."

"Don't let it, Lieutenant. Me and the men can install it in two days after we get it."

"This morning, Sergeant, I received the schedule for Mr. Khrushchev's visit. The president and the Soviet premier will be arriving from Washington by helicopter on the twenty-fifth."

"And here we are with six gaping holes in the fence," Kellerman said.

"Well, let's keep an eye on them, Sergeant, especially if they are not fixed by the twenty-fifth. We'll probably want to include something specific in Special Orders that weekend."

Phillips said, "Sir, what do you want done with the camera? We still are listing it as inventory."

"Have someone return it to the Thurmont police together with the shotguns we confiscated from those construction workers at the main gate. You would have thought by now they would have left them home. They know that all cars and trucks are searched and if any firearms are found they're confiscated."

Leaving the guardhouse with Fergurson, Kellerman said, "I agree, sir, and the jerks had them hanging in front of the rear window of their pick-up trucks."

"I want to tell you something, Norm, I know where I saw that guy with the camera."

"Did I hear you right? You're kidding me—you're not. Where was that?"

"On some beach on the Adriatic coast in Yugoslavia."

"You're sure of that? What the hell were you doing there?"

"In fifty-six, I was with the Marine detachment on the Ranger and we went ashore to rescue a couple of hundred Hungarian refugees."

"That was three years ago, Lieutenant. They all looked alike from what I remember from the newsreels."

"No, not this guy. You see, a storm was on its way. We had to get off the beach in a hurry and I remember these four people—two or three of them were hurt and were way behind the others. I went back for them. Hell, our pilot, a major, chewed my ass out for holding up the aircraft. I was just a new, ninety-day wonder, a Second Louie and way out of line. But I just couldn't see leaving them there."

"You've got balls, sir. I like that."

"You can say that now, but what if we hadn't got off? No, it was, I suppose, reckless."

"That's what it's all about. You've got to stick your neck out and it may get chopped off. No, I like that kind of spirit. But, Jesus! You know what the chances are for you to run into this guy again? And here? A million to one."

"I know. And what really bothers me is why would he lie about his name and nationality? And what the hell was he doing out there in the first place?"

"Maybe he was just scared and didn't want any trouble. You know how foreigners tighten up when they see someone in uniform."

"I'll tell you one thing, Norm, I thought for a second that he recognized me. I could see it in his cold blue eyes. Let's plan to go to Thurmont and check out his address. I just want to make sure. Who knows, I could be seeing things."

"Wanta hold his camera?" Kellerman asked. "We can use it as an excuse to pay him a visit."

"No, we've held it long enough. Like I said, I could be all wet and he could be who he said he is."

* * *

Matt Hogan handed the memo to Rowley and said, "Here's the memo from Commander Nicholson, Chief. It seems routine. They get people coming up to the main gate all the time and they just send them on their way."

Rowley took the memo and glanced at it. "It says here, Matt, that it was the back gate. How many trespassers were ever found there—none, if I recall—now we've got this guy who maybe lives in Thurmont and is of German descent."

Hogan was taken back by Rowley's interpretation and said, "Well, that's not out of the ordinary—most of the locals in the area are in one way or another from Germany."

"I suppose. You know, this is interesting," Rowley said. "The fellow had a camera—a 35 mm with a telescopic lens. Now why would he be way up in the woods with all that photographic equipment? Did you read this, Matt?"

"I did, Chief," Hogan said, feeling uncomfortable that he may have overlooked something critical. "It sounded innocent enough. Lieutenant Fergurson asked him why the camera and I believe he said he was taking pictures of the fall foliage."

"Doesn't it strike you as being peculiar," Rowley said, "that if the guy was really into photographing leaves he would do so when they're more at their peak which, I believe in the Catoctin Mountains, is later this month? Also if ever the Marines found someone near the fence, ten times out of ten they would be carrying a rifle doing some deer poaching. But so far as I know, they've never picked up anyone with a camera along the fence, especially near the back gate which is a long way off the park road."

"No disrespect, Chief, but aren't you reaching on this one? Fergurson asked the guy why he was so far off the road and he said that the colors were out more on the northwest side of the mountains. You might not be aware, Jim, cooped up here in this cell, but it appears that we're having an early fall this year."

"I guess you're right, Matt. With this detail coming at us tomorrow, I'm seeing trouble at every turn. In any event, why don't you have the Baltimore office check this guy out—what's his name—Bender. Let's find out if we have anything on file about him."

"I'll get on it right away, Chief," Hogan said, getting up out of his chair about to leave Rowley's office.

"And Matt, just to show you how far afield my mind is ranging, I've even given to speculating a possible connection with Bender and the guy you saw in the auditorium."

Hogan's face lost some of its red as he moved back away from the door and said, "Chief, you don't think for one minute that there's a . . . ."

Instantly Rowley saw the look on his protegee's face and said, "No, no. It's just my own way of tying events together. The memo has no description of him."

"Two separate run-ins. A foreigner, male, who was not where he was supposed to be . . . that you can't deny, Chief."

"That may be so, but now you're getting caught up like me. Let's drop it and you better get on with a final check on security."

"Okay! But it does have an interesting ring," Hogan said as he headed toward the door for the second time.

"By the way, Matt, Nicholson's memo mentions that they confiscated Bender's camera. Let's get the folks at Camp David to send it to us."

CHAPTER 16

"Good God, Chris! Look at the size of that thing," the president said to his secretary of state as they watched the giant TU Illusian 114 touch down on the runway at Andrews Air Force Base. "I can see why they couldn't bring him in at National. I'm not sure he has enough runway."

Landing at one hundred sixty knots, the sleek, silver turbo jet rapidly consumed the runway and it appeared that if it did not slow down and come to a halt soon, it would go straight through the four-foot steel stanchions at the end of runway one-five.

When Khrushchev had arrived at the 1955 Summit among world leaders in Geneva, his aircraft was small and uncomfortable. What was most humiliating was that it was not an aircraft that in any way was commensurate with his position as the leader of a world power. To avoid any such future embarrassment, he had his country's engineers design the TU 114. The plane's swept-back wings, spanning close to two hundred forty feet, with six extra fuel tanks hanging from the outer wing tips like gigantic melons from a fruit tree, had enabled the plane to fly non-stop for fourteen hours from Moscow's Military Airport to Washington.

Taxiing the TU 114 back from the remaining hundred feet of runway, the Russian crew guided it to the runway crossover, and the plane's width almost prevented it from keeping the plane's wheels on the concrete. Coming to a stop in front of the arrival party, several Air Force personnel guided out a motorized set of steps for debarking the largest passenger aircraft in the world.

The noon day sun reflected brightly off the aircraft's fuselage. Observing the proceedings several yards from the end of the red carpet with the president and his secretary of state were Henry Cabot Lodge, the U.S. Ambassador to the United Nations, and joining them was Ambassador Menshikov, the Soviet Ambassador to the United States, who was not one of the president's favorite Soviets for Menshikov had over-reached himself in having set up the visit of his boss.

Standing ten yards behind the official greeting party were several dozen dignitaries from the governments and military of both countries. Stretched out in four platoons beyond the greeting party were a twenty-four man honor guard, each in full military parade dress, flanking the color guard. Beyond them were the cordon of military flag bearers, each holding up one of the flags of the fifty states, including the newest state flag—Hawaii.

Quietly awaiting the arrival and first glimpse of a Soviet leader and standing behind a six-foot chain link fence were over a thousand military personnel and their families, and below the platform were three hundred members of the international press corps with their movie cameras rolling and flash cameras popping pictures of this historical event unfolding for the first time on American soil. Twenty-five feet up on a plywood platform were fifteen network news cameramen aiming their cameras at the arriving plane. Their vantage point—like that of a hunter in his 'stand'—was directly behind the seven-man color guard.

"My God! I hope this isn't a sign of how the next twelve days will be going," the president said out loud, watching the Air Force ground crew begin to roll the mechanized steps away from the plane because the plane was too high and the top step fell several feet short of the doorway.

"Sir, I'll bet that Mr. Khrushchev will have a comment about this," Herter whispered in the president's ear.

"Just think, Chris, if he had to make his way down from the aircraft on a ladder in front of all these news people," the president said, watching the Air Force ground crew roll up a larger set of mechanized steps to the plane's door.

As the plane's door came open, a member of the Soviet flight crew pushed the heavy door back to the fuselage and took up a position in front of it. The United States Army Band struck up John Phillips Sousa's "Washington Post March."

Chairman Khrushchev stepped out of the plane onto the platform. Dressed in a dark navy blue suit with white shirt and a light colored tie, the Soviet leader did not wait for the rest of his party to join him before he started descending the stairs.

"Welcome to the United States of America, my Comrade Chairman," was the greeting from the Soviet Ambassador, engaging his boss in a bear hug and each man pressing a kiss to the side of each other's face.

"Comrade Chairman, the president of the United States, Mr. Eisenhower," Ambassador Menshikov said, introducing the president.

The Soviet leader stretched out his hand and joined the president in a hearty handshake.

"I'm pleased to meet you again, Mr. President, and most welcome the opportunity to be here in America. By the way, your airfield almost didn't accommodate our landing. You probably never expected the Soviet people to have built such a machine."

Alex Akabovsky, the president's interpreter, had moved in closer to the two leaders and listened carefully to Mr. Khrushchev's remarks. Hearing the translation, the president held his temper in check. Having been previously counseled as to the quick wit and dry humor of Khrushchev, he said, "Your country's accomplishments since the War, Mr. Chairman, are outstanding and remarkable. The American people are very proud that they were able to keep military and economic aid flowing to Murmansk during the darkest hours of the War."

It was now Khrushchev's turn to reply to the president's counter and every bit the crafty politician, did so with a wide smile.

Escorting Mr. Khrushchev to a set of standing microphones at the end of the red carpet, the president said, "Mr. Chairman, in the name of the People of the United States, I welcome you to America." Reading from his prepared notes he continued attempting to speak over the cheers and clapping of the small but enthusiastic crowd in front of him.

He did so at a slower pace so that Mr. Troyanovsky, the Soviet interpreter, would not miss a word.

"Mr. Chairman, let us continue your journey for peace by agreeing that we agree to disagree and to allow trust to be our guide," the president concluded as the sun shone brightly upon the faces of both men.

* * *

"You know, Sarge, this chow isn't all that bad," Corporal Mullins said to Kellerman, who was sitting opposite him in the Camp David mess hall.

"Let me tell you something, Mullins," Kellerman said. "This here mess is probably unlike any mess hall in all of the military. Where else do you get a family-style atmosphere, five to a table, and in front of that huge fieldstone fireplace? You tell me, and I've been in the Corps ten years and I've been to more mess halls than you've been to movie houses."

"Don't get me wrong, Sarge. I'm not bitching one bit. In fact this place reminds me of a ski lodge I once stayed at in Vermont. Matter of fact, this place—with its views out the window and the paneling—is like being in a New England inn."

"It's on T.V. now, Sarge," Corporal Phillips shouted. "The arrival ceremony."

All became silent as everyone in the hall turned to look at the television monitor.

"Well, there's the enemy, Sarge. He doesn't look so bad; just look how much shorter he is next to the president."

"Hey, look guys—there's the First Platoon," Private Arnold shouted as the news camera panned the arrival area. "God! They're sharp-looking, aren't they, Phillips?"

"Not bad, but they still don't hold a candle to us," Phillips said.

"I wouldn't go that far," Arnold replied.

"Sarge, if we don't get off this hill soon—the First will be a lot sharper than we are," Phillips said. "It's been nearly a month since I picked up a can of Kiwi polish. I'm not sure I can do any 'spit and polish' work any more."

Kellerman said, "In two weeks, Phillips, you'll be back in Washington with your ass on your locker box and your finger wrapped around a cloth, moving polish around your shoes and all along wishing you were up here, so stop bitching."

Still focused on the television as others came in to watch as well, Arnold said, "I don't think I've ever seen an arrival on television before—impressive."

Ignoring Arnold's comment, Kellerman asked, "Oh! By the way, Phillips—did you ever send that film off to Washington? You know, from that Kraut camera?"

"Yeah—it went out in the mail pick-up a couple days ago. I sent it to Special Agent Hogan in Washington. The Lieutenant gave me his address. The only thing I hope I didn't do was expose it when I unloaded the camera. That Zeiss 35mm with that telescopic lens, Sarge, is a beauty and worth many bucks. What are the chances we tell the German it got lost or something?"

"Just get it delivered to the police tomorrow, will you? It's too late now, but you should've put the film in the Camp's priority mail pouch to the White House instead of just mailing it. I got the impression from the Lieutenant that the Secret Service was anxious to see it. Oh well, let's get going and check posts."

* * *

Secret Service Agent Deeter Flohr had moved the 1949 Lincoln convertible limousine on to the runway, a few yards from where the two leaders moments before had made their addresses.

Washington, D.C. license plate PB900 was the car's identification. Many thought it should be number one, but in deference to the Secret Service's wishes to have the president's car not so conspicuous when he was not in it, the present plate was used. The car's deep black shine was outlined by oversized chrome bumpers, and fastened to the front bumpers were the American flag, with the Soviet pennant on the driver's side.

As the arrival party moved to get into the open car, there was almost not enough space in the back seat for the president, Mr. Khrushchev, and his wife, Nina. Interpreter Troyanovsky was relegated to the jump seat and Agent Rowley rode up front with Agent Flohr. KGB and other Secret Service agents, led by Hipsley, took up positions in and around the convertible and in the car directly behind the president.

Wedged in the back seat between Nina and her husband was the president. Not wanting to take up his one-third of the seat, Eisenhower gave Mrs. Khrushchev room for her wide girth together with the three bouquets of flowers she was still holding, thus the president's right side was wedged into his guest's left chest.

If Khrushchev minded the tight squeeze, he did not show it. He was involved in waving and looking at the people, who only moments before had given him a cordial and warm response to his remarks.

The president was not looking forward to the fifteen mile ride into the Capitol, especially being crammed into his own car—and even more so, from having heard the Chairman's boasts:

"I have come here, Mr. President, representing a nation of people who only three days ago launched a rocket that, when its journey is completed, will be on the moon."

141

Eisenhower was reminded of his vice president's comments about this man now sitting almost on top of him: "He will come offering peace but creating fear."

Agent Flohr's steady foot on the accelerator moved the huge Lincoln. The Army band played John Phillips Sousa's "Semper Fidelis." The motorcade, now nine in number, taxied along the airport apron to the sprawling Air Force base's west gate.

Exiting the base, the motorcade traveled a short distance. The sign before the ramp read "Suitland Parkway—Washington, D.C. fourteen miles." Flohr turned right and headed up the ramp.

The Khrushchevs did not see grand monuments or beautiful homes or buildings as they sped along Suitland Parkway. Curiosity seekers, well-wishers, and the unemployed were along the route, but not many. The Khrushchevs saw a new motel under construction as well as a small public school where most of the students were Negroes. They flashed by Ace Van and Storage Company, not far from the Church of St. Vincent dePaul, which stood majestically overlooking the freeway.

"So, where is all of the wealth I keep hearing about, Mr. President?" Mr. Khrushchev said, shouting the words to his interpreter who was holding on for dear life in a jump seat that wasn't designed for conversation and with the limousine's top down and the limo traveling at sixty miles an hour. "For miles I see nothing but poor housing and unkept yards that grow not grass or vegetables."

"I ask that you draw no conclusions about this great country, Mr. Chairman, until you come back to Washington from your visit across it," Eisenhower said testily. "In the meantime, keep in mind that our system of government does not guarantee wealth and prosperity, but does provide the opportunity to reach for it."

Along the route from Andrews Air Force Base into Washington were the fifteen thousand man security detail; the District of Columbia's military, local police, and government building security guards, together with members of the Secret Service and FBI. Their presence could be seen as the motorcade moved under and over bridges and through crowded intersections. The guard detail increased as well as the crowds when the procession crossed the Potomac River and made its way onto Independence Avenue. For the president, their approach onto Pennsylvania Avenue was a sight for which he could not have waited much longer. It would be three minutes before the motorcade, now led by Washington motorcycle policemen, arrived at Blair House. They drove by the Willard Hotel, up Fourteenth Street, turning left and passing the U.S. Treasury Building and the Riggs National Bank.

The remaining minutes were an eternity to Eisenhower. He digested the translator's interpretation of the Soviet Premier's remarks: "Mr. President, I know it is not on the agenda for our talks while I'm here in Washington or next weekend at Camp David, but I want to discuss these over-flights of our country by your so-called U-2 spy planes."

* * *

Hanna awoke early on September 15th. Unlike the others, she was able to sleep during the ten-hour drive from Arlington, Vermont, to Mrs. Gropp's house.

"Laszlo, Janos, Nina—come here! Look at this!" Hanna shouted as she stood in front of the twelve-inch television console. "He is here, he's in Washington right now. Look, there's the White House, he is going right by it. How can this be happening?"

Laszlo was listening to the T.V. commentary as he slowly walked down the stairs from his bedroom, still in his shorts, and said, "Calm down, Hanna. Sit down and try not to let what you see upset you."

"But he is fifty miles from here, don't you see?" she said hysterically. The others, still half asleep, stood in silence watching the events unfold, listening as the scene was being described by Howard K. Smith.

> *The Soviet leader, his wife, together with their two daughters—Yuliya Gontar and Mrs. Rada Adzhubel and her husband, Aleksei—will be staying at Blair House, directly across from the Executive Office Building. Also staying there will be Mr. and Mrs. Andrei Gromyko, Minister of Soviet Foreign Affairs, together with G.T. Shuisky and A.S. Shevchenko, assistants to Mr. Khrushchev. And now the president's car is approaching and will . . . ."*

"I can't stand seeing him, and he's here in America," Hanna said.

"Nina, please take Hanna upstairs and have her rest," Laszlo said. "Janos and I will continue to watch this, but it is just too upsetting for her."

"Did you know that he was going to stay in the Blair House?" Janos asked his brother-in-law, watching his wife help Hanna. "What kind of place is it? I never heard of it before now, and it does not look like an Embassy."

"I heard of it, Janos. It's like an ordinary townhouse along any street in Washington for that matter."

"Listen to what he is saying, Laszlo," Janos said.

. . . is the local name given to what sometimes is referred to as the President's Guest House. Other times, the house, which in fact is four houses, is called America's Number One Hotel. It was built around 1820, and added to several times since. The house has over one hundred rooms, can sleep twenty-five in separate bedrooms, and is located diagonally across Pennsylvania Avenue from the White House.

Nine years earlier in November of 1950, during the reconstruction of the White House, a group of Puerto Ricans attempted the assassination of a world leader, which nearly occurred when President Truman was living at Blair House.

* * *

As the Lincoln convertible approached the curb just opposite the front door of Blair House, Agent Rowley recalled that fateful afternoon nine years ago when Oscar Collazo and Geisallo Torresula, from New York City, attempted to kill President Truman. Rowley thought how close they had come and how, in the process, they had killed one of his own men, Leslie Coffelt. The brass plaque hanging from the wrought iron fence was the public's reminder of what had taken place. But, to Rowley, that incident needed no reminder. Given his present responsibilities, he could not afford to dwell on the past.

"Welcome to Blair House, Mr. Chairman," President Eisenhower said to his guest as Rowley leapt out of the front seat of the limousine, surveying the watching crowd. At the same time, he observed the coverage being provided by his men and scores of military and Washington police.

"I hope you and Madame Khrushchev will enjoy your stay here and find the house comfortable and relaxing," Eisenhower said as he helped Mrs. Khrushchev out of the car. "I look forward to meeting with you at three-thirty across the street."

"Thank you so much, Mr. President. We are so pleased to be here," the Soviet leader replied. "My! You live in such a big house, but why is it so gray when everything else is so colorful?"

Noticing that his guest was looking at the old Executive Office Building, Eisenhower said, "No, it's that house—the White House—where the president and his family reside. When you come over after you have freshened up, I'll be pleased to show you around."

CHAPTER 17

The arrival of Chairman Khrushchev had the White House staff bustling. He would be arriving shortly. The activity in the office of Ann Whitman, the president's secretary, was no exception. She had never seen a day like this before.

"Ann," the president snapped, "I want to see the vice president, secretary of state, Allen Dulles, General LeMay, and Haggerty right now."

"They're already in there, Mr. Pres— . . . ." the slamming door cut her off.

"I'm sure Dick has told you what I heard coming across Fourteenth Street," the president said. "What I want to know is how in hell do the Soviets know about the U-2? What are we to do about continuing the flights? And how do we deal with Khrushchev's wanting to discuss it next weekend?" Eisenhower was pacing behind his desk. "I also might add, gentlemen, that in two hours we and the Russians are to have our first meeting, and Dick, you know as well as anyone that Khrushchev is not one to stick to an agenda—am I correct?"

"That's correct, sir." Nixon said. "But for the moment, I believe it's not important to dwell on how he came to discover the U-2s, but on how we are to deal with the issue. I, for one, believe the bastard is bluffing and that he does not have one scrap of evidence to support his country's intelligence regarding the U-2. Mr. President, from his perspective he's developing an issue for which he has little or no facts, just to put you off from the real issue of the meeting—Berlin."

"I agree with Mr. Nixon, sir," General LeMay said, chewing on what was left of his cigar. "Mr. Vice President, there're only a handful of people in our government who know about these flights—how they're made, from what airfields, the type of aircraft, and, most importantly, the results we get from the photographs taken—by God, even the pilots don't know that."

Angrily Chris Herter said, "I am completely unaware of any of this. Why?"

"It was necessary, Chris, I'm sorry," the president said, "but, Allen, you gave me and the others your highest assurances there was no possibility for the Soviets to know about these flights. So why does Khrushchev whisper in my ear and tell me he knows all about our U-2s?"

The craggy-faced, old-time Washington bureaucrat was not one to be faced down by this president nor did Mr. Eisenhower expect his CIA director to flinch one bit as others might easily have done.

"Tell him they're nothing more than high-flying weather reconnaissance planes, Mr. President," Dulles said. "If he doesn't believe you, well, tell him to shoot one down—if he can—and see for himself and, in the meantime, get him to stick with the agenda. Our people in Moscow know that the Soviets have no specifics on the U-2s. They never did."

* * *

Shandor Tackas was well-known throughout Vermont's Bennington County. For almost twenty years he had been employed by the State's Fish and Game Department and, at times, was also a law enforcement agent, overseeing hunters in Vermont. It was his animal husbandry skills and knowledge that were called upon by farmers which made Tackas proud of his occupation. His love for animals was a close second to his other love—his Hungarian heritage. Escaping from Hitler's onslaught over Eastern Europe in 1941, a youthful Tackas had joined the Vermont Game Department as a trainee.

It was on a crystal clear Tuesday morning in mid-September that Tackas was called up to the Pelm farm by Mr. Smyth.

Swinging his large frame out from the driver's seat of his green Ford pickup and seeing his old friend, Ian Smyth, Tackas said, "What can I do for you, Ian? Where's everyone?"

"That's just it, Shandor. I don't know. I came up here to see how the boys were doing because I'm supposed to pick up a thousand birds this week. When I was here last week, they had mites. Come with me and I'll show you."

Tackas took Smyth's lead and followed him up the well-worn path to the pens. When they arrived at the wire mesh fencing, Tackas said, "Mites are not unusual. Especially with the weather we had in July." Tackas turned his head away from Smyth and looked over the farm.

"I agree, and I gave Laszlo and Janos some ideas on how to get rid of them, and they said they would move right on it. Look for yourself; not one of these birds has been dusted with the pesticide or are there any boxes of dust set out for the hens to lay in and dust themselves. Look here, there's no water or feed in the fly away pens and, at the other end, there're about a hundred dead ones."

"What the hell's going on here?" Tackas said. "Laszlo and Janos would never allow their birds to be in this condition. I've known them since they settled here from Hungary; I've helped them on many occasions, and they're good poultry growers."

"Well, I share that opinion too, Shandor. They grow the best birds that I buy and they're a pleasure to do business with. But this—I can't explain it."

"You've been up to the house, Ian? Is there no one around? How about Hanna or Nina?"

"No one—not a soul. It just seems like they took up and left. You get that impression from out here, and you'll see for yourself when you go inside the house."

As he started to walk away from the pens and toward his car, Tackas said, "This bothers me, Ian. It is not like them to just pick up and go—Jesus, they never took a vacation since they came here, and you mean to tell me with thousands of birds ready to be delivered that they would just leave and not tell anyone? That's not like the Pelms; something's happened."

"Where're you going, Shandor?" Smyth asked.

"I'm calling in the State Police. Something is wrong here—terribly wrong."

* * *

Hogan and Rowley were looking across the White House front lawn at the large crowd gathered near Blair House. "Chief," Hogan said, "Hipsley is asking for more uniform guys as well as a dozen more agents to surround Blair House. He says things are starting to get ugly there

149

with the protesters. Cries of 'Butcher go home! Butcher go home! Butcher go home,' can be heard five hundred feet away."

"You know, Jim, you just have to ask yourself what in God's name is he doing here?"

"Matt, it's our job to protect the bastard while he's here and that we'll do. And there better not be any incidents either," Rowley said, looking through his binoculars at the demonstrators. "Just as I expected, Matt. Look at those two on top of the truck—there at the corner of Jackson Place and 'H' Street."

"Yeah, I've got a fix on 'em—a man, looks like a priest, and a woman, she's holding the bull horn now."

"The priest is Monsignor Tomas Padula, chairman of the Hungarian Committee, and if there ever was a Khrushchev hater, there he is, Matt. In a letter to the Boss he said his group will abstain from undisciplined demonstrations."

"Well, we'll wait and see," Hogan said.

"The lady standing alongside him is Anna Kethly," Rowley said.

"Who's Kethly? I didn't see her name on the Bureau's watch list of agitators."

"But she did make the State Department list of known anti-Communist leaders who were once in power in Hungary."

"I'd say she was pretty high up, then," Hogan said.

"For awhile she was minister of state under Premier Nagy back in fifty-six. Those two can be real trouble. They're filled with hate for Khrushchev and can charge up a crowd in no time."

"I'd bet most of those in the crowd are refugees from Hungary and with the two on the truck fought in the revolution," Hogan said.

"And look just to Padula's left—that guy with the black arm band—Brent Bozell. He's with the Committee for National Mourning," Rowley said.

"I see. And it looks like they got the Senate and House out there with them. I see Margaret Chase Smith and Bob Byrd and look, behind Tom Dodd is John McCormack and Walter Judd."

"I should've made a stronger case, Matt," Rowley said, shaking his head. "This demonstration is just a prelude to what's coming. The boys in New York telexed this morning that we can expect the American Friends of the Assembly of Captive Nations to hold a big rally at Carnegie Hall on the twentieth. And the Federation of Hungarian Former

Political Prisoners are calling for a huge demonstration on the seventeenth at the Economic Club of New York. This is what I was afraid of—these groups. And it's just possible that someone from within the group will want to stand out, and that's trouble for us, Matt."

"Well, at least, Chief, the Old Man won't be there with Khrushchev, but Hips will have his hands full."

"So let's get Hips his extra men and in the meantime get the D.C. police to move the crowd back to the other side of the Park—over to Madison Place and to 'F' and Seventeenth."

"I'll get right on it," Hogan said as he and Rowley turned around and headed to the West Wing entrance of the White House.

"Matt, did you ever get that camera from Camp David?"

"No, just the film. It's on its way, Chief. Unfortunately the Marines sent it out by regular mail and returned the camera to the Thurmont Police."

"God, how stupid. Well let's get it developed ASAP. Who knows, maybe there's something on those pictures after all."

* * *

Now in their fifth day in Thurmont, Laszlo and Hanna were being treated to a second beginning of fall. As the two walked on the shoulder of Roody Road, the morning sun burnt away the remaining fog that had hung over the valley since daybreak like a soft, gray blanket. The sun's brilliance lit up the eastern side of the Catoctin Mountains. And, as was the case only weeks before in Vermont, the fall colors were working their way down the mountains' flanks.

Nearby Owens Creek meandered and was crossed by a covered bridge.

"Look, Laszlo! Doesn't that remind you of the covered bridge in West Arlington? You know, the one by Norman Rockwell's old house?" Hanna said.

"Yes, it does. America is a beautiful place, Hanna. It has been spared the ravages of what we have witnessed in Hungary. It's hard to realize that a hundred years ago major battles of America's Civil War were fought right here."

"I know, dear."

151

"How did you know that? I didn't know that you knew anything about the American Civil War."

"I don't, you wonderful fool," she said squeezing his hand as they sat on the creek's grassy bank. "Poetry, my love, is how I know this area. I read John Greenleaf Whittier's poem about Barbara Frietchie: 'Up from the meadows rich with corn/ Clear in the cool September morn/ On that pleasant morn of the early fall/ When Lee marched over the mountain-wall.' It was just about this time of year that General Jackson met Barbara," Hanna said. "She must have been a beautiful person, so courageous to do what she did. 'Up rose old Barbara Frietchie then/ Bowed with her fourscore years and ten/ Bravest of all in Frederick town/ She took up the flag the men hauled down.' Not many people would stick their head out the window and fly their country's flag as a conquering army rode into town, but she did."

He put his arms around her shoulders, pulled her close to him, and said, "I think Whittier could have been writing about you, my dear. Your courage on the barricades was just as heroic as the ninety-year-old Barbara. I only wish I could write a poem about you and what you have done for Hungary. And, no matter what happens, you must always know that my love for you is as deep as my love for our country."

"Laszlo, let's not do it."

"What are you saying, Hanna," Laszlo said, releasing his embrace and getting up from the grassy bank.

"That it's not our work to kill Khrushchev. Yes, I would wish him a horrible death. God forgive me for saying it—but not from us."

"Well, if not from us, who!" Laszlo shouted.

"Open your eyes and your heart, my dear. See what surrounds us. This beauty—it's us, our lives, our future. There's no way for us to escape. You know it as well as I. Why must it be us and why here?"

"Hanna, this from you who suffered so much."

"Yes, I did suffer, and I suffer everytime I think about Hungary. But I want to put it behind us. Laszlo, I'm going to give you a child—a child that will want to see its father. A child that should not have to be raised in a home full of hatred for a man that our child never knew. Do you see, my love, why I want you to take us back to the farm? We still have time—we can start all over—please! Let's go home."

Kneeling in front of her with his huge hands gently holding her face and feeling tears in the palm of his hands, he said softly, "Hanna, don't you understand—he killed my father, he killed your whole family. How will I live with you, our child, and myself knowing that I did nothing?"

"Don't you realize, Laszlo, what God is doing for us. He knows you have lost your father. Now He's giving a life back to you. A life that is part of both of us. Laszlo please, please don't turn your back on Him. Let us leave and not think anymore of Khrushchev."

"Please, Hanna, do not speak to me of what God is about to give me. It is not just my father He took—it is my country, our country, and that He will never be able to give back to us, that is why I—we must do what we came here to do. Please give me your hand and don't be upset. We must get back. Janos and Nina will be home soon from Baltimore, and if they were able to obtain Maryland license plates, we have to put them on the truck and the car right away."

The eastern slopes of the Catoctin Mountains were completely engulfed in the morning sun as Laszlo, with his arm around Hanna's shoulder, walked across the covered bridge and up Roody Road toward the village.

* * *

Oscar O'Dea did not possess the popular image of a Vermont state trooper, with all the trimmings of spit 'n' polish. He was not tall or well-built nor did he wear a neatly pressed uniform. He was stocky, five-foot eight with long, snowy hair and a round, red face. A transplant from Dundalk, Ireland, he had been patrolling the hills and valleys of southern Vermont since 1924, and then on horseback.

As he slowly emerged from his dusty Ford patrol car, O'Dea said, "Well, Shandor, when your call came into the switchboard Martha said you wanted me here in a hurry. Where's everybody?" He spoke with an Irish brogue.

"That's just it, Oscar. No one's here. Gone! Vanished! Disappeared!" The game warden said looking at the fly-away pens and the thousands of pheasants, many of whom were using all of their energy just to stay on their feet.

The stronger ones were randomly pecking at the weaker birds when Smyth said, "It seems like they took off in a hurry. Some clothes taken, both the car and truck are missing, but I just can't seem to

153

understand why they would leave the pheasants. It's not like Laszlo or Janos to do this."

O'Dea's interest was not in the welfare of the birds but the fate and whereabouts of the Pelms. O'Dea lost no time as he moved up the porch steps and swung open the screen door and entered the kitchen. He observed that the kitchen was as neat and tidy as always.

The maps and cut-up newspapers on the kitchen sideboard received a parting glance from the trooper as he moved into Laszlo and Hanna's bedroom, where he found partially packed suitcases and an opened steamer trunk.

"What do you make of all of this, Oscar?" Shandor asked, standing in the living room with Smyth.

"I can tell you that the place seems normal enough . . . there's certainly no sign of a struggle or a break-in. You know those girls are two of the most meticulous housekeepers I've ever seen. I'll admit, I'm somewhat puzzled over those open trunks."

"I've been here since early this morning," Smyth said. "Long before I called in Shandor, I was hoping they'd be back."

Surveying the gun rack over the stone fireplace, O'Dea said, "Look here. Didn't Laszlo keep a half dozen guns—couple of .12 gauge shotguns and, if I remember, two or three 30.06 rifles? The only weapon here is that Remington .22. Why would the other guns be gone?"

"It's too early for hunting," Ian said. "It's possible, Oscar, that the guns were stolen, wouldn't you say?"

"I don't know one way or the other," Oscar said, "but I don't want you to touch a thing. I wanta get the Criminal Investigation boys up here; this whole place is gonna have to be photographed and dusted for prints. Something smells here, Ian, and it's not coming from those dead birds out there. It's in here."

O'Dea started to pick up the telephone receiver when he noticed two savings account passbooks from the Factory Point National Bank on the desk's blotter.

"See here—September 12, 1959. All the money in these accounts has been withdrawn, all one thousand four hundred dollars," O'Dea said to the two men now looking over his shoulder.

"God," Shandor said, "why would they take out all of their savings?"

Getting up from the desk and moving quickly toward the kitchen, O'Dea said, "I didn't pay much attention to it a few minutes ago, but I saw some newspapers in the kitchen, and I wonder if they can help us unravel this mystery."

Smyth and Tackas were close behind O'Dea, and Smyth said, "I saw those papers too, but I didn't touch them."

Opening up the folded newspapers, O'Dea said, "It seems like anywhere there's a mark or cut out it has to do with Khrushchev's visit. See—the papers go back to August—'White House announces visit to the United States by the Chairman of the USSR this Fall . . . .' And look, the cut out was the Khrushchev visit timetable of each day he'd be here. And the maps here, they're of Maryland, Washington, D.C., Pennsylvania, New York City—why would they want them, and why are these places circled? See?"

"Maybe they're on vacation, Oscar," Ian said. "These maps would help them get there. You know they've never been out of Vermont since they came here."

Oscar snapped back, "No. No. That can't be. They wouldn't go on vacation and leave the pheasants the way they did, draw down all their savings, take their guns, and leave this place a mess. And why the concern about Khrushchev's visit? What would their interest be up here in Vermont? They never once made a political statement, did they now, Ian?"

"I've known them as long as you two, and you're right, Oscar. I don't know what party they support. You know, they still aren't U.S. citizens, but I do know that they're working on it."

"I think they would have had a keen interest in Khrushchev's visit," Shandor said. "Don't you two remember how they came about to be here? It was their escape from Hungary in 1956. And who was in charge of the Russians moving into Hungary? Khrushchev. Oscar, I think you better make that call to the barracks and get those guys up here."

"I still don't know for sure why I'm calling in, but I'd better let them know."

Straightening out a piece of crumpled paper he had picked up from the kitchen floor, Shandor glanced at it and said, "You better take a look at this first, Oscar."

"What is it, Shandor?" Oscar said, looking over the paper. "Can you read it? It's in a foreign language."

Shandor began to read:

"His Eminence, Joseph Cardinal Mindszenty, American Legation, Budapest, Hungary, c/o U.S. State Department, Washington, D.C.

"My dear Uncle Joseph, . . . "

"Any more? Is that it, Shandor?" Oscar asked.

"That's all—it just stops," Shandor said. "Laszlo once told me he was the Cardinal's nephew, that his mother was Mindszenty's sister."

"Ian, I believe we have a most serious situation here," O'Dea said. "Khrushchev arrived a few days ago and will be in the United States for two weeks. I would ask that you and Ian look after the pheasants. I must call the Secret Service. I have this terrible feeling that our good friends, the Pelms, have embarked upon something dreadful."

"Oscar, what do you think is going on?" Ian asked.

"Ian, four people just don't up and vanish. The trouble is I don't know what's going on. So, I'm asking you, and you too, Shandor, to not breathe a word of this to anyone. Let's just get to the bottom of it first. Okay?"

* * *

Using his key to open the front door of Aspen Lodge, Commander Nicholson said to Fergurson, "You've been here long enough so it's about time you were given a tour of Aspen."

"I wasn't aware, Commander, that we're allowed into this house."

"Once each day, Mike, as Camp Officer I must open the Lodge and make a complete sweep of each room, check the heating, electrical, and other mechanical systems, and, yes, inventory the booze closet—very important. And if, for some reason, I'm unable to do so, the job falls on the Camp's Communication Officer, Warrant Officer Staly, whom you've met. And, I might add, if he's not around, the job of inspection goes to the Marine officer of the Day, but that's rare—maybe once or twice in the last few years."

"I would be less than honest standing here, on the carpet of the president's house, sir, if I didn't say that I've got goose bumps."

"I share the feeling. I've been doing this every day for months now, and I still get bumps. I don't think you can ever get over it. Let's face it, this very spot has held Roosevelt, Churchill, Truman, MacMillan, and others, not to mention President Eisenhower. And, Mike, in a week, right where you're standing, will be Chairman Khrushchev."

"It's just an awesome feeling, sir. That's all I can say. Will Khrushchev be staying in this house when he comes here? Or in one of the cabins?"

"He'll be in here, along with the president, of course, and I understand that Foreign Minister Gromyko and Secretary of State Herter will each take up residence here as well.

"Come on down this corridor, and I'll show you the layout. Keep in mind this place is a far cry from the Washington Willard. Matter of fact, what struck me the most when I first came through was just that—how plain and simple this place is considering who resides here. I have to tell you, Lieutenant, I've seen more opulence in captain's quarters aboard ships than what is here, but keep that to yourself."

"Based on my six months on the Ranger, I would attest to that," Fergurson said.

"As you can see, Lieutenant, Aspen Lodge is divided into three areas—the sleeping quarters on the right wing where there're four bedrooms, the service/utility section on the left, and they are separated in the middle by the living room. Those over-stuffed arm chairs you saw flanking the three sofas were put there by Roosevelt and so was that large stone fireplace. In a way, it's laid out poorly."

"Why's that, sir?"

"When you enter the front door you're immediately in the living room and looking straight out the screened-in porch, assuming the drapes aren't closed on those sliding doors."

"What's behind the fireplace and bookcases?"

"In there is the pantry and storage closets for dishes, linens, and flatware. And through the pantry's swinging doors is the kitchen with its customary complement of appliances, more like the operation's center of a restaurant rather than a private home. Lieutenant, nowhere is the simplicity of Aspen manifested more clearly than in these bedrooms that feed off this corridor."

As he peered into the room Fergurson said, "Who would have ever thought they'd be so small?"

"Except for the small guest room that looks out onto the front path, all of the rooms have magnificent views of the Cumberland Valley, giving easy access to the stone patio and rock gardens, but a nightmare to the Secret Service—too many doors."

"What are those trap doors for? I also noticed one in the hall and one in the living room to the left of the fireplace."

"They're escape hatches," Nicholson said as he made his way out the front door. "In case of an emergency, they're opened and lead down to the tunnels you were in last week. If the Camp was attacked and we needed to get the president and his family and guests to safety, the hatches are opened and he would be evacuated into the tunnels by the Secret Service and everyone would go to the area known as L.A., or lower Aspen."

"Well let's hope they never have to be used. And thanks for the tour sir."

CHAPTER 18

The president sneezed, wrestling with the symptoms of a cold.

"Bless you," the secretary of state said. "From the way Cabot Lodge has described it, Mr. President, Mr. Khrushchev's visit isn't going too well. There's been some rough sledding as he puts it, and there're eight more days to go."

"Be more specific, Chris," Eisenhower said.

Sipping coffee and not appearing to be very interested in the lobster bisque lunch, Herter said, "Mr. President, you know the way he acted at the meeting the afternoon of his arrival. Our response to him that the over-flights were mere weather observation planes and not as he thought, spy planes, was categorically rejected by him at that time and he's now more convinced that we are flying reconnaissance planes over his country while he's here touring ours. He thinks of his country as being in a technical state of war with his host. His visit with Senators Johnson and Dirkson at the Senate Foreign Relations Committee hearing was awful. They were rough on him regarding the Russians' treatment of the captive nations. Khrushchev responded by saying they were not captive but free to do as they like. His appearance the other day at The National Press Club was by no means a picnic for him either. The press went at him in the same way, as if he were a candidate for office. You put all of these confrontations together and you can see why he's saying that we're not being very hospitable toward him."

"Where's he now, Chris?" Eisenhower asked, who, unlike Herter, was devouring his lunch.

"Fortunately he's in the air, flying to Los Angeles. He left New York's Idlewyld Airport at eight-fifteen this morning, and Lodge is hoping that a trip to the other side of the United States, specifically Los Angeles and San Francisco, will be more to his liking."

"From what you've told me, Chris, it's not all that bad. I think you all are being too sensitive. Sounds to me like he's got everyone walking on eggshells."

"It is the little things, Mr. President, that seem to get under his skin."

"For example?"

"When he arrived in New York's Penn Station, he was confronted by thousands wearing black arm bands and shouting that he go home. We knew that it might happen and it did, and Buckley made good his threat and dumped red vegetable dye in the Hudson from the deck of the George Washington bridge, and with help from the Assembly of Captive Nations, led by Monsignor Tomas Padula."

"Well, that's Buckley—true to form, I'd say."

"Khrushchev was told that the American Dental Association wouldn't move their convention from the Waldorf, so he wound up at a third-class hall to meet with business, labor, and New York's political leaders. And when he heard that his neighbors at the hotel were temporarily moving away, that set him off—felt he was being snubbed."

"Who were they?"

"General MacArthur, Cole Porter, President Hoover, and the Duke and Duchess of Windsor."

"Christ, you can't blame them for leaving. I wouldn't want to put up with all the hoopla. And the last thing you and State would want is a confrontation between MacArthur and Khrushchev."

"He was, however, cordially received during his visit with the member countries of the United Nations and was well received at Hyde Park by Eleanor Roosevelt."

"Well, that doesn't surprise me in the least."

"Lodge is wondering, sir—if you would make a statement to the press asking the American people to show more enthusiasm and respect for the Soviet leader while he's here."

"Chris, are you nuts? This administration has taken enough heat over this visit, and now you want me to go public and act as a God-damn cheerleader for this son-of-a-bitch? I don't believe what I'm hearing from you." Eisenhower was now on his feet, pacing back and forth in front of the fireplace.

"Please, do not misunderstand me, Mr. President, I—we—both, Henry and I, just want the Chairman to feel welcomed here, that's all."

"If Mr. Khrushchev wants to be loved by the American people, then he should have stayed the hell out of Hungary three years ago, stop trying to bully his way into countries that do not want him or his communist ideology, and let his country and those of Eastern Europe enjoy the freedoms that he is witnessing on his journey across America. No, sir—this president is not going to tell the people how to behave and, for that matter, I'd better not hear anyone in this administration say anything to that effect, either," the president said, glaring at Herter as his press secretary come into the room.

Jim Haggerty, out of breath, said, "Mr. President, the Secret Service wants Khrushchev's visit to Disneyland canceled. They believe that there're four, and possibly more, would-be assassins who are plotting to kill him and right now are on the loose and their whereabouts unknown. And, I might add, Mr. Secretary, your people are furious over this cancellation. They think the Russians will interpret it as a ploy—using security as an excuse to disrupt and prevent Khrushchev from going where he wants to."

"Mr. President," Herter said, "in light of what we have been discussing, I don't think we need to have the Secret Service attempt to wreck this visit."

* * *

There was a feeling of confinement in Rowley's office as Baughman, Rowley, and Hogan were there together.

"Jim," Baughman said, "I'm afraid that when the secretary of the treasury informs the White House that we want Mr. Khrushchev's visit to Disneyland canceled, the people at State will become belligerent, and so let me have what you've got on this."

"Chief, I wanted Matt here to brief you. Matt's been working with our other offices as well as the State Police in Vermont," Rowley said.

"Well, Matt," Baughman said, looking very intently at Hogan, "you better have something good and it better be supported."

Matt Hogan, glancing at Rowley, walked toward the flip chart and began his presentation. "Chief, what we know at this point is that four Hungarian refugees who came to this country in late fifty-six and took up farming in a small village in Vermont have all of a sudden disappeared. What makes this a concern of ours is that in doing so they abandoned over nine thousand pheasants, withdrew their life savings from the local bank, and vanished with their hunting rifles."

"That's all very interesting, Matt. Who are these people?" Baughman said, sounding impatient.

"Laszlo Pelm, one of the four, is the nephew of Cardinal Mindszenty," Hogan said. "He's traveling with his wife and brother-in-law and his wife. All four lost relatives in the Hungarian Revolution. Pelm lost his father, who was the Cardinal's brother-in-law."

"Dear God," Baughman said. "Matt, do you know who Mindszenty is? He's the Catholic Church's top Cardinal in Eastern Europe. He's considered a living martyr and a hero to millions."

"I know, sir. We've prayed for him at Mass every Sunday," Hogan said.

"So do we," Rowley added.

"Who's up there for us?" Baughman asked.

"Albertson, out of New York City." Rowley said.

"He was doing a field inspection when the call came in."

"Do we have anything more specific on them at this point, Matt?" Baughman said.

"Not yet, sir. Albertson's working on it. He's trying to get photos from passport control and from immigration. There must be something, at least a photo."

"Well, keep working on that anyway," he said. "In the meantime, have Albertson check their long distance calls. Find out if they were in contact with any radical group."

"Albertson's onto that as we speak," Rowley said.

Baughman said, "Jim, I still don't see why we're suggesting to State that they cancel Khrushchev's visit to Disneyland because of some connection Cardinal Mindszenty has with a nephew in Vermont, who by now is thousands of miles away from here . . . away from Vermont."

"We don't know they're that far apart, Chief. They left Vermont five or six days ago, in two vehicles—a car and a pick-up truck. And before you ask, yes, we have a nationwide alert out for both vehicles," Rowley said. "Chief, if I might add a point on security, our people in Los Angeles feel that of all the places Mr. Khrushchev will be visiting in California, Disneyland ill affords us the level of security that we want."

"That might be so, but tell me, was there anything else in the house, Jim?" Baughman said. "Anything at all that might tie them into some plot?"

"A lot of dead pheasants, sir," Hogan said. "And according to the game warden, the abandonment of the birds is very out of character for these people. And, by the way, we did find a Rand-McNally atlas."

"What about it?" Baughman asked.

"It had a couple of routes highlighted between Vermont and Washington and western Maryland."

"So, why do you think they'd leave a map book around, Matt?" Baughman said.

"I think to throw us off, sir, if their Vermont house was found out," Hogan said. "Their real aim is to get Khrushchev in California and that's why they left when they did."

"Matt's got a point, Chief." Rowley said.

"I don't disagree with you, Matt," Baughman said, "but it is important that we cover all bases. And, for now, Khrushchev is in California and that's where we must put our focus. Whose idea was it to pull the plug on Disneyland anyway?"

"Hipsley's, sir," Hogan said. "And our Los Angeles people agreed."

"And, for what it's worth, Chief, Elmer Hipsley will not be too welcomed by State when he returns next week," Rowley said.

"Well, if Hips is not wanted by those eggheads at State, I'd be glad to have him back with us," Baughman said.

"On the other hand, Hips is more concerned that if there is any attack on Khrushchev it would be at the Garst Farm in Coon Rapids, Iowa."

"Why?" Baughman asked.

"Three things," Rowley said. "First, there's a bitter strike being played out in Rapid City with the employees of Swift Meat Packing Company. Also, the area to be visited does not lend itself to protection—it's too open and too casual. Last, Coon Rapids' close proximity to Chicago, where there's a large population of Hungarian refugees residing."

"Christ, it seems like every place he goes it's going to be bad news," Baughman said.

"Matt, let's get with it," Rowley said, not responding to Baughman's statement. "Instead let's focus on the four Hungarians. And the first thing is, do we know what they look like? And let's not wait for immigration, that can take forever. How about any newspaper article about their farm or their arriving in Vermont? You know . . . ."

"We haven't checked that out. I'm not sure that we want to arouse any suspicion with the press. At least not up to now, anyway."

"I'd go along with Matt on that, Jim," Baughman said. "We still have very little to go on. And, Matt, I don't for a minute mean to take anything away from your report and conclusions."

"I understand, sir."

"But we must get hard facts that these four are out to do harm to Khrushchev and the president," Baughman said, motioning Jim Rowley to pass him a cigarette rather than one of Rowley's cigars.

"Disneyland, Chief, is it on or off?" Rowley asked.

"Let's kill it. You've got enough here. I'll brief the secretary so he knows why. I'm sure he'll be getting a call from Herter, if he hasn't already."

"Chief, with your permission I'd like to contact our people in Budapest so that we can speak directly to Pelm's Uncle, Cardinal Mindszenty," Rowley said. "We must ask the Cardinal if he knows anything about this threat. Also we need to know if he feels his nephew could, in fact, carry out a plot to kill Khrushchev."

"Jim," Baughman said, "State will go through the roof if they know we're dealing directly with their people in Hungary. His residing at the legation is sensitive stuff with those guys and I don't think they would ever allow the Cardinal to speak to us. You know how they feel about these political asylums. They'll pretend he's not there so they and their counterparts in the Hungarian Foreign Ministry can ignore the reality of the Cardinal's plight."

"Chief," Rowley said angrily, "we have in front of us the possible makings of a plot to wipe out a world leader and possibly two and I'm supposed to find out if it is real or not. But in doing so I'm not to step on any toes at State for fear of creating a little problem for them?"

"Jim, calm down. The last thing we need now is the Station Chief to lose his cool. God and I know you were never the diplomat, but on the other hand, for my sake, I do thank God you're not," Baughman said.

"Gentlemen," Hogan interjected, "I believe I have a solution. Let's get Hipsley to call our Chargé d'Affaires at the legation in Budapest. Hips works for State, knows the situation all too well, and appreciates the bind we're in."

"Matt Hogan, you are a genius. I know I did the right thing by bringing you back here from—where was it?" Rowley said.

"Omaha, Chief. And thanks."

"That's brilliant, son," Baughman said. "Jim, let's get Hipsley on the horn. By the way, Matt, you by chance wouldn't know the name of the Chargé d'Affaires in Budapest now, or would you?"

Hogan said, "Yes, sir. His name is Gerrit B. Ackerson."

* * *

"Where did Laszlo go, Hanna?" Janos asked, sitting in the dining room of Mrs. Gropp's house on a chilly, damp Thursday morning, trying to shake off the effects of boredom. It had now been nine days since they had left Vermont and Janos knew that unless his pheasants were found they would all be dead. And every time he thought of his birds, his bitterness and anger only increased.

"He went to the police station to pick up his camera," Hanna said, showing the signs of strain as well. "I don't know why he went there. It's too dangerous. What does he need the camera for anyway?"

"Laszlo felt it would be attracting attention if someone left such an expensive camera at the police station. That's why he wanted to get it, Hanna."

"Come in and join us, Nina. You didn't sleep very long," Hanna said.

"I could not sleep. Instead I lay there and kept thinking if it would make sense to contact Monsignor Padula or Anna Kethly and let them know what we're going to do. Someone should know and maybe they could be of some help to us, especially to escape back to Hungary."

"No, Nina," Hanna said brusquely, "we must not bring anyone else into knowing what we're doing; it only further compromises our mission."

"But they have connections, Hanna," Nina said. "And their bitterness toward the Soviets, and especially Khrushchev, is no less strong than our own."

"I agree with Nina," Janos said. "Why should we not share the mission with someone we can trust? Also, Hanna, the Hungarian Committee has always said that upon the downfall of the Communist regime, Anna Kethly will have a dominant role in any new government. She can't do anything but help us."

"Brother, the four of us have done well so far by doing it by ourselves."

"What do you mean, done well?" Nina asked. "So far we have done nothing but come here to this house."

"Nina, we have done more," Hanna snapped. "Hasn't Laszlo had us follow the route into Camp David so we will not be found out like he was? He's shown us the high school. Each day we have practiced. What more do you expect?"

"I'm sorry, Hanna," Nina said. "It's just that my nerves cannot take being cooped up here much longer."

"To bring others in at this late stage could seriously disrupt our plans and possibly have them exposed," Hanna said. "We already have a fifth person who now knows about what we are planning to do."

"What are you talking about!" Janos asked.

"Uncle Joseph knows," Hanna said. "Just before we left Vermont, Laszlo sent him a letter, as he usually does, to the Hungarian desk at the State Department where they get it to Uncle Joseph by diplomatic mail."

"What did Laszlo tell him, Hanna?" Nina asked with concern.

"I didn't know until yesterday that Laszlo had sent such a letter. When we were walking back from the covered bridge he told me what he had done."

"But why, Hanna? Why would he do it if he was so sensitive about security?" Janos said.

"Laszlo wanted his uncle to know that we had not forgotten him or the Hungarian people. He also wanted him to know who it was that carried out the attack on Khrushchev in the event anything should happen to us and the attack is never made public. Laszlo did not say this, but I also believe that he was writing to his uncle to request his forgiveness."

"What if someone at the legation opens the letter before it is given to Uncle Joseph?" Janos asked dejectedly.

"They never have before, brother. Why would they do it now?" Hanna said.

"Here comes Laszlo now, Hanna," Janos said, "and he looks upset; something must have happened."

"Please, both of you, don't say anything about the letter. Laszlo did not want you to know until after the mission was over. So let him tell you."

Janos got up and opened the front door for Laszlo and said, "Laszlo, come in and warm yourself. Why are you looking so grim?"

Pulling his sweater over his head, Laszlo said, "When I retrieved the camera at the police station I opened it and the film was missing. Someone removed the film from the camera."

* * *

Twenty-two hundred hours was the time of night to which many in the armed forces looked forward. The sound of the lone bugler playing taps meant that the day was over. It was also a time to reflect on events of the previous day, now quietly passing into night. And in Fergurson's area at the west end of the squad bay, the stillness and peace at this time of night was no exception. If anything the serenity of taps had an even greater effect at Camp David. Out of respect and habit, all conversations were carried out in whispers—it was peaceful and tranquil.

Fergurson cherished this time and on this particular night he decided it was time he wrote his parents a letter telling them what he had been doing these past months.

Placing several sheets of stationary on his desk, a desk consisting of two wooden foot lockers stacked one on top of the other, Fergurson thought for a moment before he began to write.

Camp David
Thurmont, Maryland
22 September, 1959

Dear Mom and Pop,

If ever there was a more peaceful place, it certainly must be where I am now, Camp David, the presidential retreat high in the Cumberland Mountains of Maryland. Pop, if you remember, the Cooley mountains just outside of County Meath, on the way to Newry, remember our seeing them when you took us back to your family's home—well, that's what the Catoctin Mountains are like.

How I was ever chosen for this assignment I'll probably never know or be able to find out. The part of being the platoon officer of the Ceremonial Guard in Washington is awesome. Mom, what

167

ever you thought of the Queen's Black Watch Unit from Scotland, they don't hold a candle to these young men who make up the USMC drill team, band, color guard, and bugle corps. I know, Mom, you taught us never to brag, but this detachment is a sight to see and when we march by a reviewing stand and the Marine Band strikes up the Halls of Montezuma, *the Marine's Hymn, I have goose bumps up my spine and I get this enormous feeling of pride that I am an American and a Marine.*

Kevin was a platoon sergeant for one of these platoons when he was stationed here. And I remember how proud we were of him. I used to tell the kids on the block about my older brother and how he was a guard to President Truman. I just wish he was still with us. I miss him and think of him often, especially when I'm with the men on the Eighth and I parade field.

Here at Camp David my role and that of my men is different. Our assignment takes on enormous responsibilities. We are no longer playing out the role of ceremonial Marines in dress blues; instead we're directly responsible for the security of the President of the United States.

I have been given a platoon of Marines most of whom are not yet nineteen years old, none of them ever set foot in college, and five did not complete high school. I've never seen a more dedicated, loyal, and splendid group of people than these twenty-four Marines. In a few days all of us will be put to the test. I'm sure you must have read that the president and Chairman Khrushchev will be coming here to engage in three days of talks, the outcome of which will have far-reaching effects on whether our two countries can look to live in peace with each other. During the three days, my platoon will be providing the security for these world leaders.

I must go now, but before I do, I just want to tell you how much I love you both and appreciate all that you have given me.

I don't know if Kevin ever told you, but all of the enlisted Marines go through their basic training at Parris Island. I understand there is a monument in the area where they train the drill instructors (D.I.s) that has on it a bronze plaque with an inscription: "Let no man's ghost ever come back to say, if only you had done your job!"

Mom, Pop, you both have done your job, now it's up to me. And I pray that I'm up to it.

Love and Semper Fidelis,
Mike

CHAPTER 19

Getting around Washington by car at four o'clock on a weekday afternoon requires unique driving skills, tenacity, and, above all, patience. However, on September twenty-fifth, all but the latter skill were useless. Traffic in and around Washington was grid-locked. If the Soviets wanted to win over the hearts and minds of D.C. motorists, their planners should have chosen an off-peak time for Khrushchev to arrive back in to Washington from Pittsburgh. Legions of Washington workers were scurrying to get home after a long day turning the giant wheel of government bureaucracy. Many felt that it was time for the Soviet Premier and his entourage to go also.

From the Oval Office window the president said, "Chris, judging from the fact that not a single car has gone by in the last few minutes, something tells me Khrushchev is about to arrive at Blair House."

"His arrival," Herter said, "gives us about an hour before you and Mrs. Eisenhower meet the Khrushchevs at Ambassador Menshikov's reception. I don't believe you will get into any 'deep' discussions regarding the issues on the Camp David agenda."

"Chris, it wouldn't surprise me if he started to lay down his country's demand for nuclear disarmament right at the bar and in front of a couple hundred guests."

"With him, that is a real possibility," Herter said. "However I'm certain he'll want to let you know how disappointed he was in not being able to see Disneyland. It's just unfortunate that Dillion's people overreacted."

"Well, let's not be too hard, Chris. They were only doing their job. I hear they're onto something about some Hungarians and it sounds real enough, but we shall wait and see."

"His trip to the Garst Farm, sir, was a big hit," Herter said, sensing that the president was not interested in his comments on security. "He enjoyed the crowd and Mr. Garst. It was a welcome relief for all of us

171

after the episode at Universal Studios. After viewing the dancers in the *Can-Can* he became terribly upset with those responsible for the trip."

"Well, he should just relax. Anyone tell him that? I bet Frank Sinatra and Shirley MacLaine did."

"Pittsburgh gave him what he wanted. Large crowds, a lot of labor people, despite the strike at U.S. Steel. From what I've been told, he's in much better spirits."

"Well, that's just dandy. I'm glad he's in good spirits because I'm not. So, Chris, let's get ready to meet the enemy. The way I feel now I can't wait for the next seventy-two hours to be over with, and maybe we can get back to some degree of normalcy."

* * *

The Carrier air conditioning unit hanging half-way out the window was working on overdrive in its attempt to cool the air in Rowley's office. The ten-year-old unit was just too tired to make the room comfortable and was no match for the ninety degree day.

"This thing sounds like it's on its last leg, Matt," Rowley said, glancing towards the air conditioner. "And, if we don't get our act together and find them soon, we'll be on our last leg—and out the door—what have we got?"

"What we've got is the fact that nothing has occurred out of the ordinary up to now, and that narrows the threat to Washington and Camp David. And, for the life of me, I can't figure which."

"It's not your life I'm worried about at the moment, Matt, and let's narrow the threat locations by hard evidence and deductive reasoning. There'll be time for 'gut' reactions later," Rowley said moving over to the office's window, having heard the sirens from the Khrushchev motorcade.

"With the tripling of the guard across the street, we reduce the likelihood that we'll have a repeat of 1950 at Blair House. However tomorrow Khrushchev is slated to tour the city and go for a helicopter ride with the president before they go to Camp David, which is to be by limo—and I want that changed."

"I'll work on it," Hogan said.

"How about any photographs," Rowley said. "Any luck in that area?"

172

"Yes, sir. Your suggestion paid off. We were able to locate a newspaper article in the *Manchester Journal,* a local, Vermont newspaper that about a year ago did a feature on the Pelms and their pheasant operations. Here's a copy. It arrived just before I came in and shows all four of them with the pheasants. Shandor Tackas, the game warden, told one of our men that Janos, the one on the left, has longer hair now but the photo is still a good likeness of all of them."

"Jesus, how young they look—and so innocent," Rowley said examining the photograph. "So this one is Laszlo Pelm?"

"Wait a minute, Chief."

"What's the matter?"

"I think I've seen him somewhere," Hogan said.

"What do you mean you've seen him? Seen him where?"

"I'm trying to remember, damnit. He looks younger in the photo, but it's him all right. I remember, the high school in Gettysburg. You know, the guy that came in that night to take a leak. Remember I mentioned him and how lax things were up there."

"You're sure of that? Be real careful now."

"I'm sure, Chief. That's him all right—I remember those eyes. Laszlo Pelm was as close to me as you are."

"That changes everything, Matt. We now know where he'll—they'll strike—during the press conference at the high school. I want that photo shown to everyone in Gettysburg—and I mean everyone. Check out hotels and motels and summer rentals. If they're not in Vermont, then they're down here. Get this on the wire right away."

"Consider it done, Chief, but only to our field offices, 'code red.' Don't want it in the press without your blessing."

"We want this out to all police authorities between Vermont and Virginia. We now know that the threat is for real, and there's only one location. Don't low key it, just tell them that we want these people held for questioning and they should approach with caution—they're—Come in, Hips, come in. Yes, it's open . . . ."

"Matt, don't leave, stay a minute and hear what State has for us."

"But before you begin, Hips, we've got some good news. Matt was . . . ."

Interrupting, Hipsley said, "I hope you do, Jim, because I've got bad news—all bad."

"Hips, hold your's for a minute," Rowley said. "Matt identified Laszlo Pelm as being in Gettysburg. We're now sure of it. There's a direct connection between the four in Vermont and a possible attempt on Khrushchev and Eisenhower at the Gettysburg High School during the press conference."

"Now what? The bad news, Hips. We can deal with both," Rowley said.

"Good job, Matt, but I'm afraid all I have is bad. We've got to act quickly," Hipsley said, using his Ronson lighter to light a Lucky Strike cigarette.

"I wasn't able to speak to Cardinal Mindszenty. He would not come to the telephone and talk with anyone outside of the legation—only to his sister. However I did get Gerrit Ackerman up-to-date on what we have here. I gave him a list of questions to put to the Cardinal. The Cardinal has been in touch with his nephew off and on ever since the nephew came to America. They write to each other about every six months. The Cardinal said he did get a letter a few days ago which was unlike any of the others; this latest letter deeply disturbed him. He feels that the Pelms and Horvaths—that's Nina and Janos's last name—are committed to carrying out an act of revenge. The letter describes a mission they feel they must execute and one from which, in all likelihood, they'll not be returning."

"Hips, did he say where the mission is to take place? Did he say when? Anything!"

"No. The Cardinal didn't say where. It was clear from the letter that it was Khrushchev they were after and in no way are they out to bring harm to President Eisenhower or his family."

"Did he say what's motivating them to do this?" Matt asked.

"He did," Hipsley said. "It has to do with their parents being killed, the fighting in Budapest. He went into a lot of detail, but I'll save you all of it, for now. I certainly can feel for them."

"Jesus save us!" Rowley said. "Is that it?"

"You have it all."

"Matt, I want photographs of the four in all the newspapers. We must get more help in locating these people. Let's move on it right away."

"Going now, Chief," Hogan said as he headed for the door.

* * *

174

"Chief, look at this!" Hogan shouted as he came into Rowley's office. "What is it? And, for Christ's sake, calm down."

"These are the photographs that were developed from the camera the Marines confiscated a few weeks ago," Hogan said, as he laid the dozen black and white photographs on Rowley's desk.

"What camera, Matt?" Hips asked, now on his feet looking at the photographs.

"The Marines apprehended a person with a camera near the back gate at Camp David a few weeks ago," Hogan said. "They questioned the guy, and I bet it was probably Laszlo Pelm, and confiscated his camera. They were satisfied that he had strayed off the main park road and was only taking pictures of the fall colors."

"Look!" Hipsley said. "This one is showing the fence line on the Camp's west side. There isn't one that shows the detail of any leaf."

Rowley said, leaning back in this chair, "The most obvious point here that blows this so-called Mr. Bender's story is if he were in fact photographing the foliage, why use black and white film and not color?"

"I'm sure it's this guy Laszlo Pelm from Vermont, the same guy I saw at Gettysburg. And now he's spotted outside the fence at Camp David."

"Matt, I want you to take these newspaper photographs by helicopter to Camp David. Tell Fergurson and Kellerman to stand-by to identify Laszlo Pelm as the guy in the woods—the so-called Mr. Bender. You know, maybe it wasn't a German accent after all. Unless you've lived in Europe, when we hear guttural languages, we often think it's German. But what if it were Hungarian instead, and how do we know the guy was from—where did he say he was from? Here it is, Thurmont. He's a dairy mechanic on a farm north of town."

"Chief, I don't mean to argue with you but that seems to be a waste of time—we know it's Pelm."

Hipsley could sense a little uneasiness developing. It was the same with his old boss, Agent Mike Reilly, fifteen years before. And for now he wanted to see how this young and intelligent agent was going to handle himself.

"Matt, for Christ's sake, stop and think for a minute," Rowley said, somewhat agitated. "Don't run off half-cocked. If you're right, you'll know it when the Marine's ID Pelm. That will nail it."

"Chief, the chances are it is Pelm."

"I'm not dealing in chances, Matt, or coincidences. I want facts. You heard U.E. He'll go to the president only if he has facts. What I'm afraid of here is the possibility of two separate groups working independently of each other."

"You see, Matt," Hipsley said, "why he's the Chief. He's always thinking. Ain't that so, Jimbo?"

"Hips, you're a big help, you know that?"

"I know, Jim."

"Chief," Hogan said, "maybe its not the High School after all, but Camp David. Can you believe they'd actually think of coming in there?"

"Matt, I can't answer that. All I know is that this guy is showing up in too many places. Jesus, the president and Khrushchev will be leaving for Camp David in a few hours. Matt, get going!"

"Hips, you're not going to like this, especially after Disneyland, but I'm going to ask the Chief to have the president and Mr. Khrushchev hold their meetings here in the White House," Rowley said reaching for the telephone.

* * *

"Laszlo, why the sudden change in plans?" Janos said, watching him weave the pick-up truck through the tourists and reporters who were using Thurmont's Main Street for a sidewalk.

"We had to leave, Janos. When I came back from the grocer I did not want to disturb Hanna any more than was necessary. I just wanted us to get packed and leave."

"Disturb her from what!" Janos said.

"Our picture is on the front page of the paper. They know who we are, Janos, and they're looking for us."

"How were they able to get to us so quickly? Do you think they know we're here?"

"If they did, they would have picked us up by now. I did not want to take any more chances," Laszlo said, inching the truck onto the entrance ramp to Route Fifteen and glancing at the rear view mirror to see if Nina and Hanna were still in their car behind him.

"Are they still with us?" Janos asked.

"Yes, about four cars behind; this was as good a time as any to leave. The German Festival began at noon and at seven o'clock, the papers said, President Eisenhower and Khrushchev will be arriving at Camp David."

"So why are we heading north? Where are we going?"

"To the Shrine. We're going to stay there until it gets dark and then you and I will unload our equipment and bring it into the woods."

"What about the girls? What are they to do?"

"They'll drive the truck and the car up to Gettysburg and leave the truck at the Civil War Cemetery. You know the one, between Eisenhower's farm and the high school. Then they'll drive back in the car and meet us at the Shrine."

"Laszlo, is it going to happen tonight?" Janos asked, turning around to see if the women were still behind them. "Stop!" he shouted, "they're not behind us. Pull over, Laszlo. I don't see them!"

"I can't do it now. There's no place to pull over. They must of gotten stuck in the traffic."

"We must stop!" Janos pleaded.

"Don't worry, Janos. Nina knows where we're to meet. It's too dangerous for us to stop. Someone will become suspicious of what we're carrying. They'll recognize us—no, we must get to the Shrine. They'll be along, don't worry."

* * *

"We don't have much time, Lieutenant," Matt Hogan said. "The president will be here at 1900 hours. Is Kellerman going to be here?"

"The men are going to Condition Orange at 1700 hours, sir," Fergurson said. "Here comes Kellerman now."

"How are you, Sarge?" Hogan said as all three men moved into the guardhouse.

"The men are ready, sir," Kellerman said. "They're to move out to the bridges in ten minutes. That's going to strip us of twelve guys and we just don't have enough relief."

"Hold up a minute, Sarge," Hogan said. "I wanted both of you here to identify some photographs. You remember the guy in the woods a few weeks ago? Bender—Henry Bender?"

"Yeah, the German," Kellerman said. "We stopped him by the back gate. Said he was looking at the colors."

"I remember him as well," Fergurson said.

"Well, let me ask you—and be very careful, take your time—is this Bender the one on the left?" Hogan said showing them a blown up photograph of the Vermont group.

Fergurson felt his stomach moving up to his throat as he handed the photo back to Hogan. He almost did not hear Kellerman shout out, "That's him all right. A little older, but that's him. You agree, Lieutenant?"

"Fergurson, are you all right? You look lousy," Hogan said.

"Yes . . . I'm fine. That's the same man we saw, that's Bender," Fergurson said quietly. "But why the interest?"

"We have reason to believe that this guy, Bender, whose real name is Laszlo Pelm, together with three others are plotting to assassinate Mr. Khrushchev."

"How do you know that?" Kellerman asked.

"It's a long story, Sergeant, and right now there isn't much time to waste."

"Mr. Hogan," Fergurson said, "by any chance is this Laszlo Pelm Hungarian? And the other three—are they also Hungarian?"

"They are," Hogan said. "Why do you ask, Lieutenant?"

"Because I was part of the Naval Rescue team that picked them off the beach in Yugoslavia in fifty-six."

"That wasn't in your report, Lieutenant. Why didn't you tell us that?" Hogan said.

"I wasn't sure—I wasn't sure then, but I am now. I met all four of them once before."

"I'll need to speak to you later on this, Lieutenant, but for now we go to 'Condition Red.' I'll call Rowley and let him know what you've told me. In the meantime, expect the Second Platoon here. They're on the way up now."

"So you've known that this guy was not Bender?" Kellerman said.

"Pretty much, Sarge," Hogan said. "And, incidentally, I also met him. He was at the high school in Gettysburg the night we were checking it out. And, by the way, don't send out bridge guards. The boss is coming in on Marine One."

* * *

Dusk was beginning to fall over the campus of Mount St. Mary's College when the dusty Chevrolet pulled up alongside the pick-up.

"Where have you been?" Laszlo snapped, keeping his voice low, not wanting the few remaining visitors to the Shrine who were now getting into their cars to hear him.

"We could not help it," Nina said. "The police car pulled us over because our license plate was falling off."

"Jesus, how careless of us," Laszlo said in disgust.

"Laszlo," Hanna said, "he was suspicious. He was calling our license plate in to his station when he was told to get back to town. It sounded like there was some commotion going on there that was more urgent. So he let us go. Laszlo, I was frightened."

"And so was I," Nina said. "We must get rid of this car."

"We will," Laszlo said. "It's dark enough. Help us unload the truck and then take it to Gettysburg. But instead of leaving the truck, leave the car."

"Laszlo," Hanna said, "are we moving into the Camp tonight?"

"Yes but worse than the license plate, I left the compasses back at the house," Laszlo growled. "We will need them. We left in such a hurry that I did not pack them."

"Nina and I will go back."

"But only after you drop off the car," Laszlo said, watching Janos move the last of their equipment onto the path to the Shrine.

"You will wait for us, Laszlo," Hanna said. "Nina and I will never be able to find you and Janos if you move too far into the woods."

Holding his wife in his arms and beckoning Nina to come into his embrace, Laszlo, now joined by Janos, hugged each other.

Whispering, he said, "I love you both dearly, and I hope you can understand and forgive me."

"Laszlo," Hanna said. "What is it you said? I could not hear it."

"I said I love you—I love you both and now you must go."

* * *

"My God, Nina, look at all the people in town," Hanna said as Nina turned the truck down Walnut Street. "Why have you been so quiet, Nina? You haven't spoken a word since we left Gettysburg."

179

Nina slowly brought the truck to a stop in front of 129A, switched off the motor, and turned to Hanna and said, "I'm worried, Hanna. Laszlo was different back there at the Shrine. He was not the Laszlo I know."

"I don't know what you mean," Hanna said as she and Nina got out of the truck and walked quickly up the front path to the porch.

Unlocking the front door and stepping into the living room, Hanna said, "Deep down inside, he can be . . . ."

"Don't turn on the lights—I'm a friend. Don't be alarmed."

"Who's there?" Hanna screamed.

"Be quiet, don't speak," the stranger said. "Just get inside and close the door."

Nina drew out a knife from her handbag and said, "I'll slit your God-damn throat if you do not tell us who you are—what do you want with us."

"Hanna—Nina—I'm Monsignor Tomas Padula," the stranger said, still hidden in the room. "Do you recognize my name?"

"Yes, Monsignor," Nina said totally embarrassed. "We know you—why are you here? How did you find us?"

"Girls, come over to the couch and sit down, but don't turn on any lights," Padula said. "I'll explain everything to you. But I must say we don't have much time. We must leave when I'm finished."

"No one knew we were here, Monsignor," Hanna said. "And what do you mean we must leave—we've got to get the compasses back to Laszlo and Janos."

"Hanna—you and Nina are to come with me."

"What are you saying?" Nina snapped. "Go with you—our husbands are waiting for us right now. They're in the woods. Do you have any idea what is going to take place?"

"I know all too well, Nina," he said. "And I wish I didn't have to know. Your picture is on the front page of every newspaper in the country. A few minutes ago I saw you on the television news. The police and FBI are out looking for you, so please . . . ."

"You still have not told us how you know, Monsignor," Hanna said.

"You see, my child," the priest said, "Laszlo called me the day after you told him that you were with child. That revelation by you convinced him that you and Nina would not be going. Yes, he told me all about what the four of you had set out to do. Only now it's just him and Janos. And I'll tell you what I said to him—I vehemently disagree with what he's doing—it is wrong—in the eyes of God and in the eyes of man. No matter what you or any of us, for that matter, thinks about Khrushchev."

"Why did he feel that way?" Hanna asked. "He never told us how he felt about our being with him; we just assumed all along that we were part of the mission—they needed us."

"Laszlo told me, Hanna," Padula said, "that he saw in your eyes and in your heart that you did want to kill Khrushchev."

"What about me, Father," Nina said sarcastically, "what did he see in me, or did he tell you?"

"The same, Nina," he said. "You wear your resentment and hatred well—on the outside—but inside you are no different than Hanna. He also wanted you to be together, especially if he and Janos don't return."

"Return to where?" Nina said. "Where can they go if we're not here. Certainly not back to the farm! Where?"

"Tonight I'll be driving you to Canada. I left my car near the ballfield. We're eight hours from Toronto. We will stay there overnight and in three days we will be in Port Burwell near Hudson's Bay. Plans are now being readied to have you taken out of Canada by ship—at this time I can't tell you anymore than that—we just didn't have time to plan."

Placing Hanna's head on her shoulder as she held back her own tears, Nina said, "Does Janos know, Monsignor?"

"By now, my dear child, he does," Padula said, now holding his arms around the two sobbing girls. "They're deep in the woods and will stay there overnight. Nothing is to happen until tomorrow. When they camp for the night Laszlo will tell Janos what I've just told you. Please, we must leave now."

* * *

The brilliant light reflecting off the Harvest moon enabled Laszlo and Janos to make considerable headway as they moved deeper and higher into the Catoctin Mountains. But still, Laszlo was finding it difficult to stay on the path, now covered over from the fallen leaves.

"Just ahead we'll make camp for the night, Janos," Laszlo said. "There's a small clearing off the path and it will be far enough away from Cunningham Falls. Any hikers tomorrow will not notice that we're here."

181

"Laszlo," Janos said worriedly, "we have come too far. We're miles from the Shrine and Nina and Hanna will be waiting for us. When are we going to go back for them?"

Not answering Janos, Laszlo angled off the path and headed to the clearing and began removing his knapsack and rifle.

"Laszlo, did you hear me?" Janos said, a little louder, not wanting to shout.

Placing his gear on a flat rock, Laszlo said, "I heard you, Janos. Put your things next to mine and let's stop and rest for the night. I will open some wine. It's going to be cold and we will not be able to make a fire."

"Laszlo, the girls. What about Hanna and Nina! We have to go and bring them here. They have our compasses."

"My dear and trusted friend, it is now only you and me. I have the compasses, I always did," Laszlo said, placing his hands on the smaller man's shoulders. "We will not be going back for Nina nor Hanna. By now they are well on their way to Canada with Monsignor Tomas Padula."

CHAPTER 20

Condition Red had placed every Marine of the Third Platoon on guard duty. Many posts were double-manned. The president and Mr. Khrushchev were airborne and on their way to Camp David. The squad bay was dark and deserted, except for the small desk lamp that was on in Fergurson's room.

Fergurson felt that he had to have a few minutes to himself, to think. The revelation in the guard house was too much. Sitting on the edge of his bunk with clenched fists holding up his chin, he wondered if his career was washed up. Was he the reason the Camp was now at Condition Red? Would he be held responsible if harm came to either the president or Khrushchev? Why had he not spoken up sooner?

"Lieutenant, the Second Platoon—sorry, sir. I didn't mean to interrupt," Kellerman said.

"Go ahead, Sergeant. What is it?"

"The Platoon just arrived at the main gate, sir. What orders do I give them?"

"Have them stand by in the squad bay. They'll go on duty at midnight."

"Lieutenant, I know something's the matter, and it has nothing to do with what we left out of the goddamn report."

"I know it, Sarge. It's more than that."

"Sure, it's more than that—it's those Hungarians—the four you met on the beach. And what if we see them here? I'll tell you, Lieutenant, you'll do the right thing, just like you did then, when you went back for them."

"You're very savvy, Sergeant."

* * *

Alex Akalovsky, Eisenhower's interpreter was sitting between the two world leaders as Marine One was approaching the ballfield landing area at Camp David and said, "Mr. Khrushchev says this is a fine machine, Mr. President. He wishes his country's helicopters provided such a smooth and quiet ride."

Speaking above the soft, but constant, murmuring of the engine on the VH34-D helicopter, President Eisenhower said: "This machine was built by one of your former countrymen—Igor Sikorsky, in Stratford, Connecticut. I believe it was in 1939 he made the first flight in one of these, Mr. Chairman."

"Yes, I'm familiar with Sikorsky, he came from Kiev," Khrushchev said. "I'll tell you something, Mr. President, that you may not know about Igor Ivanovich. In 1913 he built 'The Grand,' the world's first four engine airliner."

"No, I wasn't aware of that," Eisenhower said.

"Oh yes," Khrushchev gloated, "it even had a catwalk outside the cabin enabling the passengers to walk outside while the plane passed through the clouds. It's just too bad he left us in 1919 for America."

"Well, we're glad he decided to come here."

Looking out the window and seeing the dust being blown up by the descending helicopter, Khrushchev said, "Indeed, Mr. President, your country deserves the credit for developing the first helicopter. But perhaps you will give the Russian people some praise for having put the world's first spacecraft on the moon last week."

"You seem to like to have the last word, Mr. Chairman."

"Sometimes, yes."

Four Marines were holding their fire hoses at the ready position and watching the helicopter land, as clouds of dust swirled around them.

Seconds later the two leaders descended the aircraft's steps and Commander Nicholson said, "Welcome to Camp David, Mr. President, Mr. Chairman. I hope you had a pleasant flight from Washington and that you were able to get a glimpse of the colors."

"That we did, Commander," the president said, returning a salute. "A beautiful sight, indeed."

"Right this way, gentlemen; we have a Jeep for you, and I wish you a pleasant visit here at Camp David."

* * *

"Chief, we have positive identification," Hogan said over the telephone from Laurel Lodge. "Pelm was the guy in the woods according to Fergurson and Kellerman."

"I figured they would I.D. them," Rowley said. "And just as well, now that we don't have the fingerprints from the camera. What else have you found?"

"You won't believe this," Hogan said. "Fergurson ran into Pelm three years ago during rescue operations off Yugoslavia. I asked him why it wasn't in his report and he said he just wasn't sure until he saw the photographs."

"I bet he feels pretty lousy about that," Rowley said. "Matt, let's get to the real issue—the boss should be there in a few . . . . "

Interrupting, Hogan said, "He's here now, Chief."

"I won't keep you, then. I'll be up there later."

* * *

Laszlo set out on the blanket all of the items he had carried up the mountain: rifle, shells, wire cutters, tape, flashlight, rope, and gasoline. He was still pulling more items out of his pack when he said, "That must be them coming in now. The newspapers said they would be here at seven."

"Laszlo, if that's so why must we wait until tomorrow night?" Janos was sitting on top of his blanket. "Surely by waiting we give them more time to find us—I don't understand."

"It will be too dangerous tonight," Laszlo said. "There'll be too much moving around inside on the first night. No, tomorrow night it is."

"Tomorrow, the next day, what's the difference?" Janos said sarcastically.

"What are you saying?"

Not looking up at him, Janos said angrily, "You've led us into a trap. Your sick revenge has consumed you. Because of it you've abandoned your wife, your unborn child, Nina, me, and even God. You're not doing this for Hungary . . . you're doing it for Laszlo. You have become fanatical and suicidal. And ever since you told me that you lied about the compasses, I've got nothing but contempt in my heart for you and this dreadful mission."

Kneeling on the blanket, Laszlo said, "My God, Janos, what have I done to you? You know . . . you must know that I would never . . . Yes, I'm full of rage—we all should be."

"Did you ever stop and ask us—me—how I felt?" Janos said.

"No, Janos, I did not. But I don't ask you to feel as I do. I know you can't. Your heart has always been full of love, your faith teaches you to love and forgive your enemies. But can't you see—I've lost my faith, years ago when we lost our country and our church to Communism. Even many of our own people sold their souls and minds to it. You and the others didn't. Instead you tolerated it and waited until the revolt. I've never been willing to wait."

"Laszlo, listen. Just listen to yourself," Janos pleaded.

"If you want to leave, Janos, you know you can. The truck is still at the house. Go if you want to and I'll do what I have to do—with or without you."

"Laszlo, I'm trapped. I can't leave you. How would I live with myself? I know what is going to happen if I go inside with you. No, I don't harbor the hatred you do for this man. Instead, I have so much love for you that I could never leave you, no matter what. Tell me what is it you want me to do."

* * *

"Lieutenant Fergurson, Sergeant, meet Vladimir Burdin," Hogan said, watching the Soviet security chief get into the Jeep that Kellerman was driving.

"Pleased to meet you, Mr. Burdin," Fergurson said, moving to the back seat. "We're pleased to have you . . . ."

Interrupting, Burdin said, "How many men do you have out, Lieutenant? And did the reinforcements come here yet?"

"I can answer that, Mr. Burdin," Hogan snapped. "There're twenty-two on posts and another twenty-six came in an hour ago."

"Very well. Six of my people will join them shortly," Burdin said, as Kellerman maneuvered the Jeep back on to the Camp's main road. "Can we go to Aspen? I don't want to be too far from Comrade Chairman Khrushchev."

"Take us to Aspen, Sergeant," Hogan said, noticing the radio light begin to flash on the Jeep's dashboard.

186

Picking up the radio's receiver, Kellerman listened briefly. "Mr. Rowley wants you to call him right away, Mr. Hogan."

* * *

Pushing the guard house door open, Hogan called to the corporal at the desk and asked, "Where's the phone, Corporal?"

Following Hogan and Fergurson into the building, Kellerman whispered, "Lieutenant, the culvert pipe was delivered at 1600 . . . it's too late to do anything with it, so I had it stored at the maintenance shed."

"That's just great, Sergeant," Fergurson said sarcastically. "Make sure the men keep an eye on those culverts, especially the ones by the helicopter pad."

Hogan slowly placed the phone back onto its cradle, "Lieutenant, you better come inside and hear this."

"What's up?" Fergurson asked, moving into the Officer of the Day's office.

"Rowley told me the police found an abandoned car in Gettysburg that belongs to the Pelms."

"Does that mean that this is not the place?" Fergurson asked.

"I can't say. We just don't know," Hogan said. "We also have a tentative identification from the operator of the Esso station in Thurmont and from the postman who gave Pelm directions but can't remember to where. He did say it was a street with a house number that the guy was looking for and not a tourist spot."

"How long ago, Matt? Was it about the same time Kellerman and I saw Pelm in the woods?"

"About that time—a day or so earlier. The chief believes they have a safe house somewhere between Thurmont and Gettysburg and we've got everyone out there looking for it."

"He gave us an address, Matt. It's in our report."

"I wonder if Rowley remembered it or maybe it was a fake. I'll let him know, anyway."

"You know what I think, Matt? I think they're coming here. I believe they've gone up and down this mountain, day and night, a dozen times. Your people are looking for their truck, the safe house . . . when you locate them, they'll be gone, for sure."

"What's your point, Mike?" Hogan said testily.

"Matt, I believe they're out there in the woods. And that we shouldn't wait here for them. We should be sending patrols to flush them out."

"Mike, with all due respect," Hogan said, "do you have any idea how many square miles of forest you've got? A couple of hundred, I'm sure. And right now you've got just about enough men to man the guard."

"Then let's call Quantico for help. Hell, in three hours we could have a thousand Marines in those woods."

"Yeah, and I hope not shooting at each other," Hogan said. "On the other hand, the idea has some merit. I'll run it by Rowley."

CHAPTER 21

"Janos," Laszlo said, "you haven't eaten or spoken a word since last night—we don't have much time before it gets dark. I know how you must feel, but we have to plan or we will surely fail."

Sarcastically, Janos said, "What plan? We're dead, or don't you know?"

"Look, I have a map of Camp David and I know how we can get in without being seen."

"Where did you get it?"

"Yesterday, it was on the front page of *The New York Times,* just like the time schedules."

"God, how open . . . ."

"Never mind that now," Laszlo said. "You see this spot? This is where I was stopped by the sentries."

"Is that where we're to go tonight?"

"No. We're about here. On the far side of the golf course. It's not a very big course and you will go here, in a westerly direction."

"To the helicopter landing?"

"Yes, but you'll be outside—here. It will take you twenty minutes to get there. You've got to stay close to the outside fence and just follow it around."

"It seems like I'm to cross this road."

"You will, that's the main road into the Camp and there's a guardhouse about here. At that point you will be out in the open for a few seconds."

"What am I to do when I get there?"

"That's why we hauled the petrol up here. You are to set a fire, Janos—for two reasons. The smoke will conceal your entry through the fence. Right here where you'll cut the wire and go to the interior fence and do it again."

"And the second?"

189

"The fire will create a diversion. But remember to set it up wind so the smoke will blow in your direction when you're cutting the fence," Laszlo said, pointing to the spot Janos was to go from.

"How do you get in?"

"Remember I told you about the water furrows? My plan's to go up through them. There's one here and it created a huge ditch under the fence. I just hope it hasn't been fixed since I was here. I had overheard the Marines on Jeep patrol say that they might be doing the repairs soon."

Looking up from the blanket, Janos said, "Do you hear that singing?"

"I do, it must be those girl scouts going back down the mountain before it gets dark—don't worry, they're far enough away."

"They weren't far away when they came up the mountain this morning."

"Please, Janos! Concentrate on the map. You'll need to know where you are when you get inside. Look, once you get clear of the inside wire we each will have the same distance to cover to get to this spot—Aspen Lodge. This is where Khrushchev is staying."

"How do I get by these buildings?" Janos said, running his finger by the Camp's dining hall and dispensary.

"It'll be late, Janos. No one should be there. Just get by it and head in a southerly direction to this point and work your way to the pond in front of Aspen. Hide there in the woods and I'll find you."

"Why must we split up if we're going to meet again?"

"In the event one of us does not make it to Aspen Lodge."

"And later," Janos said, "how do we get out of here?"

"We'll go out the way I came in. We won't go down the mountain the way we came up, however. Instead we'll go to Cunningham Falls."

"Why there?"

"There's a path down from the Falls that leads right into Thurmont. And once there, we can get the truck and leave for Canada."

* * *

"Mr. Rowley, I'm Lieutenant Fergurson. For the duration I've set this cabin up as our operation's center."

"This'll do fine, Lieutenant," Rowley said, glancing around the one room log cabin and nodding his head with a hello to Matt Hogan who

190

was also in the cabin. "I see we're only a hundred yards from Aspen. I can't believe that nothing happened last night. What communication do we have, Lieutenant?"

"The Army guys got us hooked into Aspen, the main gate, and a direct radio hook-up to your office in D.C."

"Tell them I want a direct line to Colonel Sutter's field van in Emittsburg. I want that as soon as possible."

"Will do, sir," Fergurson said.

* * *

Under the cover of darkness, Janos and Laszlo crawled behind a boulder close to the Camp's exterior fence.

"Laszlo, those helicopters—do you think Khrushchev has left? So many of them."

"I think . . . I believe they've landed troops below us, Janos. Probably at the College. There were many of them. They're most likely working their way up the mountain. We have no choice—but to go in. You know what you have to do."

* * *

"Who's Colonel Sutter, Chief?" Hogan asked.

"That's him you heard a few minutes ago in those helicopters. He's in charge of two Marine companies from Quantico. They should be on the ground by now at Mount St. Mary's College."

"The tie in to the Colonel will be in place in a minute, sir," Fergurson said, putting the phone down.

"This son of a bitch is going to hit this place," Rowley said. "And it's tonight, I'm goddamn sure of it. And, Lieutenant, we've put your suggestions to bring up more Marines into action. I only wish we had done it sooner."

"Why not have them here, Chief?" Hogan asked.

"Because at four this afternoon we found the safe house and their truck—right in Thurmont under our goddamn noses. From what we found inside the house, we gather that they've been planning this route, up from the Shrine for two weeks."

"Lieutenant, see if that line is up and get me the Colonel."

191

"How much of a head start do they have, sir?" Fergurson asked, waiting for the call to go through.

"Hard to say; the neighbors say they didn't see any of the Pelms all day. So it would seem that they left sometime yesterday."

"How about the owners of the house, Chief?" Hogan said. "Are they connected?"

"So far, we think not. An old lady—German descent—goes away this time each year, leases out the house."

"Colonel Sutter, sir," Fergurson said, handing the telephone to Rowley.

"What's your status, Colonel," Rowley said, running his hands through his hair. "That's good. Anything happens, get me up here. You've got a direct line. In the meantime, the word is that it's fair game out in the woods, but once at the fence, no shooting—okay?"

Watching Rowley's face as he placed the phone down, Fergurson asked, "Where are they, sir?"

"Over three hundred of your guys are beginning their way up the mountain, Lieutenant. We've got the bastards trapped. They're in a vise and they don't know it. Okay, so much for that. What's the situation here, Matt?"

"Quiet, sir. The president and Mr. Khrushchev are doing all right. I heard meetings went well. Mr. Khrushchev wanted to see a movie—a Western at that—'Shane' with Alan Ladd. They must have known that he wanted it; Deeter Flohr dropped it off a little while ago, after he brought Mrs. Eisenhower and Mrs. Khrushchev to the farm."

"Try and keep things that way, Matt. In the meantime, Lieutenant, I want a Marine inside the back gate, and I want one of the Jeep patrols to have their Jeep block the main gate."

Fergurson appeared puzzled by Rowley's order and said, "I understand the reason for a sentry at the back gate, but why take a Jeep off patrol and have it at the main gate? We have a Marine, one of your people, and a KGB agent there as well. Why remove the coverage from the woods? I've got four miles of fence to cover with sixteen Marines, we're thin enough as it is, sir."

"Aren't you forgetting something, Lieutenant? There're two fence lines out there, with lights and a roving Jeep in patrol in the middle."

"I don't mean to be argumentative, Mr. Rowley, but there are gullies—open water courses—breaking the security of both fences. This afternoon the conduit pipes finally came."

"Yeah, I'm aware of those holes, Lieutenant. They've been there for years and up until now no one's shown any initiative to fix them except you. But let's not worry about them now."

"I just want to point out this exposure we've got, sir."

"Lieutenant, these people not only take to the woods, there's a chance they might attack in a car and ram through at the gate, and don't even ask where the car might come from. So let's get that Jeep there and make sure your people have their thirty-caliber machine gun mounted and pointing down the access road. These are city people, Lieutenant, they fought the Communists in the streets of Budapest and they're not one bit afraid of driving straight through the gate barricade. To them it's no different than a Soviet tank."

"Consider it done, sir," Fergurson said.

"And just so you know, Matt—because it doesn't mean a hill of beans now—Chief Baughman went right to the boss and tried to persuade him to call off this visit to Camp David. U.E. said the president was adamant that the weekend visit must take place if Mr. Khrushchev's stay here in the United States was to have any success at all."

* * *

Laszlo and Janos were in luck. The darkness was deep. There was a chill in the damp air. There would be no moon tonight. They could just make out each other as they stared silently alongside the fence. Neither one said a word. The crickets were putting on a symphony. High above them they could hear the sound of a four-engine aircraft. Intermittently they heard the faint sound of cars making their way up the mountain road. The immediate silence was broken when Janos whispered.

"We split up here?"

"Yes," Laszlo said softly, placing his arms over Janos's shoulders. "I won't say goodbye, my friend, because I'll see you again—whatever happens . . . ."

"Laszlo, I won't let you down, I never have. I will be there. And together we will go to Canada to be with Nina and Hanna," Janos said, his head buried in Laszlo's shoulder.

193

"Thank you, my friend. And now you must go, and Janos—God bless you."

Janos vanished into the darkness and Laszlo hunched over and, in duck-walk fashion, followed the water course up to where it went under the fence. Taking off his pack, he placed it behind him and laid down in the stream bed and waited.

* * *

Fergurson had just gotten to his desk in the guardhouse when the field phone rang, "Fergurson here. What is it?"

"This is Mullins, Post Number Three, sir. We have a fire in the woods outside of the perimeter fence on our side of the park road. If you don't get people down here, it could become a big one."

"Kellerman, get Hogan on the other line," Fergurson said hurriedly. "Mullins, what direction is the fire moving?"

"Hogan's on the line, sir."

"Tell him to hold for a second."

"Looks like its south, southeast, sir. Toward the truck parking area. And it's moving faster now!"

"Mullins, stay on the line. Don't move," Fergurson said. "Matt, we've got a fire near Post Number Three."

"Was it set?" Hogan said.

"I believe so. Fire's moving into the wind, smoke in opposite direction."

"I'll tell Rowley. Get some men over there and don't take anyone off their guard posts, not yet, anyway."

* * *

Along the Camp's perimeter half of the fence-line sentries had become aware of the fire, particularly those on the Camp's north and west sides. They could smell the smoke, the fire now within a few hundred yards of the Camp's access road.

Not far from the main gate the sentries at Posts Thirteen and Fourteen could see the flames, and their attention was drawn to the fire, not to the fence line they were guarding. Twenty feet from the interior fence, Laszlo lay in the ditch and watched the sentries. He had no trouble

194

working his way through the exterior fence. "It was too easy," he thought. He began to inch his way on an angle toward the interior fence, cradling his 30.06 rifle in his arm. He froze as to his right he saw the sentry, M-1 in hand, walk slowly along the path, just inside the second fence. "He didn't see me. The light from the fence lamp was weak. Thank goodness there was no moon. He's moving away." Laszlo raised his head like a woodchuck, then heard the Jeep approaching and knew he had to move quickly. "But to where?" he thought. The hole under the fence was packed with new wire. He had heard the same motor before; it was the patrol.

The Jeep patrol was almost on top of him. He had to get inside. Rapidly he dragged himself along the gully on his elbows. Sharp stones ripped into his legs, tearing the skin on his thighs. "How long can it be," he thought, sliding his rifle ahead of him. In seconds he was next to the barbed wire that was stuffed into the gully. There he lay motionless as the two-man patrol roared by with the Jeep's passenger nearly ejected as the vehicle bounded out of the ditch.

The Jeep was not far away when he pulled out his wire cutters. The sentry along the path could be returning. How soon he did not know. He should have watched and timed his movements. It was too late to think of that now. Before the pliers bit into the wire he listened and looked for the sentry. He wasn't there. The wire broke cleanly and quietly. It was not strung tightly. It was also new. Quickly he made a half dozen more cuts. The wire was loose. He pulled it back away from the fence. It still clung to the fence. One more strand had to be cut. Pulling himself back up to the fence, he froze once again. The sentry was lumbering back up the path. He was fifty feet away. He wasn't looking left or right—just straight ahead and at the ground so as not to stumble. Laszlo watched him disappear. Laszlo got up and went over to the stubborn strand that did not want to come loose. He pulled out his shirt tail and wrapped it around the wire. He cut his shirt and the wire. The wire broke. He had muffled the noise. He pulled the wire packing away and crawled through the culvert. He was in. Aspen had to be directly in front of him through the trees; he could see the lights. Concealed behind a bush, he saw the Post Thirteen Marine make his return walk down the fence path.

* * *

195

"Matt, Fergurson here. Diversion it is! They're inside the Camp. Mullins found a cut in the fence. The fire was spreading south because it had been ignited by gasoline."

"Get those Marines off the fire detail, Mike, and set up a perimeter guard from the barracks to Laurel Lodge. And keep that Jeep by the gate. We still could be in for more diversions."

CHAPTER 22

Laszlo, catching his breath standing just inside the tree line along the fairway, saw a light come on less than fifty yards in front of him. Moving closer to obtain a better view, he saw a sentry exit what he thought was a privy. Instantly he remembered seeing similar structures—the day he was stopped by the marines.

As the Marine adjusted the sling on his rifle and moved away into the darkness, Laszlo waited, looked, then darted toward the building, from which the light had come.

Carefully he opened the door. Not too much, not to let the light be conspicuous. He was thankful that the opening was toward the woods. He entered and closed the door.

"It's not an outhouse at all; it's an entry to some tunnel." He glanced around and saw the multi-colored wall map enclosed in a glass picture frame. Quickly he moved to examine it and noted the red arrow with the words, "You are here." His eye followed the broken line as it trailed off to Witch Hazel Lodge and then, making a right angle—to Aspen Lodge.

* * *

The buildings' large red cross painted above the double door entrance was sufficient for Janos to realize he had just passed the Camp's dispensary. He crouched behind a garbage dumpster to get his bearings.

Laszlo was right; there had been no one around the two buildings by which he had passed. "I must keep going—I must keep going. Laszlo will be waiting—he should have given me more time."

* * *

Khrushchev and Eisenhower walked slowly down the lighted path from Laurel Lodge back to Aspen. They were surrounded by three KGB agents and a like number of Secret Service men. In Laurel Lodge they had watched the hit Western movie "Shane."

"Alan Ladd is one of my favorite actors, Mr. President," Khrushchev said through his interpreter. "He portrays that in the end good will always overcome evil."

Both men were oblivious to the events unfolding around them. The wind had moved the smoke from the fire in the opposite direction and the moonless night prevented them from seeing Marines move into position alongside Laurel Lodge.

* * *

Janos gently pushed the pine branches out of his way and moved in the direction of the pond. The pine needles softened his footsteps as he continued. Reaching out with his left hand and pulling back a large branch, Janos stopped still. There was no mistake—it was him! "That's Khrushchev walking with the president. Where's Laszlo? Am I going to have to kill Khrushchev myself?"

* * *

"'Shane, come home. Come home, Shane.' How can you ever forget those words, Mr. President? Please thank Mr. Ladd for allowing me to view his copy of the movie."

"I certainly will, Mr. Chairman. We were very fortunate that we could get it here. I was told it was your favorite."

"Mr. President, for security reasons," Hogan said, "we would like you and Mr. Khrushchev to move quickly back to Aspen, sir."

"Nonsense, Matt. This place is as safe a place as any. And please, don't be alarming Mr. Khrushchev," who already had had Hogan's remarks translated for him and, unlike the president, appeared to take the agent's comments more seriously.

* * *

Private Wilson and Corporal Schaffer had, over the past year, spent countless hours crisscrossing the Camp David tunnel complex to the point that it had become routine; they had become careless. They were oblivious to what was taking place topside. Laszlo took advantage of this. It was not hard to hear the whistling. The sentry was not alert. He had not seen Laszlo back up against the wall at the intercept of Witch Hazel and Aspen tunnel connections. He didn't see the butt of Laszlo's rifle. It smashed into the side of his head. However his fall was not without noise. He went down along with the table and chair that were near him. Corporal Schaffer, hearing the noise, shouted, "What the hell's going on, Wilson? Keep it down."

Laszlo quickly moved to the other wall. He could hear the other Marine running down the corridor.

"Jesus, Wilson. I could hear your stumbling a mile aw . . . ." The butt of the rifle caught Schaffer in his stomach, just above his cartridge belt. As he fell forward, Laszlo brought his rifle up and smashed it into the back of Schaffer's head. He lay lifeless on the floor. Blood was spilling out of the wound.

Laszlo took their side arms, saw that they were unconscious, left them, moved up the tunnel, and realized, when he saw the tunnel's comforts, that he was getting close to Aspen.

* * *

The moviegoers were approaching the front of Aspen. Mr. Khrushchev was chatting about the movie with his security aide, Vladimir Burdin. Hogan, close to the president's side, was anxious to get him and Khrushchev inside.

"Is that smoke I smell, Matt?" Eisenhower asked.

In speaking to the president he did not see the figure rise on top of the rock wall that surrounded the pond. "Yes, Mr. President. We've got a small fire in the woods near the helicopter pad. It's under control, sir."

"That's good."

The stillness of the night was broken by a passionate cry: *"Szabjads'agot a magyar n'epnek!"* *"Freedom for the Hungarian people!"*

Hidden in the trees, Fergurson shouted, "Drop your weapon, you're under arrest!"

The command from Fergurson was ignored. The blast from Janos's twelve gauge shotgun smashed the kitchen window and cedar siding of the Lodge.

With the shot, Hogan threw his arm around the president's shoulder and pulled him to the ground while yanking his .45 automatic out of his gun holster and aiming at Janos.

At the same time, Agent Burdin had thrown his arms over Khrushchev's back, pushing him forward. The other KGB agents fell on top of them.

The sound of the blast brought Elmer Hipsley instantly to the front door of Aspen. Gun drawn he rushed out of the Lodge and over to Khrushchev.

The second blast from the double barrel gun struck the path. Gravel flew into the air, showering Chairman Khrushchev, Burdin, and Hipsley.

Janos was reloading, not seeking cover behind the wall, when Hogan's shot caught him in the chest and he fell forward into the pond.

As other agents provided cover, Hogan helped the president up and wondered where the other Hungarians were. He rushed to the front door of the cabin and pushed the president inside, where two Secret Service agents had taken up positions. Behind Hogan were three KGB agents and Hipsley carrying Khrushchev to shelter.

A swarm of agents surrounded the pond, guns pointed at the floating body. It lay lifeless in the water, which was already showing the signs of blood.

Hogan shouted as he ran along the path on the south end of the house, "Flohr, take some of the men around to the other side. Burdin, Fergurson, come with me. Hips, stay with them inside."

"And for Christ's sake, Lieutenant, if you pull your weapon, shoot it! Where the hell are the other three?"

"Who the hell knows?" Fergurson said, shaken.

"I must stay with the chairman," Burdin said.

"Colonel Burdin, our problem is out here," Hogan said testily, "not in the house. There're three more and they have to be close by."

"Mr. Hogan, why was the KGB not informed of these people? You seem to have known that they were coming. You knew it all the time."

"Mr. Burdin, right now I've got no time for that."

"Lieutenant! Lieutenant!" Kellerman called, joining the others on the footpath.

"What is it?"

"Just before he had heard the shooting, Post Number Thirteen saw a light coming from 'Baker Five.'"

"What is Baker Five, Mr. Hogan?" Burdin asked, uneasy about not knowing what the Sergeant was referring to.

"Considering how close our countries' leaders have come to being assassinated, you'll soon find out what Baker Five is," Hogan said.

* * *

"Matt, it makes no sense for us to go to Baker Five," Fergurson said. "If they're in the tunnel, we can cut them off by going down through Baker One, just off the first tee. Schaffer and Wilson will have them boxed in from the other end."

"Good point, Mike. You and Kellerman go in at Baker One and Burdin and I'll go back to Aspen. It could be that we now have them in a trap."

"Mr. Hogan, I've got Chief Rowley on the radio," Kellerman said. "He wants you."

Hogan said, "I'm here, Chief. All hell has broken loose. President and Khrushchev are safe, in Aspen with our people and the KGB. I'm coming back to Aspen. The others are in the tunnel under Witch Hazel. Chief, we can't wait for them, we've got a positive that they went in . . . just three . . . we killed one at the pond. I did. Thanks."

"Any change, Matt?" Fergurson asked anxiously.

"No, I'm to meet him back at Aspen. He wanted to know if we should wait for Colonel Sutter's men. They're almost to the outer fence. Too late. We've got to get going, so let's do it."

* * *

The sound of the removal of the hatch cover at the Baker One tunnel entry alerted Laszlo—he was no longer alone.

He placed his rifle on the carpeted floor; the gun was clumsy, not effective. He pulled from his belt the two .45 automatics he had taken from the sentries and raced down the tunnel toward Aspen, using the barrels of the guns to knock out the bulbs in the overhead lights.

* * *

"Quiet!" Fergurson snapped. "Listen—just ahead—that popping."

"It's the bulkhead lights, Lieutenant," Kellerman said. "He doesn't want us to see—it doesn't matter. The emergency lights will go on, and he can't break them."

* * *

Laszlo knew the pursuer was close. "I can't go back," he thought, standing at the first step of the ladder way directly below the Aspen hatch cover.

His breathing became rapid, he could hear it. He also could hear the running. "How many are there?" he wondered. "They won't see me, it's too dark."

* * *

"I'll be against the wall, Lieutenant. Hug that side and stay low," Kellerman said, with his .45 cocked and raised.

They sprinted down the carpeted corridor, their footsteps muffled. As they approached a slight turn in the tunnel, Fergurson could not slow down. The momentum carried him to the center of the passageway and away from the wall.

"I'm a dozen steps to being inside Aspen. If I run up will they shoot me in the back, or should I stay here and fight? Janos, where are you? I can't wait for you, I must end this. You may have been right, Janos. It's madness, but now I must do something," thought Laszlo.

* * *

"Lieutenant," Kellerman said excitedly as he shoved Fergurson back against the wall, "get back. You're too far . . . ." The blast from Laszlo's gun interrupted the warning. The force from the high velocity bullet spun Kellerman around. He dropped to the floor.

* * *

"Listen up, everybody. We can't use the escape tunnels," Rowley announced as he stood in the living room, gun drawn.

202

"What's going on, Mike?" the president said, visibly shaken, as was his guest. They were sitting on a sofa surrounded by KGB and Secret Service agents.

"The Marines are down in the tunnels, sir. We believe there're three more in the gang. Shots have been fired."

* * *

Fergurson dove to the carpet, gun pointed in the direction of the shot. His finger held the trigger back in a vise-like grip. His bullets were spent in an eye flash, all eight rounds went wild. He could hear them ricocheting off the metal pipes and ladderway.

Fergurson reached down to his belt for his replacement clip and heard Kellerman gasping, "Lieutenant—I'm hit."

* * *

"Mr. Rowley, how did they ever get this close?" Herter, pale and shaken, asked, sitting beside Andrei Gromyko.

"Mr. Secretary, at this time I don't know. I'm sure there'll be a follow-up investigation. However, in the meantime, we still have to . . . ." Rowley never finished his sentence. Eight shots rang out from below. "Everyone outside! Now!" Rowley shouted. "Matt, move them to Laurel. Get more men here."

* * *

The emergency power pack provided just enough illumination. Fergurson turned and saw Kellerman. He knew instantly that his platoon sergeant was gravely wounded.

He spun around, and crept over to him. The carpet was soaked in blood. Its light green color had been transformed to dark brown. Fergurson lifted Kellerman's head and heard him whisper, "Get him, Lieutenant . . . get the bastard . . . you have to do it . . . ."

"Norm, don't say a word. I'll get help!"

"No you won't." Laszlo guided the muzzle of his gun inches away from the back of Fergurson's head. "Leave him there. You're going to get me in to Khrushchev."

"In a pig's ass, I will—you bastard—Pelm, Laszlo Pelm."

"Who are you," Laszlo snapped. "Stand up and leave the gun on the ground."

Fergurson slowly rose to his knees—his eyes were still on his wounded friend.

"Get up and turn around—slowly, or I shoot you too."

Fergurson got to his feet and turned. He was facing Laszlo. In the light, what little there was, he saw in Laszlo's eyes the expression of someone who had just seen the devil.

Startled, Laszlo said, "I know you."

Hesitating, giving him time to get a longer look, Fergurson said, "You bet you know me, you son of a bitch, and it wasn't just in the woods. I should have left you and the others on that goddamn beach three years ago."

"I thought you might of recognized me that day in the woods. I'm sorry it has come down to this."

"I bet you're sorry. Are you sorry for that?" Fergurson said, pointing to his wounded platoon sergeant.

"I didn't mean to shoot him."

"The hell you didn't."

"I swear, I—we came to kill Khrushchev—only him. I didn't kill the other two back there. I could have, but I didn't."

"Look, Pelm, I don't give a shit, not one bit for you or your goddamn cause. You're sick—all of you are."

"I'm not asking you to concern yourself with our cause."

"When you came into Camp David, you made it my cause. There's no way I and my men are going to permit you to harm the president or Mr. Khrushchev, no way. Do you understand?"

"That's very interesting, Lieutenant. Very brave—but I've got the gun. And you're going to lead me to Khrushchev. Right up those steps. You're going to tell the guards that it's you—and I'll be right behind you."

"What if I tell you to go to hell? Which is where your brother-in-law is right now."

"What are you saying?"

"I'm saying give it up—now, while you and the women still have a chance."

"Our wives are long away from here, Lieutenant. They never came, they're in Canada by now, and you can't reach them. Janos is close by."

"Janos is dead."

"You're lying. Janos is waiting for me."

"Yeah, in hell—and if you don't give me that gun, you're going to join . . . ."

The blast from the direction of the floor sent a bullet into Laszlo's shoulder. Crying out in pain, he let the gun in his right hand drop to the floor. Before he could release a round from the other .45 automatic, Fergurson sprang at him, and slammed him into the wall.

Laszlo's head rocked against the rows of iron steam pipes. Stunned, he lunged at Fergurson, who now had his hands around the cocked automatic.

Fergurson called on all the strength he had and turned Laszlo's arm, forcing the muzzle toward Laszlo's stomach. Laszlo's right arm was useless, hanging like a partially severed tree branch. He raised his head back as far as he could. He brought it forward, attempting to butt his way free. Fergurson pulled the trigger.

The lifeless body slumped over and fell onto Fergurson, who guided it gently to the floor. When he let go, his hands were trembling. He turned and looked at the dying Hungarian's face. He saw that his lips were moving, he was saying something. Fergurson moved closer, he put his ear next to Laszlo's lips and heard: *"Isten meg fogja nekem bocsa'tani amit tettem." "God forgive me for what I have done."*

* * *

Agent Flohr slowly opened the hatch door just beyond the living room; five agents had their weapons pointing in his direction.

"Don't shoot, it's me," Fergurson said, pushing the hatch cover open. "It's all over. The women never came in. Laszlo Pelm is dead, Sergeant Kellerman is down there, he's been shot and needs help," he said gripping the fireplace mantle for support, sweat pouring down his blood-stained uniform.

Flohr shouted, "Tell the chief it's over. They can come back."

* * *

Khrushchev and Eisenhower came into the room, followed by Gromyko and Herter. They all looked shaken. Hogan was on the phone calling Dr. Snyder.

"Help him before he collapses!" Mr. Eisenhower ordered. "What is your name, son?"

"Lieutenant Michael Fergurson—Marine Corps, Mr. President."

"Well, Lieutenant, I owe you my life, and so does our guest—Mr. Khrushchev."

Through his interpreter, Mr. Khrushchev said, "Young man, the Soviet people are grateful for your heroic act. I hope you are given a medal. And here I want you to have my medal. It was given to me after big war—the Order of Lenin."

Khrushchev then turned to Eisenhower and said angrily, "Mr. President, I wish to leave at first light for Moscow. What has happened here tonight, and the other indignities my party has received in the course of our visit, compels me to want to withdraw my invitation for you to visit the Soviet Union."

"Mr. Chairman," Eisenhower said, his voice still showing signs of strain, "I would hope that after a good night's rest you would reconsider your statement. What has taken place here tonight should never have happened. We never thought that there could be an attack at Camp David!"

"Nevertheless, Mr. President, I'll be leaving in the morning."

CHAPTER 23

THE PRESENT

The effects from the cold and damp night had been neutralized by the heat coming from the logs burning in the fireplace at Camp David's Witch Hazel Lodge.

Professor Fergurson, wearing an Irish wool sweater, a pair of corduroy slacks, and slippers, was sitting at the desk sipping a scotch and water. He pushed the chair up on its back legs and glimpsed the dozen or so handwritten sheets of notepaper that were scattered on the desktop.

He was starting to feel tired. The day had begun fifteen hours ago, when he had left his room at the Willard and met the president in the Oval Office. He was grateful to Commander Hoyt and his wife for dinner and the offer to spend the night.

His report, almost finished, had to be delivered to the president in two days. He was determined to complete the first draft before retiring.

He placed the drink down, brought his chair closer to the desk, picked up his pen and continued.

Immediately after the incident had occurred, President Eisenhower placed a cloak of secrecy over it.

Chairman Khrushchev made good his threat. He canceled President Eisenhower's invitation to the USSR and left the next morning. The following year, he raised havoc at the Paris Summit and at the United Nations. However, he never revealed what had taken place at Camp David.

The world remembers the weekend at Camp David in the phrase that Chairman Khrushchev spoke when he boarded his plane to Moscow: "The Spirit of Camp David." In their minds, it was the U-2 affair and the Gary Powers nightmare that brought about subsequent and unfortunate relations with the Soviets and not the attempt on Khrushchev's life, which only a handful of us knew was the real reason.

As for the Marines that were involved, miraculously Kellerman survived the gunshot wound. He was given a commission in 1960. He and Schaffer were killed in Viet Nam during the Tet offensive. Wilson, the other Marine in the tunnel, was killed in an automobile accident in 1968.

Matt Hogan left the service soon after President Kennedy's assassination and is a Professor of Law at a university in New York.

The two girls came back from Canada in October of 1960. Because there never had been an official investigation, they returned to Vermont and continued to operate the farm. Their husbands were secretly buried at Camp David, just outside the back gate. President Eisenhower had ordered that a headstone be placed over their graves. I saw it today and it has on it an inscription:

"Itt fekszik a negy
magyar hos ketto
maradvanya"

The translation is:

"Here lie the
remains of two
Hungarian Patriots"

Their uncle, Cardinal Mindszenty, with help from President Nixon, gained his freedom in 1972. He died in the mid-seventies in Austria. He never lived to see his homeland become free.

Notwithstanding my confrontation with Laszlo Pelm in the tunnel, the Marine Corps' senior staff believed that I could have prevented the incident. Not coming forward

208

sooner regarding my recognition of Laszlo Pelm was, to them, a breach of command responsibility. It was with deep regret that soon after that I resigned my commission.

It wasn't until today, when I stood over their graves that I realized why I never came forward. For thirty-five years I've searched for the reason for my inaction, my hesitation.

Mr. President, these were good people. They tried, no matter how wrong they might have been, to change the world for the good of mankind. The enormous events that have recently taken place in Eastern Europe and in the Soviet Union has proven them right. Whether consciously or subconsciously, I felt this back in 1959 and, like them, I too was wrong. But who of us was to know?

Mr. President, you may have noticed my anxiety when you gave me the assignment to report on what had happened here thirty years ago. I beseech you, let it stay that way, for the world, . . . and for those of us who were involved, let it remain the secret of Camp David.